KINDRED SPIRITS

A NOVEL

STUART FABE

Author's Note

IT'S ALWAYS CURIOUS TO ME what I choose to write about. In some ways my random thoughts are like stars scattered across a night sky that eventually coalesce into constellations, bringing definition and form to an otherwise abstract realm.

I never set out to be an author, and it never dawned on me that I would become a storyteller. I just never gave myself credit that I could actually pull that off well. Yet, as I get older, I must confess that it's enormously gratifying to go in new directions and see where they lead. After all, why not?!

It's been said that authors write stories based on personal experiences, and I generally agree with that belief. In my previous story, *The Write House,* I took the liberty of using my world in Putnam County, Indiana, as the major setting for my book. I was able to construct much of that story around familiar locations that still exist today, and to give respectful mention to area landmarks that are no longer around. I'm pleased that many of my readers enjoy my paying homage to places that they know as well.

Kindred Spirits is a sequel to *The Write House,* with the Engel Family again playing a prominent role. Over twenty-five years have passed since the first story, and Caroline and Delano Engel's daughter, Aurora, has matured into a fine young woman who takes a leadership role in her community. She also marries a loving and complex man named Ben Witt. What ensues is an intriguing story filled with mystery and a struggle against frightening threats to the Engel family and their hometown, Greencastle.

I have also chosen to write this story as a supernatural mystery for two main reasons: The concept of an other-worldly realm is highly entertaining to me personally, and it gives me an opportunity to portray life in my hometown as having mystical elements. In *The Write House* I used the magical Book of Tamberg as the spirited medium that provided guidance to my heroes, Delano and Caroline Engel. In *Kindred Spirits* it's a sentient old school bell that offers similar guidance to help my heroes avert disaster for themselves and their beloved community.

Kindred Spirits is my ninth novel, and I sincerely hope that you enjoy reading it as much as I entertained myself by researching and writing this spirited mystery set in America's heartland.

— Stuart Fabe

Dedication

To the Kennedy Family
of Cloverdale and Lafayette, Indiana,
Whose Bell Collection Reverberates With History

and to

Anita Barr McEnulty
A Fine Friend Who Started Me on
A Memorable Path

Prologue

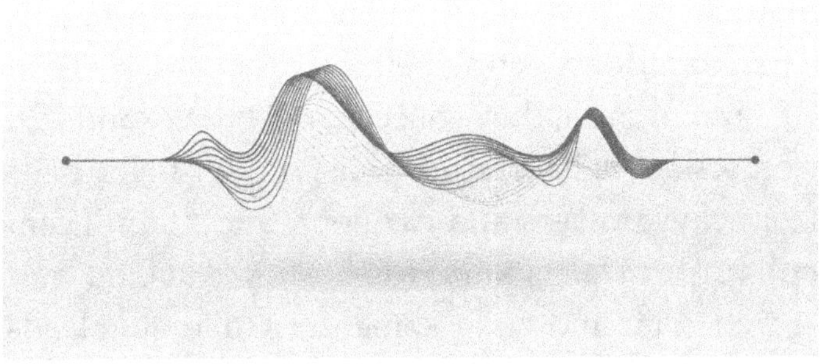

Putnam County, Indiana

1935

For Max Kindred and his brother, John, the only consoling thing about living during the Great Depression was that nearly everyone they knew was enduring similar financial hardship. The stock market crash of 1929 hadn't immediately affected the bachelor brothers' livelihoods, but over time very few people had the money to purchase their livestock and grain. Fortunately, Max and John grew their own food on their modest central Indiana farm, and they had very little need for material possessions, with one major exception … a passion for collecting bells.

You name it, they collected old bronze and cast iron school bells, church bells, dinner bells, bells from clock towers and carillons, and magnificent bells from trains and ships. They traveled and searched far and wide; sometimes following leads from folks they met along the way, other times just being free-stylin' brothers on the road looking for vintage bells wherever that road led them.

Many of the "ringers", as Max liked to call them, came from foundries in New York and Boston, but even more came from Cincinnati, Chicago, and St. Louis. If they were in good condition and gave a sonorous peal, they bought 'em and displayed them all around their property. What started out with the purchase of a single bell so the mailman could announce his arrival, turned into a massive private collection of over three hundred bells. They hung from wooden posts and fences, from sheds and corncribs, from porches and barns, even trees. And, they never sold them. They just kept adding to their collection, and before long their property became known as the Kindred Bell Farm. They may have been living during the depths of the Great Depression, but the Kindred brothers felt as rich as anyone could feel. Wealth, after all, is in the eye, ear, and heart of the beholder.

"C'mon, John, or we'll be late for that estate auction in Cloverdale. Sure don't wanna miss an opportunity to find us another gem."

"No sir! Heaven forbid someone else would find a big ol' bell and outbid us. Though I gotta admit, Max, I prefer we get someone to help us load whatever we buy into the truck this time. Seems to me we have a knack for buying the heaviest bells, and my agin' back isn't what it used to be."

"Yeah, well, I'm older than you, so I hear you, brother. After gettin' darn near three hundred bells, you'd think that we'd have our fill of collecting these dang things, but they just have a special way of talkin' to me. Hard to explain, but every once in a while when I ring one, it just sorta vibrates into my very being like it's communicating with me, or something. I know, it sounds batshit crazy, but I swear it's true … just hard to explain."

John looks at his older brother quizzically. "Well, Max, while you're trying to figure out that nutty notion, I'll go get the truck, and we can head over Cloverdale way."

Max watches his younger brother adjust his faded felt hat against a stiff breeze that's just come up and amble across the barnyard toward a large weathered shed to fetch their old Diamond T pickup. The northerly breeze picks up briskly, and Max watches as the trees begin to sway as if animated by some unseen force. He watches John as he pulls open the shed's heavy wooden doors and disappears into the dim light within. The force of the wind causes old corn sheaths and last winter's fallen leaves to dance around him, and he hears the clappers from a few nearby bells begin to strike their heavy metal sides in a chaotic, atonal rhythm. He approaches one of the bells nearest to him hanging on a gnarly wooden post by an old ship's chain. Both the bell and the chain are covered with lichen from disuse, and the bell's deep ringing seems to impart an unusual cadence within his bones and teeth. He stops in his tracks to try to recall if he's ever felt that sensation before, but his pondering is interrupted by the rumbling sound of John approaching in their truck.

"Better hurry up in here, brother," John calls out to Max. "Looks like we may have a goose-drowner heading our way." Max reaches his hand out to touch the ringing dinner bell before departing and feels its vibrations reach deep within his body before dissipating into near-nothingness. He opens the passenger side door of the truck and hears a vague, resonate sound in the wind, almost like a breathy voice, just before he closes the door ... *"Hear ... Feel."* Once inside he peers curiously at the old weathered bell not knowing exactly what he just experienced as John puts their Diamond T into first gear and they slowly pull away.

John steers the pickup onto County Line Road and then makes a left turn heading west on State Route 42 toward Cloverdale. He looks over at Max who is vacantly staring out the front windshield watching droplets of rain splatter between the swooshes of the wipers.

"You're awful quiet over there, brother, cat got yer tongue?"

Max glances at John with a momentary smile. "Naw, not really, but something weird happened back there in the barnyard when I was waitin' for ya."

"Oh? Did ya git hit by lightning, or sumthin?"

"Naw, nuthin' like that. It's just that … you ever git a feelin' that there's more to life than meets the eye?"

John grins and shoots his brother a skeptical look. "Yeah, darn near every day when I'm sweatin' in my skivvies out in the fields!"

"Yeah, I git that, but …"

"But what? You're not gittin' religion on me now, are ya, Max? Gittin' hit by lightning can do that to a fella!"

"Naw, course not. It's just that … oh, never mind. Let's just go find us a bell."

John drives over the steel truss bridge crossing the Mill Creek and comes upon the Smith place on the north side of the road. "Looky there, Max, that young couple's collectin' a few bells too. I knew we'd have some competition eventually."

"Yeah, well, if they're nutty enough to pay good money and haul those heavy ringers, more power to 'em, I guess. It's not like we don't have a good head start on 'em!"

They pass the Vann family farm, and some three miles later they come to a crossroads and hang a right onto U.S. Route 231. The soaking rain has abated to a light drizzle, and John accelerates and dodges a few potholes as he passes a slower-moving tractor. Just before entering the main drag of Cloverdale, the brothers turn left into the soggy grounds of the local auction barn. There are already several vehicles parked near the entrance to the barn, but they find a spot nearby under a small grove of mature walnut trees.

"You ready for this, brother?" John asks as he excitedly exits the truck and promptly steps into a puddle.

"Yup! Keep your eyes and ears peeled for any ringers we can find before the bidding starts. Let's split up. You go left, and I'll go right and we can meet in the middle of the barn. How's that sound?"

"Sounds like the same strategy we use every time. Sing out if you see something worth our biddin' on!"

The Kindred brothers enter the auction barn and part company. The interior is filled with a myriad of household items and sundry collectibles from the Estate of Willa and Charles Pemberton, folks who'd lived in Putnam County all of their eighty-plus years and entered the kingdom of their lord within a week of each other. Both of them had devoted their lives to music. Charles was the music teacher at Cloverdale High School his entire career, and Willa led their church choir for nearly forty years and gave private piano instruction in their home. They'd had no children of their own, so they received satisfaction and joy by filling their world and the lives of others with song and scripture.

John slowly meanders down a row of tables, carefully scanning every inch above and below. He sees lots of furniture, knickknacks, kitchen utensils, photographs, garden tools, and reams of sheet music, certainly nothing of interest to him. He moves along and sees a few interesting hand-crank organs and an antique Edison Home Phonograph, but he abides by a collecting rule that he and brother, Max, had agreed upon a long time ago, stick to collecting bells. He passes down another row and then another growing a little weary not finding what he's looking for when he hears the resonant sound of a cast iron bell from up ahead. He quickens his pace and sees Max with a huge grin on his face admiring a lovely ringer that he'd lofted up onto a stout table from beneath a tarp on the ground.

"Ain't she a beauty?!" he sings out to John as he appears by his side. "She's intact and has a wonderful verdigris patina! I almost missed her, but then I heard, actually felt, a weird vibration and looked under the tarp and saw this great ringer."

"Well, Jumping Jahosafat! Who made it?" John asks with equal enthusiasm.

They both examine the old school bell and see the maker's mark, *Virtue Bell Company, Cincinnati, Ohio.*

"Virtue, huh?! That's quite a venerable company. Ya know, of all the bells we've got, I don't think we've ever had one of those which is kinda odd since the Virtue foundry's been around a long time and Cincinnati isn't that far away. Always wanted one of those."

"Yep, she's a beaut!" John echoes. "I think we ought to try and git her. Anyone else showing any interest?"

"Not yet, but I reckon we'll find out once the biddin' starts."

As if on cue the auctioneer announces that the bidding will begin in a few minutes and asks everyone who hasn't done so already to register and pick up a bidding card. The brothers agree that John'll take care of that while Max keeps a watchful eye on the Virtue bell.

"Hmm, a Virtue bell," Max whispers to himself. "Always did want one of those." He gently runs his hand across the exterior of the bell, feeling its curvature and the rough texture of its surface from years of weather and use. As he pulls his hand away, for the second time that day, he hears and feels a faint, breathy vibration, barely a sound … *"Yours …"* And, then it's gone.

Max has a bewildered look on his face as John reappears holding their bidding card. "What?!" he asks Max. "From that goofy look you're sportin' I swear you look like you got hit by lightnin' again. You sure you're okay, brother?"

"Huh, oh yeah, I'm fine," Max fibs. "I think maybe my sugar diabetes is catching up with me again. C'mon, I think the auction is about to start."

During the course of the next several minutes, the auctioneer begins at one end of the auction barn and goes, item by item, the length of one row of tables. He takes a brief break to allow people to pay for and retrieve their items. When he starts on the final row of tables, many folks have already gone home with their winnings or memories of things that got away.

"Looks like the bell is up next," John states the obvious to Max.

The auctioneer describes item number seventy-three as an old school bell made by a company in Cincinnati, Ohio. He opens the bidding at twenty dollars, and immediately there's a bid from the back of the barn. Max and John turn to see who it is and notice that it's their neighbor down the road, young Ansel Smith.

"Well, I guess we know who our competition is," Max asserts. He promptly offers a bid of twenty-five dollars which is swiftly met by a counter bid by Mr. Smith of thirty dollars. Over the course of the next few minutes Max Kindred and Ansel Smith go back and forth until the bidding is at seventy-five dollars, a lot of money for an old school bell in those days.

"I don't know, Max, that's more money than we're accustomed to paying for an old bell. Are you sure you really want it?"

"Damn straight I want it, brother, and I aim to get it."

Ansel raises his bidder card again when the auctioneer announces an increase to eighty-five dollars, and John looks anxiously at his brother to see how he'll respond.

"One hundred dollars!" Max shouts out to everyone's surprise, including his brother, John, who is now staring at the ground shaking his head.

"One twenty!" Ansel counters in response, and then there's silence while the auctioneer allows Max or any other bidder to raise the amount. Max remains silent to his brother's relief, and the auctioneer states, "One hundred and twenty dollars going once, going twice," and then Max shouts out defiantly, "Two hundred dollars!"

Those left in attendance murmur among themselves and turn their eyes expectantly to Ansel

Smith. Young Ansel looks over at Max, thinks momentarily, and then finally shakes his head in defeat.

"Sold to Mr. Max Kindred!" the auctioneer declares, and the few people left in the auction barn whoop and holler as Max grins victoriously.

"Well, now I know for sure you got hit by lightnin', brother! I hope you brought enough cash to pay for that!"

Max ignores his brother's snarky comment and question. "C'mon, John, let's see if we can snooker someone into helping us load the ol' Virtue into our truck."

The drive back to their farm is somewhat subdued. John stares intently at the road as he drives and occasionally looks over at his brother who has a look of proud satisfaction etched on his face. Up ahead they see Ansel Smith turn into his property on State Route 42. To his credit Ansel offers a friendly wave of concession as the Kindred brothers motor past. Max reaches over to the steering column and toots the pickup's horn in a respectful reply.

A few minutes later John turns into their gravel driveway and asks his brother, "Okay, Mr.

Moneybags, where do you want to put our new, very expensive acquisition?"

"How 'bout from that heavy ship's chain hanging from the big oak tree in the front yard?" And, after several minutes of sweatin', gruntin', and cursin', the Virtue bell is securely in place.

Later that evening after John has already turned in, Max walks outside to enjoy the crisp air and admire his new bell. The earlier rains have moved off to the north and the night sky reveals a pale crescent moon and a panoply of stars.

Max approaches the Virtue bell hanging from the huge tree limb at about the same height as his head. He proudly examines his acquisition, knowing in his heart of hearts that he did the right thing buying it. He leans his face closely toward it to see the maker's mark again and is greeted by yet another breathy vibration as he gently swings the Virtue's clapper. A verbal resonance settles deep within his very being, *"Home."*

Chapter 1

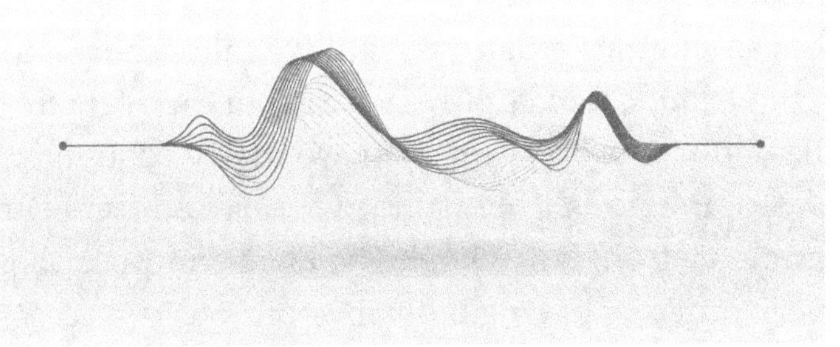

Putnam County, Indiana

Spring, 1946

THE WAR WITH GERMANY AND Japan is finally over, and it's a peaceful Sunday morning in Greencastle, Indiana. Many folks have gathered for services at their houses of worship, but Delano and Caroline Engel have chosen to remain at home to enjoy some rare quiet moments in their busy lives.

They sip from their coffee cups on the patio of their lovely Victorian-era home at the end of Carriage House Lane sequestered from the din of the world. They've lived here for over twenty-five years now and still marvel at the subtle grandness of their house and the verdant tranquility of their property.

Delano and Caroline are each in their late forties now and proud of their wonderful daughter, Aurora, who is in her midtwenties and a recent graduate from law school. The Engel family is also very proud of having built an enormously successful business from scratch.

Engel Air Corporation, which the Engels began in 1920 after Delano returned home from WWI, became a vital supplier of airplane parts and munitions for the U.S. government's war effort in Europe and the Pacific. As a result, Engel Air reaped huge financial profits during World War II which made them among the wealthiest families in the Midwest.

Along the way, they each have taken leadership roles in improving the lives of their neighbors and friends by organizing and supporting civic and charitable organizations that touch nearly everyone's life in their community. You name it, new initiatives have sprung up to meet basic human needs with jobs and small businesses, and housing, healthcare, and education. Moreover, the quality of life has been enhanced with new parks and infrastructure, an expanded county fairgrounds and animal shelter, music and art programs, a new museum, and closer town-and-gown ties with Asbury College.

Emerging from the struggles of WWII, little Greencastle is developing into a world-class town, and despite the Engels' resistance to attention and accolades, everyone knows that the supportive investments and philanthropy from Delano and Caroline are making their community shine as it never has before. It's the beginning of what promises to be a golden age for Putnam County, Indiana.

Caroline pours them each another cup of coffee, and they enjoy fresh scones and berries that she'd picked up at a trendy new restaurant on the square named Almost Heaven. With spring planting on her mind, she flips through the new seed catalog from Fox's Plant Farm, while Delano reads the news and stock market quotations from Friday's *Wall Street Journal*.

"What're you reading about?" Caroline asks as she flips another catalog page.

"Oh, you know, news about Europe. A lot of rebuilding needs to be done, not to mention the resettlement of millions of people. With the defeat of Germany, we're just now starting to get reports of the atrocities the Nazis forced upon people across the continent, and now there's serious talk of another major conflict on the Korean Peninsula. I swear, Caroline, I just don't know if we as a species ever learn anything from the horrors of war."

Caroline takes his hand and softly whispers, "I know, darling, it's awful. Do you ever have misgivings about the role our company played in the war effort?"

"Absolutely, every day. The thought of weaponry that we produced killing people, combatants and civilians alike, is not something that I'm happy about. On the other hand, if we hadn't been actively involved, I shudder to think what would've happened if Germany had won and Japan's hegemony grew in Asia. Not pretty thoughts. And now we've got to contend with Russia and China's emergence onto the world stage. There aren't any easy answers. Aside from the role of our business and others like us, the only thing that saved America from even worse conflagration was three thousand miles of ocean separating us. But even then, the Japanese attack on Pearl Harbor showed us that our geography can't necessarily save us. Like I said, 'there aren't any easy answers,' and I haven't even mentioned the terrifying nuclear thing."

"Well, that wasn't the answer I was expecting, but I understand, Del. With the exception of some big bumps and scrapes along the way, we've certainly been very fortunate to be in a position to be helpful during the war … and now."

"Yeah, and being helpful is what I want our family's legacy to be. In fact, I've been thinking about our doing even more, and that's something I want to discuss with you and Aurora when she comes home. Any idea when she'll return from vacation after passing the bar exam? And, do you think that she and what's-his-name are very serious about each other?"

"She returns home soon, and you know very well that his name is Benjamin, and yes, I think they're very serious about each other, so you might as well stop being snarky and remember his name."

They both peer at each other over their newspaper and catalog and offer the other warm smiles. "Besides, it would be nice to hear the patter of little feet around here. It's been a very long time," Caroline adds.

Delano nods his head affirmatively and smiles. "Yeah, that would be nice." They both look over at their carriage house about fifty yards away. "Remember when we had that set up as a play room for Aurora when she was little? And now, it's her own house. Hard to believe how much time has gone by."

Caroline comes over and sits on the bench beside Delano, and they look around their property at the gardens and trees that they've planted. A few pieces of stone sculpture stand as silent sentinels here and there, including an angel with a wing pointing up. Simultaneously, they lift their gazes to the house's roofline and the tower room that played such a pivotal role in their lives when they first moved here in 1920.

"Ever think about the Book of Tamberg?" Caroline asks her husband.

"How can I not?! Most every day," he freely admits. "At this point in our lives it seems like a distant dream and a nightmare all wrapped up in one huge conundrum. How about you?"

"Most every day," she repeats, "And, ya know, we've never spoken with Aurora, or anyone else for the matter, about the book's magical powers, and how we nearly lost Aurora to those weirdos when she was an infant."

"Yeah, at age twenty-six I suppose she's adult enough now to hear the truth, but I'm not overly anxious to relive those days. How about you, darling?"

"We probably should, Del. Keeping secrets is burdensome, and it was a crucial time in all of our lives. I often wonder if the magical book will ever reappear and under what circumstances. I still shake my head in bewilderment."

"Yeah, me too," are the only words that come from Delano's mouth.

After a few moments of silence, Delano stands and starts collecting their coffee cups and utensils to take inside. Caroline looks at Delano and smiles as she watches her very accomplished husband doing the most basic of domestic chores.

"Wanna take the plane up for a ride?" she encourages. "The day is young and the sky's blue. We can buzz this place again like we did with the ol' Curtiss Jenny the first time we laid eyes on it." She gives Delano that winning smile that he's never been able to say no to.

"Okay, you talked me into it. I've been wanting to get my hands back on the controls of my new plane anyway. Just been too darn busy of late. Let's get some things put away, and I'll call Bryan at the airport and ask him to get the Spartan Executive fueled up and ready to go."

A few minutes later Delano walks outside and sees Caroline already sitting behind the wheel of her 1941 Ford Woody station wagon with the engine running. "I was wondering where you were. I should've known you'd prefer to drive the Woody."

"Climb on in, Mr. Engel, my Woody might look like a delivery vehicle, but it's got a lot of heart. You mark my words, sir, this car will be a valuable classic in a few decades."

"Probably true, if it's still around, but I think you just like to drive it because it's fun and you can haul a lot of plants in it." Delano settles into the passenger seat, and Caroline stomps on the accelerator the moment his door closes. "Oh, and because it's fast too!" Delano shouts above the roar of the engine.

"Woohoooo!!!"

"Actually, I'm really glad we're driving to the airport. I'm curious to see what progress is being made with the new Veterans Highway. The mayor and I have been leaning on some of the state and federal transportation people to help improve our roads and bridges, and I think we're starting to see some results … and that's just the beginning."

"Anyway, pardon my going on and on about this, but it's very encouraging to see progress on a number of fronts because it'll make a huge difference in attracting families, businesses, and even new members of faculty to the college."

They drive into the heart of Greencastle at the courthouse, and Caroline points out some of the beautification projects she and her fellow volunteers have been working on.

"See, Del! Look at the new street lights that are going up, and the expanded green space around the courthouse. Plus, we've gotten matching funds from the government to help business owners around the square freshen up the facades of their buildings. Lots of power washing and tuck pointing the old brick store fronts and coats of bright, new paint. This summer we'll also be seeing cascades of flowers from window boxes that will adorn all the buildings. And, like you said, 'that's just the beginning'!"

As they exit the courthouse square, they hear the bell in the clock tower peal ten sonorous times announcing the hour and then they head east along Indianapolis Road, passing the new Inspire gift shop and Hadley's hardware store. From that point there's only corn and soybean fields until they see the Putnam County airport just up ahead.

"Remember how small this airport was when we first started flying the Curtiss Jenny back in the day? Couldn't really even call it an airport. It was basically a grass airfield with a couple of hangars and sheds. Now, we have a real terminal, concrete runways with landing lights, a radio tower, plus a restaurant and hotel accommodations. Before long we'll be expanding the length of the runways because of the jet-propelled aircraft that are quickly becoming the new standard of commercial aviation. We may even add a small jet to Engel Air's little fleet before too long."

Caroline pulls her Ford Woody up to their original hangar, and they see the airport manager, Bryan Hilton, emerge to greet them wiping his hands on an oily rag.

"What're working on, Bryan?"

"Oh, just trying to keep the ol' Jenny in tiptop shape, Del. She's a relic, but I think she still has plenty of flying hours left in her. So, I've got both the Jenny and the Spartan fueled and ready to go in case you wanted to change your mind."

"Your choice, Caroline. We can fly whichever one you want, dear."

"Let's take the Jenny, Del. It's such a beautiful day, and even with the open cockpits, I think we should be warm enough up there." They slip on their coveralls and goggles and climb aboard the Jenny with Caroline in the front cockpit and Delano behind her handling the controls.

Bryan gives the propeller a couple of hardy yanks, and the old Curtiss Jenny's engine roars to life. He removes the wooden blocks by the wheels and gives the Engels a thumbs-up sign indicating they're clear for takeoff.

A few moments later it's wheels-up, and Caroline yells her customary "Woohoo!" as they leave terra firma for the firmament.

Delano brings the Jenny to a cruising altitude of two thousand feet and guides the old plane in a westerly direction back toward town. He sees two other aircraft on the horizon, one heading toward Indianapolis and the other probably going toward Lafayette or Chicago, but aside from them, the skies are clear of any traffic.

With a top cruising speed of ninety miles per hour, they're flying slowly enough to make out familiar landmarks. Delano descends to about a thousand feet and buzzes the campus at Asbury College and downtown Greencastle before heading a little west toward their home. When they arrive Caroline makes a circular pattern with her finger indicating that she wants Delano to circle it a couple of times. He does as she requests, and just like twenty-five years ago their house's roof tower extends high above the surrounding trees and a bright golden sunbeam reflects off the tower's window panes. Caroline turns and looks at Delano who understands that she's thinking the same thing he is: Has the magical Book of Tamberg returned to the hidden tower room in their attic? Delano shrugs at her as if to reply, "maybe … maybe not."

After circling their house a final time, Delano veers the Jenny to the south using U.S. Route 231 as their flight line. They pass over the small town of Cloverdale and then turn east following State Route 42. They fly over the Vann family farm scattering livestock and continue over the Mill Creek. A moment later they're flying over a small farm when all of a sudden the needles on Jenny's gauges go haywire and begin acting very erratically. Thinking that some weird, errant radio signals might be affecting them, Delano drops to within two hundred feet of a secluded farm and is stunned by the cacophonous sounds of scores of loud ringing bells. He circles the Jenny to see if he can shake the interference with the gauges when the old plane's engine totally quits leaving the Engels' aircraft gliding without power. Caroline looks back at Delano and sees that he's struggling to control their rapid descent while looking for a safe place to land their plane. "Dammit!" he shouts.

The ringing of the bells grows louder the closer they get to the ground, but Delano manages to find a fallow field where he finally sets the Jenny down near the farm's old house. It's only when the Engels exit their cockpits and stand unhurt beside their plane that the ringing of the bells abruptly ceases.

Chapter 2

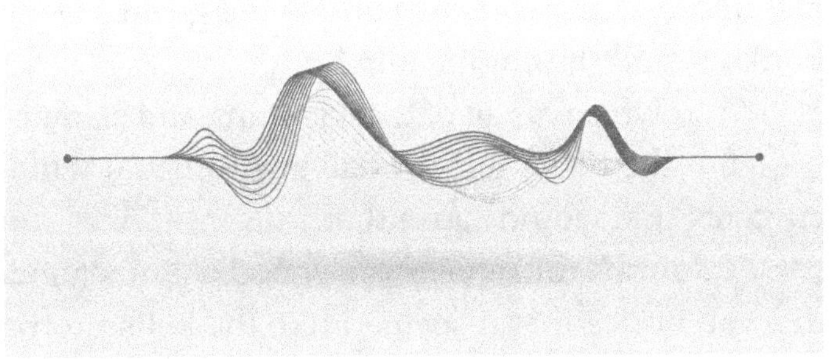

"WHEW! THAT WAS CLOSE!" He exhales as Caroline wraps him in a big hug. "Are you okay, dear?" Delano asks.

"Yeah, aside from damn near wetting my coveralls, I think I'm okay. That was some mighty fine flying you did, Del, but I'd prefer that we not make a habit of landing like that."

"I'll second that!" They take a few minutes to examine the Curtiss Jenny and find that it's in reasonably good shape with the exception of a few minor dents and scrapes.

"Any idea what happened up there, Del?"

"Not really. One minute we're cruising along just fine, and then all of a sudden the gauges went bonkers, and the engine quit."

"And what was all of that clanging and clamoring with the bells? I didn't feel any unusual wind currents that would cause that."

"I dunno. Your guess is as good as mine, and did you notice that it seemed like the bells pretty much stopped ringing the moment we set down?"

"Strange, huh?! And here I was hoping that our lives were finished with spooky stuff happening."

"C'mon, honey, let's see if anyone's home at the farmhouse. Maybe we can call Bryan and have him come get us with the trailer."

They walk about a hundred yards and enter the front yard of a modest wooden-frame farmhouse. The name on the mailbox reads Kindred, and from where they're standing, they can see scores of old cast iron and bronze bells hanging everywhere.

"Hello the house! Anyone home?" Delano calls out. They walk up on the front porch, and

Caroline raps her knuckles on the weathered door frame. "Hello!" she repeats and knocks a couple more times.

They wait a few silent moments and then turn to leave when they hear a voice from within. "Hold your horses, I'm comin'."

They look at the screen door and see a grizzled, whiskered face staring back at them. "I ain't interested in whatever you're selling, so you might as well skedaddle on out of here."

"We're very sorry to intrude, sir, but we had to make an emergency landing with our plane in your field," Caroline states in a clear, friendly voice. "We were hoping to perhaps use your phone and call for some assistance."

"What plane? Where?"

"Over there in your field, sir." Caroline says as she points in that direction.

"Well, I'll be darned. Now, that's not sumthin I see every day."

"Sir, we're very sorry to intrude," Delano repeats, "but we'd be much obliged if we could use your phone and call for assistance. We'll be happy to compensate you for your trouble, if that's an issue."

The older man steps out onto the porch to size up his visitors a little more and get a better view of the plane. "Well, hell's bells, that's not a plane. That's a damn antique. No wonder you fell out of the sky."

Both Delano and Caroline smile a bit as they size up the old man as well. He looks to be in his eighties and is wearing bib overalls with a red bandana tied around his neck. His face is suntanned, ostensibly from working outdoors a lot, and he has several days of whiskers populating his face.

"My name's Delano Engel, and this is my wife, Caroline. I take it from the name on the mailbox that you're Mr. Kindred. Am I correct?"

"Yeah, that's right. Max Kindred. You look kinda familiar to me. Do I know you?"

"I don't believe we've ever had the pleasure before, Mr. Kindred, but it's very nice to meet you now," Caroline says sweetly.

Max gives them a small smile and a bit of friendliness comes into his voice.

"Yeah, I'll be happy to let you use the phone, and pardon my grumpiness. I'm not used to people stopping by unannounced unless they're trying to sell me stuff I don't need or want. C'mon inside and pardon the mess. The phone's in the kitchen."

They step inside and see the cluttered interior of a home that they'd expect to see for an elderly man living in the middle of nowhere. "Phone's over there."

While Caroline and Max sit in the parlor, Delano places a call to the airport, and Bryan answers on the fourth ring. "What's up, boss?!"

"We ran into a bit of a problem, Bryan, the Jenny's engine all of a sudden crapped out on us, and we had to land it in the middle of a field."

"Are you and Caroline okay?"

"Yeah, we're fine, and the Jenny appears to be no worse for the wear and tear, but we could sure use your help with a trailer and a ride back to the airport."

Delano calls out to Max to get his address and directions from Greencastle which he shares with Bryan.

"Give me about forty-five minutes, and I'll come get ya. I'm just glad you're safe."

"Yeah, sounds good. Here's the telephone number in case you need to get back to me." They hang up, and Delano joins Max and Caroline in the parlor.

"Bryan'll be here before too long," he tells Caroline.

"Do you mind if we go back outside, Mr. Kindred? I caught a glimpse of some of your bells, and I'd like to hear a little about them if you don't mind putting up with us a bit more."

Max brightens at the thought that these folks are interested in his bell collection. "Sure, that'd be fine, young fella. You and the missus are welcome to take a gander at my 'ringers'."

Max leads them outside, and they step off the porch. There are bells hanging everywhere, along with huge ships' chains and very old farm implements.

As they walk Caroline inquires, "Do you mind if I ask if you live here by yourself, Mr. Kindred?"

"Please call me Max. Mr. Kindred sounds awfully stuffy to me, and yessum, I've been on my own here ever since my younger brother, John, passed away about five years ago now." He stares at the ground, and it's clear to Caroline that Max is a lonely old man.

"Neither John nor I ever married. We inherited this land from our parents and lived here together and worked the fields all of our lives. Collecting bells was just something that got into our blood, and as you can see we got a little carried away over the years. Got pert near three hundred of 'em!" He gives a hoarse laugh and then a look of sadness comes across his face. "Yeah, John loved 'em as much as I do."

Caroline and Delano are very patient as Max gives them a tour of some of his favorite bells. Some thirty minutes later they're standing by a huge oak tree in the front yard. Caroline sees a beautiful school bell hanging from one of the tree's stout limbs. "What about this one, Max? What's its history?"

"Oh, you've got great taste, young lady, that school bell was made by the Virtue Bell Company in Cincinnati, Ohio. John and I picked that gem up at an estate auction in Cloverdale about ten years ago. John always thought I was nuts, but I swear that bell talks to me sometimes. John thought I'd been hit by lightning or something, but I swear it does communicate with me at times. Hard to explain."

"Believe me, Max, I think we understand. We had an old book once that used to do that with us." Caroline and Delano give each other a brief, private glance.

Max offers another hoarse laugh. "Well, sounds to me like you two may have been hit by lightnin' too." His laugh turns into a cough, and he wipes his mouth with his red bandana.

About that time they hear a rumbling coming down County Line Road, and Bryan pulls up with the airport's truck and a trailer.

"Bryan, say hello to Max. He's been kind enough to help us out and show us around his property while we've been waiting for you."

"Nice to meet you, Max, I'm Bryan Hilton, and I manage the airport in Greencastle. So where'd you land the Jenny, Del?"

"Right over there," Delano replies as he points in the direction of the field across the road.

"Oh boy, let's go see what we can do about getting it out."

"If you need my tractor, just holler, folks," Max offers.

"Thanks, sir, but the soil seems firm, and I think I can probably get my rig over there, but please stand by just in case, okay?"

The three of them walk over to the field while Bryan negotiates the terrain and gets the trailer situated by the Jenny.

"Think it'll start, Del? If so, we can probably just drive it onto the bed of the trailer."

"I doubt it, but let's give it a try."

Delano puts his coveralls back on and climbs into the cockpit. He turns on the magneto, and Bryan gives the propeller a strong yank. Lo and behold, the Jenny's engine roars to life.

"Well, looky there!" Max shouts. "That old antique still has some life left in her."

From the cockpit Delano shouts above the thrum of the engine. "Caroline, why don't you ride back with Bryan? I want to fly the Jenny back to the airport. She seems fine now."

"Are you sure, Del?" she voices with concern.

"Yeah, I'm sure! Just because something's old, we don't want to lose faith in it, right, Max?!

"Right as rain, young fella!"

"We can't thank you enough, Max. It's been a pleasure getting to know you, and to see your wonderful collection. I hope you don't mind if we bring our daughter, Aurora, over here sometime. I'm sure she'd enjoy one of your private tours."

"Anytime, sir, anytime."

Bryan and Caroline say goodbye to Max and drive off with the empty trailer. Delano lets the engine have a little more time to warm up, and he checks the cables, wings, and gauges. He puts his goggles on and gives Max a final wave before moving the throttle steadily forward and picking up speed. The Jenny rumbles along the dry field, kicking clods of dirt hither and yon, and the old plane lifts off into the warm spring air. Delano looks around, gets his bearings, and points her back north toward the Putnam County Airport.

As Max watches Delano rise further in the sky, the clapper on the old Virtue school bell begins to sway rhythmically creating a series of strong, lively tones and vibrations. Other bells begin to ring in unison, as if offering affirmation to the Virtue bell's spirited voice.

Max turns to face the bell and lightly places his hands on its patinated surface. "Yup, I reckon we all agree, old friend, the Engel family could be ideal companions for you … and very appreciative of your sage wisdom."

Chapter 3

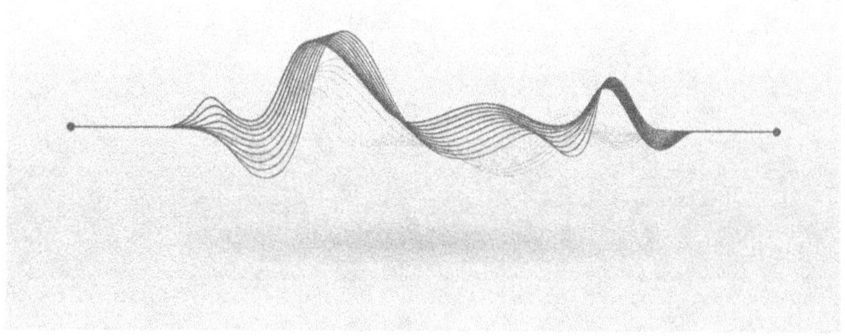

AURORA ENGEL CRUISES SOUTH along U.S. Route 231 in her yellow Lincoln Continental convertible. She's heading home after spending eight days on a well-earned vacation in Silver Lake, Wisconsin, with her charming fiancé, Benjamin Witt. Both have recently graduated near the top of their class at Northwestern's prestigious law school, and each is considering offers of employment from major law firms. The world is their oyster, as the saying goes.

Aurora's golden hair waves in the breeze as she motors along garnering admiring glances from other drivers. From time to time she changes radio stations looking for lively music by some of her favorite stars, Frank Sinatra, Bing Crosby, and Ella Fitzgerald. As she enters Putnam County she reduces her speed looking out for cops and slow-moving farm vehicles. But more than anything, she can barely take her eyes off of the stunning diamond engagement ring Ben gave her when he proposed the night before.

It's been many weeks since Aurora's been home. Between law school classes, taking the bar exam, and enjoying Chicagoland with Ben, she's been a very busy lady. And now, she and Ben need to decide about wedding plans and where they want to live and work after they're married. Very adult decisions!

Trouble is, she loves living in Greencastle, but she isn't sure if Ben can slow down his lifestyle living in a small town, and if he can feel fulfilled practicing law here. After all, he grew up in a tony part of Naperville, Illinois, and after earning his BA degree in Global Affairs from Yale, he spent two years working for the U.S. State Department in England and Belgium where he rubbed shoulders with diplomats from all over the world. And then, he decided to go to law school where he met bright, witty, and beautiful Aurora Engel, and his priorities got turned upside down.

Aurora smiles then sighs a little thinking about all of the changes coming her way. She continues on U.S. Route 231 and accelerates after she passes Detro's trailer lot, anxious to get home. She can't wait to see her folks and share the great news with them about Ben. When they parted company at Silver Lake, she and Ben agreed that he'd come to Greencastle in a few days to get better acquainted with her folks and talk about their future plans.

Aurora turns up the radio when Ella Fitzgerald starts singing a Cole Porter tune and zooms past the Wagoner Tree Farm sign. She reduces her speed as she drives down Waterworks Hill and crosses over Big Walnut Creek. She can't help but smile when she sees the Putnam County Fairgrounds on her left, remembering many summers of fun and a little teenage romance.

Two minutes later she drives past the glass-domed Putnam County courthouse, and two minutes after that she turns onto Carriage House Lane and sees the grand Victorian house where she grew up and the attractive red carriage house that's been her personal space whenever she's returned home from school.

"Aurora! You're home!" Caroline shouts as she and Delano stop what they're doing and hurry over to meet her by the carriage house. All three embrace at the same time, and then her parents help her unload her luggage and carry it inside the carriage house.

Aurora stretches her arms out wide and spins around in the center of the room. "It's so great to be home! I've missed you guys so much!"

"Well, it seems like forever since you've been home, sweetie, even though it's only been a couple of months," Caroline says. "We sure hope you can stay for longer than just a few days."

"I know, I know! There's a lot to catch up on, and yes, I plan on staying for a little while, and I've asked Ben to come down in a couple of days too."

"Oh! That'll be wonderful," Delano says as he shoots Caroline a quick glance. "Why don't you put some things away and then come join us up at the house for some refreshments? C'mon Caroline, let's give her a little space, and then we'll catch up, okay?"

They exit the carriage house, and Aurora starts unpacking her belongings, and then sits down on the edge of her bed. Unexpectedly, tears come to her eyes as she examines the interior of the carriage house as a myriad of memories of playing here as a child come flooding back to her.

"I love this place so much," she murmurs to herself. She looks from one corner of the large open room to another and then up to the loft. She wipes the tears away and smiles, thinking what a magical life she's lived so far, with parents who are about as great as anyone could hope for, and a home as grand as anyone might want. She looks at her engagement ring and a tear drops from her eye onto the shiny gemstone. "And now, my special Ben ..."

Aurora finishes placing her belongings away in the bathroom, and in drawers and closets, then gives her carriage house another admiring glance. She opens the door to leave and sees a golden light emanating from her parents' attic. Then, a rush of wind greets her as she steps outside. Like a barely discernible voice, almost like a whisper, she hears a most unusual sound in the wind, *"Bring it home …"* and then the breathy sound is gone.

She looks around thinking that perhaps someone is in the yard, but seeing no one and not hearing any further sound other than the wind, she shrugs and walks off to join her parents. As she crosses the yard the golden light from the house's roof tower illuminates her way as if welcoming her home … and beckoning her to an unknown future.

She walks inside and sees her mom in the kitchen preparing a large veggie and cheese tray, along with a selection of premium California wines.

"I bet you're starved after your long drive," Caroline offers. "Your dad's on the phone with a good friend of ours who's running for office as a state representative. He'll be along shortly."

"Yeah, that looks tasty! I stopped for a light lunch in Merrillville, but I could definitely eat more.

So, what's new with you and Dad? Busy as ever, I presume."

"Yeah, you know your dad. He's always got a couple of projects that he's juggling, and there's always someone who wants to float a business idea by him, or a well-meaning friend who has an idea to make Greencastle even better. It's the price he pays for being successful and approachable."

"Well, if I'm correct, Mom, you're no slouch when it comes to that either, ya know! I think you two are a major reason I went to law school. I want to fight the good fight for those who deserve it."

"Ah! There you are!" Delano says warmly as he joins mother and daughter in the kitchen. "Got everything squared away in the carriage house, Aurora?"

"Yep!" she chirps as she gives her pop a warm hug. "So who were you on the phone with?"

"Our good friend, Suzette Crosley. She's running for office in the statehouse, and your mom and I respect her and her husband, Jeb, a great deal. She wanted to share some thoughts with me about her campaign platform. We're supporting her campaign financially, and I think she can really make a huge difference in improving peoples' lives across the state. She's pretty progressive which your mom and I both respect, and now that the war's over, there's a lot of rebuilding that we can and need to do. Suzette's got the right mindset for moving Indiana forward."

"She sounds like my kind of woman. I look forward to meeting her along the way."

"No doubt you will, and Jeb's a rock-solid guy. She's darn lucky to have him by her side. He's a hardworking farmer and quiet, but like they say, still waters run deep. Plus, he's built his own plane which you know grabs my interest and respect. But, enough of that for now, let's grab something to snack on, and we want to hear about what you've been up to."

"Well, a lot actually. You know I passed the bar exam, thank goodness, and I've been trying to figure out my next steps."

At that point Aurora reaches her hand toward the veggie tray, and Caroline begins to choke on her sip of wine as she spies the glitter coming from Aurora's left ring finger. "You're engaged!" she blurts out. "Delano, our baby's engaged! Why didn't you tell us, you scamp?!" She grabs Aurora in a huge hug and reaches out for Delano to join them.

"Well, Ben and I got engaged just last night, and I wanted to tell you in person, so yeah, we're getting married."

"We're thrilled for you, darling," Delano says, "But, are you sure you're old enough? In my mind you're still like sixteen years old," he teases.

"Yeah, I'm sure, Dad, and you'll love Ben once you get to know him. He's wonderful, and I love him! He's coming here in a few days so we can all get to know each other."

"Oh, Aurora, we're so happy for you, and we can't wait to finally get to know your special guy."

Delano is a little quiet considering the ramifications of their baby girl getting married.

"And Dad, please be nice to Ben. He's a very accomplished guy, and I'm sure he'll be a little nervous meeting the famous Delano Engel."

"Of course, I'll be nice to him, and I'm glad he'll be a little nervous too! Boy, do I need to come up with a list of questions for him!" he jests. "Perhaps, I should treat this like a job interview!"

"Dad!!!" Aurora pleads.

"Trust me, Aurora," Caroline consoles, "Your father will be on his very best behavior, won't you, Del?!"

"Of course, darling." He winks at Aurora, and she hugs him again!

From his apartment high above the Chicago River, Ben Witt stands at his picture window admiring his panoramic view of Lake Michigan and miles of expensive glass and steel edifices as far as the eye can see.

At this point in his life, he's a very happy guy. He's got his juris doctor degree from a prestigious law school and a beautiful woman that he's nuts about. On top of that he's had excellent work experience and made some important international contacts during his time with the State Department. Life's good!

A few moments later his telephone rings, and he sets down his binoculars to answer it. "Hello," he says melodiously.

"So what're you doing? Thinking about me, huh?!" he hears Aurora's voice tease.

"Of course I'm thinking about you, darling. What else could I possibly be doing?" he tosses back at her.

"I told Mother and Dad about us being engaged, and they're thrilled for us. I told them you'd be coming down to Greencastle soon, and they're excited about meeting their future son-in-law."

"Cool! I'm excited to meet them as well and kinda nervous at the same time."

"They asked me about meeting your parents at some point, and I shared with them that they'd died several years ago in a car accident. I hope you don't mind my telling them."

"No, of course not, Aurora, it is what it is."

"My mom said she and Dad would be more than happy to smother you with love, and I told them 'thank you very much, but that's my job!'"

"Well, it's been a while since I've been a part of a family, and from everything you've told me about your parents, it'll be exciting to feel that kind of special bond again."

The two of them chatter away for a few minutes longer, and then pick the day after tomorrow as the day he'll drive down to Greencastle.

"Can't wait to see you, Aurora. I feel like half of me is missing when we're not together. I love you, honey."

They hang up, and Ben moves back to the picture window. He smiles at his good fortune, and says out loud: "Wow! I'm getting married."

The phone rings again, and he picks up. "Let me guess, you wanted to hear me say I love you again, right?"

"Uh, Mr. Witt, this is General Wendell Grossman from NATO Command calling. Perhaps you'll recall our meeting a couple of years ago in Brussels. I'd like to schedule some time with you to discuss something sensitive. Are you available tomorrow, say around 10:00 AM?"

Chapter 4

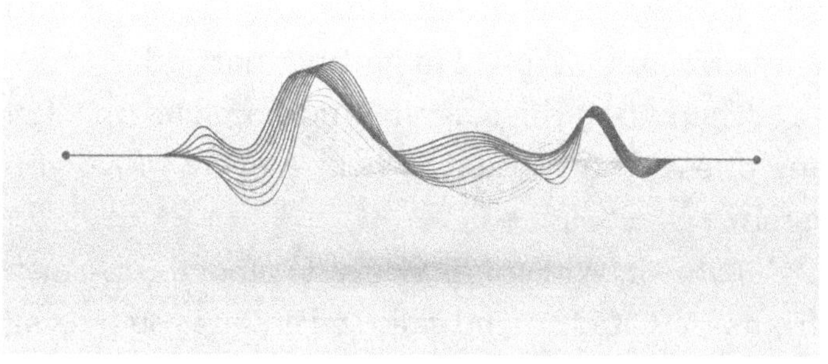

TWO DAYS LATER BEN follows the same route to Greencastle that Aurora had taken home from Silver Lake. The traffic through Chicago isn't awful, but it isn't great either. He's read that President Truman is pushing hard for Congress to fund an interstate highway system, but for now Ben has to contend with two-lane state roads connecting a myriad of small Indiana towns. He's relieved when he finally reaches Lafayette and can make up time on U.S. Route 231. Ninety minutes later he enters Greencastle and drives past the courthouse to Walnut Street. He hangs a right and goes about a mile until he spots the sign for Carriage House Lane. A hundred yards down the lane he sees the Engels' home set amid a lovely grove of ash trees. He pulls his Studebaker coupe into the driveway near the red carriage house, and Aurora comes running out to greet him and jumps into his arms.

"You made it!" she states the obvious and plants a big kiss on her fiancé. From their parlor window Caroline and Delano get their first glimpse of their future son-in-law, and Caroline leans sweetly against Delano, happy that their daughter's in love. "He's a very nice looking young man, Del." Light brown, wavy hair with a kind face and an athletic six-foot plus build.

"C'mon, Del, let's go greet our new son!" They walk across the lawn toward the carriage house, and Ben straightens up when he sees them approaching.

"Mr. and Mrs. Engel, Hi I'm Ben, it's so nice to finally meet you."

"Well, it's a pleasure to meet you as well, Ben!" Caroline replies warmly. "We've certainly been hearing a lot of glowing things about you."

Delano extends his hand to Ben. "Welcome, Ben, I'm Delano, and we're delighted that you're here. Let's drop the formality though. My wife and I would much prefer that you call us Caroline and Delano, okay?"

"Absolutely, sir! It sure looks like you have a very lovely home."

"C'mon inside the house, Ben, we've got a guest room ready for you," Caroline encourages. "You can put your belongings away and then we can grab a bite to eat and get acquainted. How's that sound?!"

"Sounds perfect, Mrs. Engel, I mean Caroline." He looks over at Aurora who is beaming like a cheshire cat. "I'll give you a hand, Mom."

As they head up to the house, a warm breeze follows them and Delano looks skyward and notices a bright, golden light emanating from a window in the roof tower. He glances over at Caroline and sees that she's observing the same ethereal thing. She looks back at him briefly but neither comments about the radiant light that they haven't seen for many years now.

Aurora shows Ben to the guest room, and once behind closed doors, she leans into him, and they enjoy a passionate lip-lock or three.

"My, my! Has somebody missed me?!" she chirps, and then she grabs him again. "You just wait until I get you alone later, Mr. Witt!"

"Ooh, I like that, Miss Engel, you randy little vixen!" They embrace again, and then she pulls away, straightening her hair and garments before returning to the kitchen to help her mom.

"Ben seems very charming, Aurora, and he's quite handsome," Caroline says.

"Yes, he's all of that, plus much more. I certainly hope that he and Dad hit it off well. Where is Dad?"

"I think he went into the library to finish writing a letter to the mayor. He's been talking with me about creating a special charitable foundation, and I think he wants the mayor's input on some local programs he may be interested in our funding."

"That sounds very cool. I know that you and Dad have already been pretty generous."

"Yeah, we've been fortunate to be in a position financially to be helpful. I know he wants to speak with you and get your advice as well."

"At some point he may want to talk with Ben too. In addition to his experience with international affairs, I know he has a special interest in working with families on their estates and creating charitable trusts. He made it a major focus when we were in law school."

"Hmm, sounds like his counsel could be very helpful, indeed, but let's have the two of them get to know each other first before making any suggestions or promises to Ben, okay?"

"I understand." Just then Ben appears in the kitchen. "Wow, you really do have a lovely home, Caroline. I imagine it has quite a colorful history. If only these walls could talk, huh?!"

"Yes, quite a history, indeed!" Caroline replies. "Some of it rather, uh, magical actually."

Just then Delano enters the kitchen. "What's magical?" Delano asks.

"You, darling!" she replies. "Ben was just commenting about the house. We can give him the twenty-five cent tour at some point, but let's enjoy some of these refreshments now. I hope it's okay with you two, but we went ahead and made a dinner reservation for tonight at Almost Heaven. I didn't want us to spend Ben's first evening here with us in the kitchen."

"Sure, that's fine, Mom, and later today I want to give Ben a tour of Greencastle."

"Yeah, I've heard Aurora speak so glowingly about her hometown. It'll be fun to see some of the places she's mentioned."

"Well, it's certainly not like Chicago or London, or Brussels, but small-town living certainly has some benefits that big cities can't claim. Of course, Caroline and I are a little prejudiced."

After enjoying their repast, Aurora and Ben climb into her Lincoln and drive down the lane and head back toward town.

"Your folks seem great, Aurora. I hope I'm making a good impression on them."

"I don't think you have to worry about that, Ben. I know them both pretty well, and I think I would've picked up on any red flags already. I'm sure they're curious about where we plan to put down roots which is something we obviously need to decide for ourselves too."

"You know, it's a big world out there with endless possibilities for us, but I must say that having lost my parents, and now having an opportunity to join another family, I'm open to just feeling our way and not ruling anything out at this point, including our living here."

"Really, Ben?!"

"Yes, really! Let's just see how things unfold, okay?"

Aurora takes his hand briefly, and they cruise along with the convertible top down. The afternoon sun is shining brightly and throws a warm glint off the glass dome of the courthouse. As they drive slowly past the square, the courthouse bell gives off a deep, resonate peal as if welcoming the young couple to an intersection of life and love and endless possibilities …

They spend the next hour or so with Aurora showing Ben where she went to elementary and high school, then a brief tour of the county fairgrounds and Dunbar covered bridge over Big Walnut Creek. They continue their drive through the lovely campus of Asbury College, past the Carnegie Library, and on to city hall.

"I'd love to take you to the airport and show you the hangars and main production facilities for

Engel Air, but I think Dad should be the person to do that. It's his baby after all."

They wind up the little tour back at the courthouse square where Aurora points out some of the law offices, clothing shops, restaurants, and other merchants.

"That's Almost Heaven where we're having dinner tonight, and a couple of doors down is our newspaper, *The Banner*. The editor is an energetic and fair-minded chap named Red Jergens. He and Mother and Dad are good friends, and I'm sure you'll get to know him before long. Certainly doesn't hurt to have a respected newspaper man on your side! And, I guess that's about it for now. Don't want to overwhelm you on the first day with all of Greencastle's major attractions," she jests.

"No, this has been great, Aurora. I can see why you're so devoted to your hometown. Seriously, I'm really enjoying this!"

She gives his hand another gentle squeeze and turns the Lincoln onto Walnut Street. A few moments later they're back at the carriage house, and in the distance they can hear the courthouse bell officiously ringing the hour.

Dining at Almost Heaven has become a very pleasant culinary experience ever since the owner, Gwen, expanded the menu and the seating capacity after the war ended. With servicemen returning home with a few more bucks in their pockets and the economy picking up, a larger restaurant has been a welcome change, and Gwen has been keen to capitalize on the additional patronage.

"Well, if it isn't some of my very favorite people in the whole world," Gwen coos as she welcomes Ben and the Engel family. "Aurora, it's been entirely too long since I last saw you. You're all grown up and looking terrific, and who is this fine gent? I'm sure he's not from around these parts because I'd definitely remember this handsome hunk."

"Gwen, this is my fiancé, Ben Witt. It's his first time to Greencastle, so my parents and I wanted to be sure we brought him to the finest dining establishment in town."

"Ben, welcome! It's a pleasure to meet you, and you're marrying in to a mighty fine family."

"Thanks! I know, and it's a pleasure to meet you, too."

"Caroline and Delano, it's always great to see you! Why don't you follow me? We've got your favorite table waiting for you."

Caroline and Delano exchange a few more pleasantries with Gwen as she leads them over to an attractive table by the window.

"Enjoy your dinner, folks, and please let me know if there's anything you need."

The meal is excellent, and the foursome settle in with frank conversations about Ben's interests, both professionally and personally. He talks about what led him to decide to go to law school after working for the State Department and his interest in hanging his own shingle as an attorney instead of going to work for a very large, cutthroat law firm. Privately, Delano admires his entrepreneurial spirit and his interest in doing things his way rather than chasing some other peoples' concepts of the brass ring.

"So, what was it like working for the State Department?" Caroline asks. "Seems to me like it would be fascinating work."

"Yes, it was, and it is, and while the international experience looks great on my resume, there were some self-serving people trying to get ahead at all costs, both on the American side and other countries too. I honestly didn't find that behavior very appealing. The Russians, in particular, were especially assertive when it came to trying to influence decisions and curry favor. Their aggressiveness frankly unnerves me, and I decided I didn't want to constantly feel like I had to defend against being threatened, blackmailed, or bought. Yeah, so I decided that a career as a diplomat on the world stage wasn't as appealing as I once thought."

"I don't think I ever heard you describe it that way, Ben. I'm really sorry it was such a conflict for you." Aurora consoles.

"It's okay. It's in the past. I have other more important interests now," he says as he holds Aurora's hand.

Delano listens carefully to what Ben is saying, and his respect and appreciation for the young man grows.

"And, what about practicing law?" Delano asks.

"Yeah, I love the law. In its purest form it's a magnificent tool for protecting the rights of the many as well as the few. I don't want to be a litigator because of all the constant conflict, and as I said I'm really not attracted by working in a large firm. Sure, the money could be huge, but I think that if I'm good at what I do for my clients, then I can do good and do well at the same time. So, in law school I found myself leaning toward estate work and helping nonprofits organize and succeed. I had an adjunct law professor at Northwestern named Daniel Joseph, and the man was brilliant and established a very fine career doing estate and nonprofit work. I think I admired him more than any of the other professors because he genuinely seemed to love what he was doing. So, that's what I think about when I think about practicing law, and I believe I could do that no matter where I live."

Delano and Caroline look at each other with ever-rising interest in their future son-in-law.

"And … what have the two of you decided about a wedding?" Caroline asks with excitement in her voice. "Obviously, we'll be happy to pay for whatever you choose to do."

Aurora and Ben look at each other and blush a little. "I don't know, Mom, since we just got engaged. Ben, do you have anything in mind for a ceremony and reception?"

"Yes, I do! I want whatever will make you happy, sweetheart! I know that sounds like I'm being casual about the wedding, but I'm very serious when I say that."

"Smart man!" Delano jests. "No wonder you did so well at the State Department and law school. C'mon, let's pay the check and go home and have a nightcap. There are some things Caroline and I would like to discuss with you." Delano catches Gwen's eye and motions for the check. While waiting for her to return, Delano feels a light tap on his shoulder. He turns to see Red Jergens, the editor of *The Banner* newspaper smiling broadly.

"Hey Red, I didn't know you were here. How's it going?"

"Going fine, Del. Yeah, I was at a table tucked away in the back corner trying to grab a quick meal and write tomorrow's column. Evening, Caroline, always good to see you. From what I can tell, you and your fellow volunteers are making a huge difference with your beautification projects on the square."

"We're trying our best, Red, but I sure don't want people to think that we women are just capable of making things pretty. That's why I'm working hard to get Suzette Crosley elected as our state representative. You and I both know that she's the real deal and will make a huge difference for the people of our state."

"Trust me, Caroline, I'm a fan of Suzette's. Of course, *The Banner* needs to be fair-minded with the campaign coverage, but Suzette certainly has my vote. And, is this really Aurora, looking all adult and everything?!"

"Sure am, Red! It's great to see you again, and let me introduce my fiancé, Ben Witt."

"Mr. Witt, it's a pleasure to meet you, sir! Any friend of the Engel family is a friend of mine. Where will the two of you settle after you get married?"

"Thanks, Red! It's very nice to meet you too. We're still working out the details on next steps after the wedding, but from the tour that Aurora's given me so far, I'd say Greencastle is certainly in the running."

Red looks at Delano and Caroline and raises his eyebrows in approval. "Well, that would be wonderful. I hope we have a chance to get to know each other better. Now, I'd better scoot. Gotta get this column typeset for tomorrow's paper."

As he leaves, Gwen returns with the dinner check. Delano pays the bill leaving a very generous tip. They step outside into the night air, and the courthouse bell chimes softly as if bidding them a fond adieu. They climb into Caroline's Ford Woody, and ten minutes later they're back home. As they exit the car a soft breeze picks up and a glow appears from the house's tower window bringing a subtle feeling of enchantment to their growing family.

"Let's take a little break, everyone, and then meet in the library, okay?!

Chapter 5

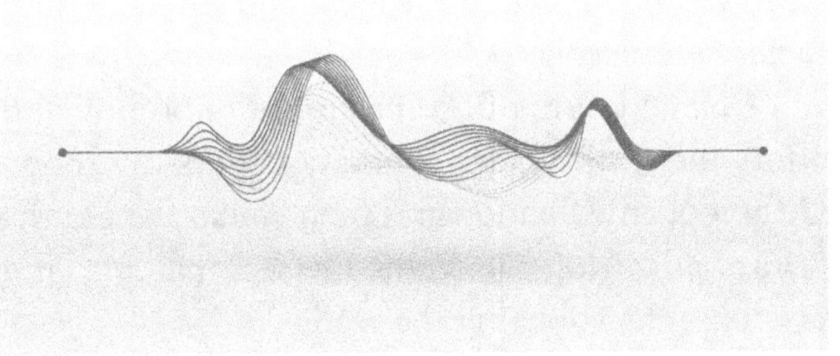

THE LIBRARY IS A VERY COZY paneled room with floor to ceiling bookcases containing various genres of literature. Centered between the bookshelves is a fireplace with a magnificent limestone hearth, brass andirons, and a carved cherry mantel. The other walls are covered with framed photographs of the Engel family, including a charming picture of a younger Caroline and Delano Engel seated in their Curtiss Jenny airplane with Caroline holding an infant Aurora. Other framed items include letters from presidents Roosevelt and Truman, congressmen, foreign dignitaries, along with Engel Air patents, and other business ephemera. Delano's handsome Wooton desk occupies one wall, with comfortable seating and finely crafted tables completing the decor.

Delano pours himself a snifter of brandy and offers the same to Ben when he enters the room. He accepts the libation and then walks around the library admiring the framed letters, patents, and photographs adorning the walls.

"Very impressive, Delano! You and Caroline certainly have a lot to be proud of."

"Thanks, Ben, we've been very fortunate to have our efforts pay off the way they have so far."

A few moments later Caroline and Aurora join the men and pour themselves glasses of ruby port. Soft cello music performed by Asbury College professor Enrique Bergman adds to the ambience. They all take seats and listen to Dr. Bergman's rich, soulful melodies. Their bellies are full and their moods are bright. It's been a good night all the way around.

"So what did you and Mom want to talk with us about, Dad?"

Delano takes another sip of his brandy, inhales its headiness, and peers at the dark amber liquid in his snifter. He takes a dollar bill out of his pocket and addresses Ben. "I want you to view this dollar as a retainer. I'll give it to you if you promise to observe attorney-client privilege regarding what I want to share with the two of you. Are you willing to do that, Ben?"

"Yes, I am provided there's nothing nefarious or illegal about it. Fair enough?!"

"More than fair. And you, too, Aurora, I'd like for you to use good judgment when discussing this. After your mother and I make a public announcement very soon, you're totally free to speak as you wish. I take it you're comfortable with that."

"Of course, Dad, but what're you talking about doing?"

"Ben, I'm including you in this discussion because in addition to your serving as my impromptu legal counsel, I view you as a member of our family. Okay?"

"Thank you, sir, I'm doubly honored. I'll be as helpful as I can be."

Delano's voice softens, and he looks warmly at Caroline. "Your mother and I have been together a long time now. We've seen a lot and *witnessed* a lot, especially in the young days of our marriage after I came home from fighting in France. We had a dream to build a company at the forefront of civil aviation, and to lead the way in manufacturing high quality aircraft and parts and products to service those aircraft. And yes, we diversified with munitions and clothing, as well."

"Aurora, I realize that you know all of this because you've grown up with it, but your mom and I want to do much more to improve the lives of others. We've been blessed immeasurably."

"Sure, Dad, that's great ..."

"So what your father is taking forever trying to say is that we want to donate $25 million and create an *Engel Family Charitable Trust* whose sole purpose will be to review applications, and distribute financial grants to charitable organizations who submit applications to us."

"Holy Guacamole!" Aurora blurts out. $25 million!"

Ben is standing there stunned at this astronomical announcement.

"Yeah, that's exactly what I was getting ready to say, dear!" he replies with a self-abasing grin.

"Your mother and I have had some very productive discussions with our financial advisor, Conrad Zyer, in Chicago, and we believe that financially we can make a commitment of this magnitude without hurting our shareholders."

"$25 million!" Aurora repeats.

"There's more!" Caroline alludes. "Tell them the rest, Del."

"We're gonna need a top-notch pro to serve as CEO of the Engel Family Charitable Trust, and Aurora, I can't think of a better person than you to serve in that capacity. We'll build a small board of directors to oversee management and business interests, and I'll serve as chairman. We can also build a second board of professional advisors to provide ad hoc counsel on programs that we're considering funding.

"I know we're really catching you off-guard about a major commitment like this, and as much as your mom and I would love to see the two of you settle in Putnam County, we're not trying to buy and keep you here. Your life is your own!"

"I agree with your father, Aurora, I can't think of a wiser, more energetic person than you to lead the charge."

Aurora looks at Ben, and the two of them begin laughing in surprise, not out of disrespect, but at the awesome enormity of running a large family foundation. The contagion of laughter quickly spreads to Caroline and Delano, and for a solid twenty seconds they celebrate their family's wanting to do a really good thing.

"How could you not take a job like that?!" Ben implores Aurora. "It's the job of a lifetime, one that would touch so many lives and also secure the Engel family's legacy. Wow! Good for you, Caroline and Delano!"

"There's more," Caroline says again. "Continue, Del!" They smile at each other enjoying the playful banter.

"As for you, Benjamin, if law is the career of your choice, and you wish to hang your own shingle, I'll be delighted to help you acquire office space and clerical support, and I know some folks who I believe could benefit from your expertise with estate planning. We'll be happy to get you started, Ben, because we also believe that you'll be very successful on your own. A little extra help at the beginning of your career might make a difference though."

"Mr. Engel, Delano! I don't know what to say. You barely know me, and you're willing to be this generous. I'm grateful beyond words, and it's a little overwhelming to take all of this in right this second. Wow!"

"There's more! Tell him, Del!" she smiles.

"We want you to serve on the board of directors for the trust and take an active role in helping to decide the directions our grant money should go. So, you can have your law practice and serve on the family foundation board too. I'm sure this is something both of you will want to think about. We know it's a lot to digest."

"Whew!" Aurora exhales. Caroline is smiling at her and nodding her head affirmatively.

"C'mon, Del, let's let these young people have some alone time."

"I'll leave the hall light on for you, Ben. Sleep well, guys!"

"Dad, I'm not sure either of us will get much sleep after our little library talk tonight," she demurs. She looks her father in the eye and warmly says, "Good for you, Dad. Good for you! Love you both! C'mon, Ben, time to walk me home!"

They step outside in the night air and listen to the peepers calling out by the pond. Lightning bugs flit along here and there. Aurora embraces Ben's strong arm as they slowly walk across the lawn to the carriage house. A waxing gibbous moon provides ample ambient light to illuminate their way, and the courthouse bell peals as if to bid them a fond good night.

"Boy, it's beautiful out here," Ben says as he stops walking, and he and Aurora hold and kiss under the stars and trees.

"So, what do you think, Ben? The one thing I know for sure is that my parents have never been overly controlling of me. And wow, and the notion of running a charitable foundation of that size is mesmerizing. I'm really more concerned about where you're coming from on this. You know, the idea of our moving to small-town Greencastle, and your opening up a law practice with my dad's help and serving on the family foundation's board. Plus, you'd be living in the same town where your in-laws live who happen to be really rich and respected. Actually, the way I just phrased that sounds pretty darn good. Yep, I'd seriously consider that offer, yessir!"

They kiss a few more times, and Aurora says, "What was it that Gwen called you at Almost Heaven tonight? Oh yeah, 'handsome hunk'! Well, c'mon mister 'handsome hunk' surely you'll protect me out here in the dark," she teases. "Or better yet, let's go inside the carriage house and turn out the lights … that way no one will know we're home … and we can hide under the blankets too! How's that sound?!" She giggles and pulls him by the arm and leads him inside the carriage house. It's dark and the rustle of clothing coming off is undeniable …

Chapter 6

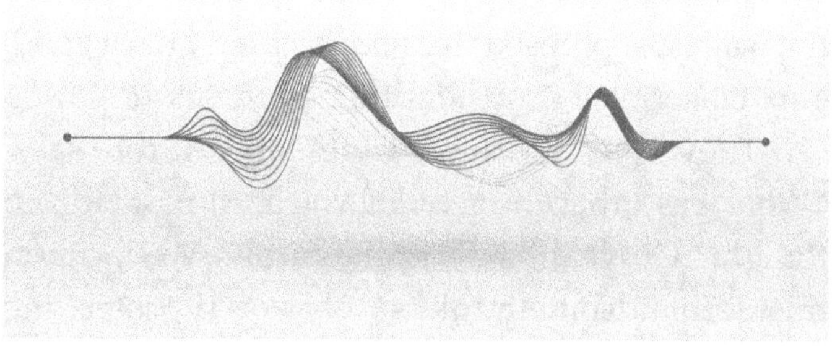

THE NEXT MORNING Ben rises early, kisses Aurora lightly on the cheek, and quietly walks back across the lawn from the carriage house and into the kitchen.

"G'morning!" he hears Delano say as he pours them both a cup of coffee.

"Uh yeah! Good morning to you too! How'd you sleep?"

"Slept pretty well, thank you … and you?"

"Well, we stayed up pretty late last night talking about your offers, and thinking about the future. You know …"

"Uh huh!" Delano replies with a sly smile. "And, have you decided anything about what we discussed?"

"I think so. It's an incredible opportunity for both Aurora and me, and we can't thank you enough. I'd prefer to wait for Aurora to be here to answer your question though, okay?"

"I'd be surprised if you didn't say that. Of course, we should wait for her."

"Good morning!" Caroline sings out as she enters the kitchen. "Looks like a glorious day ahead!"

A moment later Aurora comes inside to join them. Her hair looks like a bird's nest, and she yawns as she holds her coffee mug out to be filled by anyone near. "G'morning …" she replies, then takes a couple of sips from her mug.

"Your dad was just asking me if we'd made a decision after last night's conversation."

"Coffee, first!" Aurora offers with a little smile. "Then, adult stuff!"

"C'mon Aurora, why don't you help me prepare some bacon and eggs. Maybe that'll help you regain your, pardon the pun, wits!"

Benjamin Witt smiles at the double entendre. "Yeah, we've talked about it a lot, and your offers are enormously generous and appealing." He looks expectantly at Aurora for her input, and she looks back at her fiancé to measure the depth of his commitment. He nods and smiles approvingly at her.

"Yeah, I'm sure we'll have a ton of questions, and obviously creating the family foundation and a new law firm will be huge endeavors, but yeah, we'd love to accept your offers! Right, Ben?"

"Absolutely, we can't thank you enough, and we're anxious to get started."

There're hugs all around, and then they settle around the breakfast table to refuel and to discuss next steps.

Over the next couple of weeks, there's a huge flurry of activity. Aurora and Caroline spend a lot of time looking over wedding catalogs, considering dresses, and hiring a wedding planner. It's pretty much decided that the wedding will occur in the autumn on the grounds of their home, with large tents and dazzling lights everywhere. Aurora and Ben agree to ask Reverend Langston Bryant from the United Methodist church on Asbury's campus to officiate.

And, when she and her mother aren't contemplating the nuptials, they discuss who to invite to sit on the foundation's board of directors, its mission, by-laws, articles of incorporation, and the process to apply for federal tax-exempt status. Ben is a natural for establishing the legal structure for the foundation, and he spends a lot of time, both in person and on the phone with Conrad Zyer, their financial manager, discussing the transfer of family and corporate assets to fund the corpus of the Engel Family Charitable Trust.

And, if that weren't enough, Ben identifies office space on the courthouse square to open his new law firm and begins interviewing potential people for support staff. Finally, they schedule a meeting with Red Jergens at *The Banner* to discuss publicly announcing the creation of the Engel family's new charitable foundation.

"You realize, of course," Red begins, "that people in our county already think you've got more money than God, and now with you announcing your foundation, people will be coming out of the woodwork, virtually hanging out on your doorstep to get their hands on free money."

"That's why we'd appreciate *The Banner's* help in printing that it's only charitable organizations that can apply. We're establishing rigorous guidelines on eligibility, and Aurora and her team will assiduously follow those guidelines to the letter."

"Yeah, well, be prepared for the crazies to come out of the woodwork too."

"We understand that, Red, but it's not a reason for not doing the right thing."

"Can I qualify as a charitable organization?" Red jests. "I swear, my wife and kids are about to eat me into the poorhouse!"

"Your wife and children are lovely, Red, not to mention trim, so your request to be recognized as a nonprofit is formally and respectfully declined." Aurora declares. "Now, the homeless shelter is another story."

"Dang!' he protests. "So, how much of the $25 million do you expect to give a way each year?"

Everyone looks to Ben to answer that. "Well, in order to qualify as a charitable foundation, the trust needs to distribute at least 5 percent of its income annually. So, for example, if the trust earns 2 percent in dividends and interest that would yield about $500,000, and if the foundation made grants of only 5 percent of that amount, we'd be in a position to give away about $25,000 to worthy causes."

"Lotta dough going to a small community in 1946!"

"Yes, it is!" Caroline confirms, " And, that's if we only give away the bare minimum. We expect to make our dollars stretch and perhaps motivate others with significant assets to follow suit. We want our community to be an example of how citizens can step up and take care of its neighbors through philanthropy, and not just government handouts."

"Well, I hope you know that the Engel family can count on me and *The Banner* to help spread the word."

"Thanks, Red!" Aurora replies. "I plan for my office to regularly release stories of how the foundation is making life in Putnam County better, so you and I are going to become very fast friends."

"I'm sure we are!" he smiles.

A few days later, a major story announcing the creation of the Engel Family Charitable Trust appears on the front page of *The Banner*, with Aurora Engel identified as the chief executive officer. The buzz in the community is absolutely electric! Several local charities that have already been growing in recent years thanks to support from Engel Air Corporation grants, begin plans to grow even more in the next several years.

And, the news of the Engel family's benefaction isn't just big news in Putnam County, Indiana. Their philanthropy becomes an overnight national and international sensation. So much so, that some people even begin making noises for Delano Engel to run for president.

In the weeks that follow Aurora assembles her small staff, and they begin the review process so the foundation's new board of directors can approve and announce the first wave of quarterly grants. The only interruption to her work schedule, and that of new rising legal star, Benjamin Witt, is a little thing called a wedding.

The weather on this Saturday in mid-September is partly cloudy with effusive rays of sunlight streaming through billowing white clouds. The skies are a deep blue in color looking like a cerulean sea with a flotilla of cloud-ships navigating its waters. To Caroline, the sky and landscape remind her of an old world Dutch painting … A Vermeer perhaps.

Delano joins her on their porch as they watch a small army of workers put the final touches on the tents, tables, lighting, and flowers. Caterers from Almost Heaven scurry around making certain that the food is pristinely prepared and looking scrumptious. Well-stocked bars are scattered here and there, and Dr. Enrique Bergman practices his cello selections over by the carriage house. He'll play while the guests gather and during the processional and dinner. A hip new band led by the legendary Tad Robbins will liven things up once the newlyweds are presented.

Reverend Bryant waves to the Engels from his elevated podium covered with garlands of white flowers. He's known Aurora since she was a little girl and feels like she is one of his own.

Delano and Caroline walk through the yard smiling broadly at how lovely the scene is. Caroline leaves him to go see how Aurora is doing with her coterie of bridesmaids fussing over her wedding dress, hair, and makeup. They've sworn that she'll be the prettiest girl on the planet on her wedding day. Delano walks slowly enjoying what he's seeing, and his gaze takes him skyward to the clouds hovering over the house's roof tower. He's surprised to once again see radiant light emanating from the tower room, a light that once was all too commonplace in their lives but only seen by him and Caroline recently after many years.

"Behave yourself!" he whispers aloud, remembering how the magical Book of Tamberg played such a mystical role in their lives twenty-five years ago. "Not today!" he declares aloud. "Not during my daughter's wedding!" The bright light seems to diminish and is replaced by the distant gong of the courthouse bell.

Finally, once all of the guests are seated some thirty minutes later, and Ben arrives by the floral altar, Dr. Bergman begins playing the processional and a hush comes over the gathering as Delano enters with a glowing Aurora by his side. Caroline weeps tears of joy as she witnesses her baby walk down the aisle and take the next step in her life.

"Dear Heavenly Father," the reverend begins … and the rest of the ceremony becomes a blur of joyous emotions for Delano and Caroline. Heartfelt words are expressed, promises are made, and vows exchanged, all sealed with a kiss and enthusiastic applause at the end. Reverend Bryant shouts out, "Please welcome our blessed newlyweds, Aurora Engel Witt and Benjamin Witt!"

The Robbins band begins playing lively music, and well-lubricated guests hit the makeshift dance floor. Once Aurora reappears after having shed her wedding dress for more comfortable attire, she and Ben lead their family and friends in an evening of unbridled exuberance. Well-wishers crowd the young couple periodically between songs, several of whom place envelopes of cash in Ben's jacket pocket.

At one point Ben feels a tap on his shoulder, and his giddy expression turns into a confused, awkward smile as he sees General Wendell Grossman from NATO command grinning at him. "Congratulations, Ben, on your marriage and for marrying into a very, uh, influential family."

"Hello, General, I didn't see your name on the invitation list, but it's nice of you to come and express your good wishes to our family."

The general places an envelope inside Ben's jacket pocket. "Consider this a wedding gift … and a down payment for future services rendered. We need to meet again fairly soon."

"Yes, well, Aurora and I are leaving tomorrow for our honeymoon in Bermuda, and we're going to be awfully busy when we return."

General Grossman's smile belies his true intent. "Young Witt, I'm not sure you quite understand. This is not a request. Consider it more like a summons, and as I advised you at our conversation a while back in Chicago, do not speak a word of our conversations to anyone. It could be a tragic decision for people you care about." He flashes a reptilian grin, and his steel-gray eyes bore deeply into Ben's being, then he turns and retreats into the partying throng.

Ben blanches in shock. All of a sudden this general he barely knew at NATO shows up, hands him an envelope stuffed with cash, and a not-so-veiled threat to do harm if he doesn't meet with him soon. The other thing Grossman made very clear was that Ben was forbidden to speak with anyone about any of this … whatever "this" is.

Aurora sidles up to her new husband all aglow. She sees that he looks a little ashen. "Are you okay, Ben? Better pace yourself with the champagne, hubby, the night's young, and we have guests to entertain."

"No, I'm fine, sweetheart, I think I should put a little food in my belly though. C'mon, let's grab something to eat. The pickled herring and gefilte fish look especially good," he jests, and the two of them go trotting off to the buffet tables.

Chapter 7

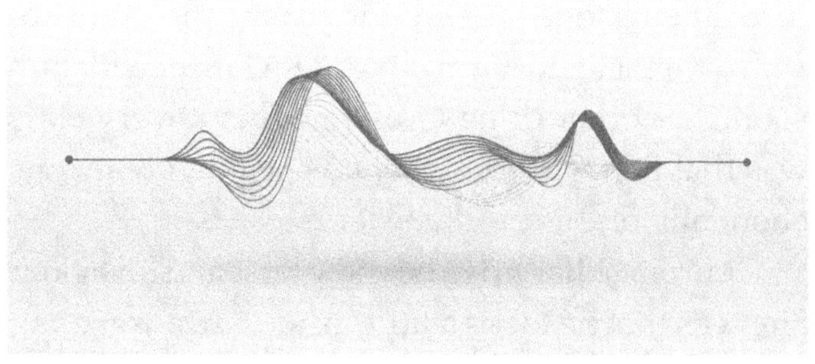

TWO WEEKS PASS AND Aurora and Ben return home to Greencastle from a wonderful honeymoon and are met with stacks of work and phone messages waiting for them on their desks. Ben's portfolio of clients has swelled ever since Delano and Caroline suggested to friends and associates that they have their son-in-law update their wills and trusts.

As for Caroline and her staff at the Engel Family Charitable Trust, the flood of fresh applications for grants is nearly overwhelming. While they're excited about making some very helpful grants, there's also a ton of work that needs to be done vetting the requests before presenting them to the foundation's board of directors for final approval.

Ben and Aurora drag home about 8:30 PM and collapse into each other's arms.

"I'm so tired my teeth hurt!" Ben says. "Maybe we can get Almost Heaven to deliver dinner to us?"

"I don't think so, darlin', their kitchen closed thirty minutes ago."

"Can we just go back on our honeymoon for the rest of our lives?"

"Sounds like a plan! Unfortunately, we made a commitment to everyone including ourselves."

"Oh that!" he deadpans.

A moment later their phone rings, and it's Caroline saving the day.

"Your father and I saw that you got home very late this evening. We've got a lot of food left over from dinner if you haven't had a chance to eat yet."

"Bless you, Saint Caroline!" Ben intones. "As long as it doesn't move, I'll eat it! We'll be right up."

Delano smiles as he opens the door for the weary couple. "Oh, to be young and invincible!" he jests. "Just look at the bright side. At your ages you only need to work like this for the next forty years."

"That's not even funny, Dad!" Aurora grumps. "Tell him, Ben!"

"I can't. I'm too busy stuffing my mouth full."

After dinner the four of them sit on the porch enjoying the cooler night air, and the young couple has recouped enough brainpower to share some of the really positive things that they're dealing with at their respective jobs.

Ben is pleased to report that efforts are underway to form a United Way in Greencastle that would seek financial support among area businesses and their employees to help meet special needs.

"I think creating the Engel Charitable Trust has gotten a lot of people thinking about hometown philanthropy. There's even talk about creating a Putnam County Community Foundation that would enable folks to establish their own donor-advised funds without having to go to the expense of paying for a trust. The more the merrier as far as I'm concerned, plus I should be able to help all of those initiatives in one way or another."

"That's great news, Ben. Caroline and I had hoped that our taking the lead with our family trust might spark a surge in local philanthropy, large and small."

"Aurora, I received a note in the mail today that's gotten me thinking about something we want to run by you."

"Oh?"

"Your mom and I had a chance encounter a while back with an older gentleman named Max Kindred. He's a bachelor farmer who lives on a plot of land just southeast of Cloverdale."

"When your father says 'chance encounter', what he really means to say is that we crash-landed the Curtiss Jenny in a field next to his farmhouse."

"You're kidding?! Were you hurt?"

"Just our pride," Delano replies. "Bryan came to pick us up, but I was able to fly the Jenny back to the airport."

"So what did his note say?" Aurora inquires.

"Well, Max is pretty well up there in years, probably in his late eighties. He and his late brother,

John, collected large bells their entire adult lives, and he asked me if it would be possible for him to donate his land and bell collection to our new Putnam County Museum as an interpretive center about the history of bells."

"You guys need to visit Max's place and meet him. Both he and his bells are quite unique, and I think it would be good to see if we can do something special to help preserve his collection. Would you be willing to our driving over to visit him and see where our conversation goes?"

"Sure! Of course, Dad, as long as it's not tonight!"

"Great, I'll call him tomorrow and see when we can schedule a time. Ben, you're agreeable too, I hope."

"Yeah! I like bells and older people, especially with a full tummy. Thanks again for dinner, Caroline."

Two days later the four of them climb into Caroline's Ford Woody and drive southeast of Cloverdale to meet Max Kindred.

"Well, if it's not the folks that fell out of the sky and landed in my field a while back, and they've brought some young people with them."

"How are you, Max?" Caroline chirps as she gives the old geezer a hug. "You know Del, of course, and this is our daughter, Aurora, and her husband, Ben."

"Oh yeah, I've been reading about you folks a lot recently. Young fella, you're that really smart attorney, aren't ya?"

"Well, I'm not sure how smart I am, and I feel like my youth is rapidly going bye bye."

"Wait until you're my age, Ben. I know my days are numbered, so you'll forgive me if I'm not overly sympathetic to your plight, young fella. And, this pretty lady is your new bride, Aurora, right? She's heading up the work with that new charitable trust fund your family set up, right?"

"It's a pleasure to meet you, Mr. Kindred," Aurora says warmly. "My parents have told me about meeting you and your fabulous bell collection. And yes, both Ben and I are very excited about the foundation."

As if on command, a breeze picks up and numerous bells start ringing and chiming.

"Wow, I see that you do have quite a collection here," Aurora continues. "Do you mind showing us around a bit?"

"Not at all, young lady. We've got pert near three hundred ringers as I like to call 'em."

"You say 'we,' Max. Does someone else live here with you?" Ben asks.

"Naw, it's just me and my ringers, but my late brother, John, and I both collected the darn things, so I guess I say 'we' out of respect for his memory." Max pauses and looks at the ground momentarily, and a somber sounding bell peals softly from a tree limb in the front yard.

"Naw, it's just me and my ringers these days," he repeats.

The five of them walk around Max's property some more looking at old school bells, dinner bells, church bells. Every few feet there's something else to notice like a huge ship bell with an enormous anchor chain and steam whistles. Both Aurora and Ben are fascinated by the huge number of large bronze and cast iron bells hanging from various perches throughout the barnyard and along the road.

"I've never seen anything like this," Ben effuses.

"I believe it's got to be a very historic collection, one that definitely needs to be preserved," Aurora encourages.

Delano and Caroline both remain quiet because they want Aurora and Ben to take the lead on the discussion with Max.

"C'mon up to the porch, folks. I've got some lemonade, and maybe we can chat a spell. How's that sound?"

"Great!" they reply in unison.

They sit and sip from their plastic glasses and look around the house's yard. It's definitely seen some better days, and Max isn't in much of a position to physically keep up with the maintenance. A warm breeze comes out of the southwest and wrangles some of the bells' clappers into an atonal rhythm.

"Max, what if we created a Life Estate Agreement," Ben begins, "where you donate all of your land and the contents, including the bells, to the Putnam County Museum, and in return you'll receive a healthy charitable tax deduction and be able to live here as long as you wish. Then, of course, at the end of your days, the museum takes occupancy as well as full ownership. The foundation will also agree to pay you a generous cash annuity for life to help you cover the cost of utilities and upkeep on the property."

"Can you do that?" Max asks naively.

"We definitely can," Aurora says. "Plus, the name of the property would be The Kindred Bell Farm in perpetuity with a large plaque and literature describing the collection's inventory and history. How would that sound?"

"Sounds like I might have a lot of people traipsing through my property while I'm livin' here."

"Could be," she says. "But I think they'll generally be respectful, and just think of all the little shavers and families you could tell bell stories to. Could be a lot of fun, Max."

Max smiles a little sheepishly and says, "Could be at that! Let me think about it a little, okay? Can we talk more in a day or two?"

"Of course. Whatever you're comfortable with, but I want you to know that we're serious about everything we've said."

"Well, okay then, I sure appreciate you all stopping by." Max begins walking the four of them down his uneven front sidewalk when he stops abruptly. "I understand the two of you recently got married. Isn't that so?"

"It is, indeed. We've been married about three weeks now," she beams.

"Well, here's something pretty special that I'd like the two of you to have as a wedding gift. It's a special school bell that John and I collected about a dozen years ago. I've always felt that this bell had very unique characteristics. It was manufactured by the Virtue Bell Company in Cincinnati, Ohio."

"It's beautiful, Max. Are you sure about giving it?"

"Yeah, I'm sure. Something tells me it's the right thing to do, so I hope you'll set it up on a stout post somewhere nearby in your yard and think of the ol' Kindred brothers from time to time."

"Of course we will! You mentioned that you think the bell has 'unique characteristics.' What do you mean?"

Max coughs a little and clears his throat. "That's a little bit hard to explain. It just has a way of talkin' to me sometimes. Not like a regular voice, but something like vibrations or tones that strike a chord within me. It's like it's talkin' to me, and even though I don't hear words, I understand what it means. Weird huh?! Maybe you can come back sometime, and tell me what you think that means. I'd be curious."

"Well, sure, we can do that. It seems to me that all of your bells have unique characteristics …"

"True, but some more than others, I assure you. C'mon lets see if we can snooker your husband and father to help loft this baby into the back of your mom's Woody."

The Virtue bell is heavier than it looks, and Ben and Delano are definitely winded once they get the bell securely stowed in the back of the car.

"I'm hiring someone to install it on a post when we get home, unless you really want to do it, Ben."

"Uh, no thank you! That ringer weighs a ton!"

They say goodbye to Max and agree to be in touch soon. Ben will contact Max once he's drafted some papers for him to look at, and Max will search around his clutter for the deed to the house and any literature relating to the history of his bells. They wave and drive away.

"This was a very special day visiting with Max," Ben says. "Thank you for introducing us. There's just no telling what people have, is there? I'm looking forward to our creating a proper legacy for Max's family … and we've got us a great 'ringer' to boot!"

Chapter 8

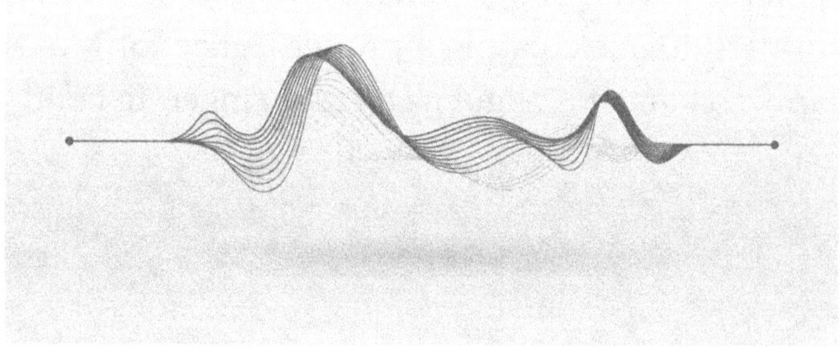

THE FOLLOWING DAYS FLY BY and the warm temperatures in October begrudgingly give way to cooler weather. The Virtue bell has been erected on a sturdy post by the carriage house's front porch with an attractive brass placard. Ben and Caroline enjoy ringing it when they leave for work in the morning and come home each evening. It's quickly become a fun fixture in their lives.

After much thought Max happily agrees to contribute his property and collection, thereby creating the Kindred Bell Farm. Ben also prepares the trust articles for Max's Life Estate Agreement, and the museum's board of directors votes to accept the Kindred property and bells into the museum's permanent collection. Once the museum board knew that the Engel foundation would financially guarantee the upkeep and curation of Max's property, their positive vote was ensured.

Days stretch into weeks with Thanksgiving coming up fast. Ben is very busy finalizing estate issues for families before the end of the year, and similarly, Aurora and the staff at the Engel Charitable Trust are working night and day to prepare grants for various charities before the tax polls close on December 31st. In a relatively brief period of time, the promise of money from the Engel Trust has swelled the size of several organizations' capabilities to meet clients' needs.

The Homeless Shelter and Food Pantry are able to serve more people than ever before, and expansion of the animal shelter has made its dream of becoming a no-kill shelter come true. With a new sense of financial security, arts organizations also thrive with visual exhibitions, theater, and music concerts springing up on calendars. Little Greencastle, Indiana, is quickly becoming known as an arts and entertainment mecca, a banner that Rick Freedman and the folks at the Convention and Visitors Bureau are more than happy to wave. A new golden era for Putnam County is in the making, and Caroline and Delano beam with pride.

Over time Ben finds himself also doing more and more legal work for both Engel Air Corporation and the Engel Family Charitable Trust because so much of their financial structures are intertwined.

"I always knew I'd end up doing more legal work for you, Delano," Ben states matter-of-factly to his father-in-law. "Not that I'm complaining, mind you, it just makes sense, and I'm having a helluva lot more fun doing this than I would've slaving away for a huge law firm."

"Yeah, it's worked out pretty darn well, and I know that Connie Zyer is relieved to be working with just you and a couple of others on financial matters rather than a large team of expensive lawyers and bean counters trying to make names for themselves and line their own pocketbooks."

"And, I don't mind going back to Chicago to meet with him regularly either. Some of my other clients live in Chicagoland, too, so I'm able to multi-task for them and the foundation."

Thanksgiving comes and goes, and finally Christmas is nearly upon the Engel/Witt household. Caroline and Aurora do some mother-daughter bonding by going to the Wagoner Christmas Tree Farm to pick out trees for their living rooms, and the four of them decorate the outside yard and gardens with brightly colored lights and swags of evergreen boughs. The Virtue bell looks like it's all dressed up waiting for Santa to arrive.

Aurora brings egg nog and cookies outside as the family puts the finishing touches on their Noel decorations.

Delano raises his cup. "Here's to a very good year, and an even better one to come!"

"Here, here!" Aurora seconds that toast, and they finish up their libations and admire what they've done. Caroline and Delano eventually bid them a good night and drift across the lawn to the house. Ben carries the cups inside the carriage house while Aurora lays a few leftover pine boughs in window boxes. She glances around admiring the decorations and is surprised by the clapper on the Virtue bell beginning to sway and create rhythmic vibrations despite a lack of any wind.

"That's odd," she whispers to herself as she places her hand on the bell's surface. The vibrations grow stronger finding their way through her arms and chest into her very essence. There's no sound other than the clapper hitting the sides of the bell, and yet Aurora feels a presence and a voice within her bones and flesh, *"Protect … Protect,"* and then it's gone. The bell sits silently once again, cast in a warm radiant glow from a light emanating from the house's tower room. She can't explain the sensations she's feeling, but there's some unmistakable connection among the bell, the light, and the Engel Family.

"Hmm, I wonder what Dad's doing up there at this hour."

She goes inside the carriage house but says nothing to Ben about the bell, lest he tease her that she'd been hit by lightning or something.

The next morning Sping Ben reminds her that he's driving to Chicago for a few days to meet with Conrad and a few clients. "I'll be back for sure on Christmas Eve, and please don't go sneaking around in closets looking for your Christmas gifts."

"Bah humbug!" she chides him and then offers to give him a little gift before he leaves. "Mom and Dad are gone, darlin'. Wanna make a baby?!"

Forty minutes later Ben tucks his shirt into his trousers, kisses Aurora sweetly, and plops down in his Studebaker coupe.

"Whew! That'll sure keep me going till supper!" he calls out to her, and then he contentedly drives away.

Delano and Caroline drop by several minutes later, just as Aurora is departing for the office.

"Ben's gone already?" Delano asks.

"Yeah, he's off to Chicago again. Promised to be home for Christmas Eve. I've got to scoot now, but I've noticed some weird things happening recently that I'd like to share with you when I come home this evening, okay?"

"Uh, yeah, sure," Caroline says. "Just come on up to the house when you get back."

Aurora pulls away in her Lincoln, and Caroline and Delano look thoughtfully at each other and then turn their attention to the tower room atop the roof of their spirited Victorian mansion. Its windows glow.

"I think it's time we had 'The Talk' with our daughter, Del."

This time of year the sun sets much earlier in the evening, so it's already dark when Aurora drives up to her carriage house at seven o'clock. She hears the courthouse bell chime seven times as she exits her car and turns to enter her home. As if on cue the Virtue bell gongs once.

"Well, it's good to see you, too, Mr. Virtue," she jests. The bell rings a second time, and Aurora reaches her hand out to feel its timbre and vibrations. "Gee, it's almost like you're purring." The bell hums a little louder and Aurora laughs in delight. She walks inside her house to drop off her work paraphernalia, then returns outside to join her parents. She stops and looks again at the Virtue bell.

"Oh, so now you're playing the strong silent type, huh?" She laughs and turns in the direction of the house and suddenly hears, actually feels, the resonant vibrations coming from the bell. *"Protect!"* She turns to look and only sees the bell's clapper gently swaying in the breeze, occasionally hitting the side. "Protect, huh?!" Her thoughts are confused as she continues up to the house.

"Ah, there you are!" Caroline says. "How was your day?'

"My day was good. I think we got a lot done. I haven't heard from Ben so far today. I assume he made it safely to Chicago and is meeting with clients. I spoke with Conrad around noon, and he said that he and Ben had met earlier, but that Ben had to cut their time together a little short because he got called to an unexpected meeting. A little unusual, I thought, but stuff comes up!"

They sit down for dinner and Delano opens a bottle of Pinot Noir.

"So, I wanted to ask you about something," Aurora begins. "Do you remember when we met with Max Kindred, and he said that the Virtue bell has 'unique characteristics'?"

"Yes, I recall that."

"Well, what do you suppose he meant by that?"

Caroline and Delano look at each other to see who wants to take the lead on this. "Well, what do you think he meant?" Caroline tosses back at her.

"He told me that sometimes the bell has a way of talkin' to him, not like a regular voice, but with vibrations or tones that strike a chord in him. He said he doesn't hear actual words, but he understands what it means. Weird huh?!"

"Yeah, that is pretty weird," Delano agrees.

"The reason I'm bringing it up is because I've had similar experiences ever since we brought the Virtue bell home."

"Has it spoken to you?" Caroline asks with curious concern.

"Not in so many words, but it's like Max said, it's like it's talkin' to me, but I don't hear words. It seemed to communicate with me just a little bit ago as I was coming up to see you for dinner."

"Do you want us to come outside to the bell to see if we can figure anything out?' Delano asks paternally.

"I don't know. I mean, I don't feel unsafe, in fact, I feel like it exudes a kind of friendly spirit. It just communicated the word 'Protect' with me, but

I don't know who or what I should protect. Weird huh?!" she says again.

Both Caroline and Delano sit in silence, and finally Aurora says, "What? What's with the awkward silence?"

Delano looks at Caroline and says, "There's something that happened here many years ago that we haven't shared with you, and your mother and I agree that it's way past time to do that."

"Whatever are you babbling about, Dad? Now you're starting to scare me a little."

They finish dinner, and Delano says, "Okay, come with us," and he and Caroline get up from the table and motion for Aurora to follow them.

"Where are we going?"

"The attic." They climb the steps to the second floor and then open the door to the attic staircase and begin walking upstairs. They reach the main room of the attic, and Caroline directs Aurora to follow them into one of the cedar closets inside the tower room.

"Okay, I think that maybe the two of you have gotten a little too cozy with the wine. Is there a reason we're inside a cedar closet in the attic?"

Aurora watches her father as he steps to the rear of the closet and pushes his thumb against a knot in the wood paneling. There's an audible click, and a hidden door slides forward a few inches. Delano pulls the door open, and the three of them step inside a hidden room that Aurora never knew existed.

"You've got to be kidding me. All of the years that I played up here, and I never had a clue this room existed."

"We had our reasons for not sharing this with you."

Aurora looks around the room and notices that there is nothing inside except a finely carved rolltop desk.

"I don't get it," Aurora states matter-of-factly.

Delano walks up to the desk and gently lays his hand on its writing surface. "There was a time a long time ago when you were a baby that a great, old book rested here. It led us to it. It was sentient and communicated with your mother and me by words magically appearing on its blank pages."

"Are you serious?" Aurora asks incredulously. "What did it say?"

"It said a lot of things and had a wisdom about it that made it clear to us that it was somehow connected to another realm, an unseen realm that transcends time and place. We learned of Christopher and Elizabeth Wright, the builders and original owners of our home, who one day up and left with nary a word to anyone. Just gone … but we saw their smiling visages briefly the day we safely brought you home. It was a mystically heartwarming experience. We still can't explain it!"

"Okay, now you're really starting to spook the crap out of me."

"And, the Van Gogh painting in our library? It was the Book of Tamberg's guidance that led us to it. Originally, a wedding gift from the artist to his cousin, Elizabeth."

"Do you two have any idea what's it's worth?" Aurora asks her parents.

"Yes," comes Caroline's prompt reply. "A lot!"

"If it weren't for the Book of Tamberg, we never would've saved you from kidnappers when you were just an infant."

"What?!" Aurora stammers. "Kidnappers?! I never knew any of this! Why didn't you tell me this before now?"

"Because it was very unpleasant and because it would've meant that we'd have to explain the magical book, and people think you're crazy when you start talking about things like that, so we just kept mum … until now."

"So, you weren't surprised when I told you about the bell 'talkin' to me?"

"No, not entirely," Caroline confesses. "Your father and I have come to accept that there's much around us that we don't understand. And, it's been twenty-five years since we last saw the Book of Tamberg. We just got used to it not being around. We were kinda hoping that inexplicable magic stuff was behind us, but it appears not."

"Well, this is exhilarating and a little terrifying at the same time! Do you think the Virtue bell and this Book of Tamberg are related in some way?"

"You mean like first cousins?" Delano jests. "We don't know, is our honest answer. And, I couldn't tell you why the Book of Tamberg disappeared, or why you've received a seemingly magic bell from Max Kindred. It is what it is."

"And, speaking of disappearances, I haven't heard from Ben. Whenever he's out of town he always calls, but I haven't spoken with him since he left this morning."

"I'm sure he'll call you in a bit, Aurora," Caroline soothes.

The three of them close the door to the secret room and walk down the attic steps. "I'm just bushed, both physically and emotionally," Aurora laments. "Between a magic book and bell, and getting kidnapped, and not hearing from Ben, it's a little overwhelming."

"We understand, sweetheart. The good news is that we're all in this together. But for now, I agree that a good night's sleep is in order."

They say goodnight, and Aurora walks across the lawn to the carriage house. As she approaches the Virtue bell, she stops momentarily to see if it chooses to communicate in some way. Its silence is deafening.

The next morning Aurora gets ready to go to the office and tries calling Ben at the hotel where he stays in Chicago. The desk clerk confirms that he's registered there, but there's no answer when the clerk connects her call to his room. She waits fifteen minutes and tries again. Still no answer. "That's odd," she murmurs aloud. "Maybe he had an early breakfast meeting with a client."

A couple of times throughout the morning, she continues calling Ben's room, but to no avail. She calls the hotel desk clerk again and leaves a message for him to call her. After lunch she phones Conrad Zyer and asks if he's seen Ben.

"Yes, Ben and I had a very productive meeting yesterday, mainly talking about the charitable trust. We discussed the trust's financial holdings and Irvin Financial Services which is the investment firm Ben wants us to have managing the assets. At this point nearly all of the $25 million your parents pledged has been transferred to the charitable trust."

"That's great news, Conrad, I'm sure Ben is tied up with clients, but would you please ask him to contact me if you speak with him before I do?"

"Sure will, Aurora." They hang up.

As the day goes by and evening approaches, Ben still hasn't returned Aurora's calls, and she's beginning to get very worried.

"Where are you, Ben? This isn't like you?" she says aloud to herself for the umpteenth time. She calls her mother to see if Ben has arrived home. Caroline looks out the kitchen window toward the carriage house and replies that she doesn't see his car.

Aurora phones the hotel one more time. The desk clerk's comments send chills down her spine. "Sorry, ma'am, but there's no one registered here named Benjamin Witt, and according to our records, no one by that name has stayed here for weeks."

Aurora sits at her desk totally dumbstruck. She stares at the phone incredulously. "What do you mean he hasn't stayed there in weeks? I spoke to another clerk earlier today, and she acknowledged that my husband was a guest at your hotel."

"I'm sorry, ma'am, but I'm just telling you what the register indicates."

"Can't you ask the other clerk to confirm what I'm telling you?"

"I'm sorry, ma'am, but I've been pulling a double shift since yesterday afternoon, and this is the first time we've spoken."

Aurora can't even think of words to reply with. She stammers and tries to utter a challenging response, but she's in so much shock that she can't even form an intelligible sentence. In frustration, she hangs up, and calls Conrad's number. He answers the phone, and Aurora barges ahead without saying hello. "The hotel says Ben hasn't been a guest there for weeks. What the hell is going on?"

"I don't have a clue, Aurora, there's got to be some logical answer, but we've got an even bigger mystery to solve right now."

"What do you mean 'bigger'? What could be bigger than my husband being missing in action?"

"How about twenty-five million times bigger?"

"What do ya mean?"

"It's gone, Aurora! It's all gone! The $25 million we transferred from your parents' accounts to create the Engel Family Charitable Trust. I just found out five minutes ago from Tyler Irvin that it's all gone, and nobody knows where the hell it is."

Chapter 9

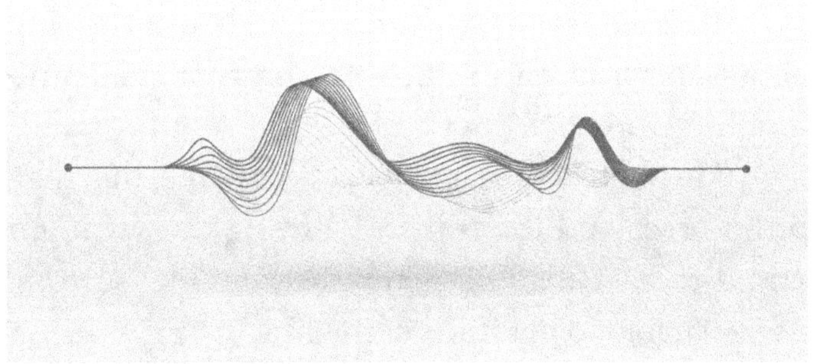

TWENTY MINUTES LATER Delano and Caroline join Aurora in her office at the Engel Charitable Trust. Everyone's facial expression shows how painful a moment this is for the family. Conrad is still on the speaker phone.

"What the hell happened?!" Delano asks trying to control his anger. "And, what are we doing about it? Twenty-five million dollars can't just disappear."

"We're working on it, Delano. I've been communicating with Irvin Financial where we transferred the trust's assets to invest for us, and they say they never received them. In fact, Ty Irvin said he was surprised that they hadn't heard from us about the transfer."

"I asked him what the Sam Hill he was talking about and told him I have a receipt for the entire amount from HIS firm."

"He politely repeated what he told me, that they hadn't received the transfer. I hung up with him and directly called Ben's number, but like Aurora, I wasn't able to get him on the line."

"So, what does your gut tell you, Delano?" Caroline asks.

"My gut tells me we need to contact the FBI and the Department of Justice immediately, and we need to make certain all of Engel Air Corporation's assets are secure. We've got to find out who's behind this theft and then go after them."

"Do you have any idea who could be behind this? I'm sure it's the first question the FBI will ask."

"Honestly, it could be any number of people or competitive companies, or a pissed-off foreign government, or just a brainy nutcase who figured out a way to steal a bunch of dough and hide his tracks. And, there's the possibility it could be an inside job too."

Those last words send a shock into Aurora. "You don't think that Ben had anything to do with it, do you? Why would he do that?"

"No, I don't, sweetheart, but I wish he'd resurface so we can definitively put that possibility behind us."

Aurora nearly loses it thinking that Ben might've been involved in some way. She shakes her head in disbelief. "No, no! That's not possible!"

"Okay, everyone, we need to try and figure out what actions needed to be orchestrated to allow this fraud to happen. The FBI will be here soon, and we should try to present various scenarios for them to consider. Then, let's follow the evidence."

"There's another thing," Delano says. "This won't stay secret for long, and the whole community is in for a major shock when people and agencies start thinking the Engel Charitable Trust can't deliver the financial grants we've promised. We should call Red Jergens at *The Banner* to see if we can draft a press release and get ahead of the turmoil by providing reassurances from our family. So, I'll call the FBI. Aurora, please see if Red's available. Caroline, please contact the Greencastle Police department and request an officer on site, just in case. Connie, please work with your contacts at Irvin Financial to see if they can shed any further light on the transfer-that-never-happened."

***

General Wendell Grossman sits alone on the patio of a posh restaurant in Georgetown DC. Recently retired from his influential position at NATO Command, he casually sips on a vodka martini while enjoying a robust Cuban cigar. The cocktail and the cigar both courtesy of his longtime contact in Russia, Yuri Tabeshenko.

"Here's to you, comrade!" the general says as he raises his glass in a cynical toast to good ol' Yuri. He briefly looks at a handwritten note that Tabeshenko had sent him earlier with the drink and cigar. *"You've done very well, my friend! As we agreed your compensation has been deposited into the Swiss bank account. Memorize this account number and then destroy this note. Until we meet again!"* General Grossman burns the note after reading it and mixes its ashes with his cigar's ash.

Grossman mutters to himself, "Goddamn Russians! The only thing good about them is their vodka and their cash. I spent my professional life fighting against communism, and here I am taking their dough."

Grossman takes another sip from his glass of Stolichnaya and thinks back on how things got out of hand during that trip to Moscow at the end of the war. World War II was over. Germany had surrendered. The Russians raped and pillaged Berlin. The allies were celebrating all over Europe, and General Grossman was caught up in the euphoria. Alcohol and women were available everywhere, and the Russians' espionage professionals made sure that Grossman was literally caught on film with his pants down with a wrinkled stash of rubles bulging from his pockets. The Russians now owned a senior member of NATO.

Grossman shakes his head in disbelief that he'd let himself get compromised so badly. It seems that the Russians had a special interest in an American named Delano Engel, and how Engel had made outstanding, sophisticated aircraft and war materiel … and along the way had become very wealthy. The Russians wanted both his secrets and a bunch of his cash to help rebuild a struggling, postwar Soviet economy. When Grossman learned that a former junior member of NATO, Ben Witt, was marrying Engel's daughter, Aurora, he recognized an opportunity to keep his Russian handlers off his back, and he seized it. Ben Witt never saw it coming.

The big sham began very innocuously. Grossman knew that both Ben and Aurora were close to graduating from law school at Northwestern and that there was talk of their imminent engagement. As a guest lecturer Grossman also purposefully attended a couple of Ben's classes, and during a class break, Grossman reintroduced himself to the young Mr. Witt. They reminisced a little about NATO and its importance in the new world order post-WWII, and Ben was flattered that someone as senior in rank as General Wendell Grossman would take interest in him.

So, when Ben and Aurora got married, General Grossman decided to crash the wedding reception and begin compromising Benjamin Witt.

And, now that they're back from their honeymoon, its time for the general to launch his assault on the Engel Family, and to use Ben as the Molotov cocktail.

"Twenty-five million dollars is a huge number!" General Grossman says aloud. "And, Benjamin Witt is going to be my new best friend whether he likes or not."

A few days later in Chicago, General Grossman schedules a meeting with Ben, and it turns out worse than Ben could ever imagine.

"Ah! Mr. Witt, how is married life treating you? Well, I hope!"

"General, I'm returning the cash you gave me at our wedding, and I don't want to have any further contact with you. And, enough with your thinly-veiled threats to use violence. Don't make me go to the authorities. Is that clear?!"

"Yes, Benjamin, you've made yourself very clear. I like that. I like clarity. It leaves nothing to the imagination, right? So, here's my idea of clarity.

You're going to use all of your brains and charm to transfer the $25 million from that new Engel trust to my own personal nest egg… and, you're going to give me the trade secrets for weaponry that Engel Air has developed! My Russian friends are especially interested in those!"

"Are you out of your effing mind? Why would I ever want to do that? This meeting's over. We're over!" He starts to get up.

"Sit down, young Witt, you haven't heard my counter offer."

Ben reluctantly sits down, and the general's eyes bore into him. "From this point on you will do everything I say. I have some very serious-minded people leaning on me, heavily. People who do not take no for an answer. We both knew some of those people through our NATO work, so I'll leave it up to you to imagine how, uh, unpleasant some of them can be. Bestial, actually …"

"So, you are threatening me!"

"Yes, of course, you'll be dead, but these 'people' won't stop there. They'll take great pleasure in torturing and executing your beautiful wife and her loving parents. Then, perhaps they'll firebomb your home and law office, and the headquarters of Engel Air, even the charitable trust. Many employees could die. Yes, Ben, you will do everything I say. No questions asked, and if you decide to go to the police or FBI, everyone's fate is sealed. How's that for clarity?!"

"You bastard!" Ben screams as he lunges at Grossman. The general manages to deflect his assault and quickly pulls a Glock pistol.

"Here is what you're gonna do," Grossman says soberly. "I have a special room for you at your hotel, and I arranged for telephone lines to be routed elsewhere. You will go to your room and await further instructions from me. Do not make any calls. Do not attempt to surreptiously communicate with anyone or ask for help. Like I said, I'm being leaned on heavily by some very serious-minded people. In the end they'll probably kill me, too, but $25 million is a mountain of dough, and if I need to give a bunch of it to my handlers and keep maybe half for myself, I view it as the cost of doing business. Giving them Engel Air's trade secrets and intellectual property is what they really want though. Might makes right, etc. etc."

"You're a damn traitor and a thug!"

Surprisingly, Ben's insults strike the general more than he expects. "I suppose that's very true, young Witt, but I hope to find solace at my sweet little beach house in Mexico where I can live out my days tanned and rich as hell."

Ben tries negotiating. "What if we were to simply give you a few million dollars to just go away and not have to worry about those other people?"

"No can do, buckaroo!" Grossman keeps his gun trained on Ben. "We're both in way too deep, like it or not. Now, get out of here and go to your hotel room and get ready to make the final transfer of assets from them to me! And remember, if you talk, loved ones die."

Chapter 10

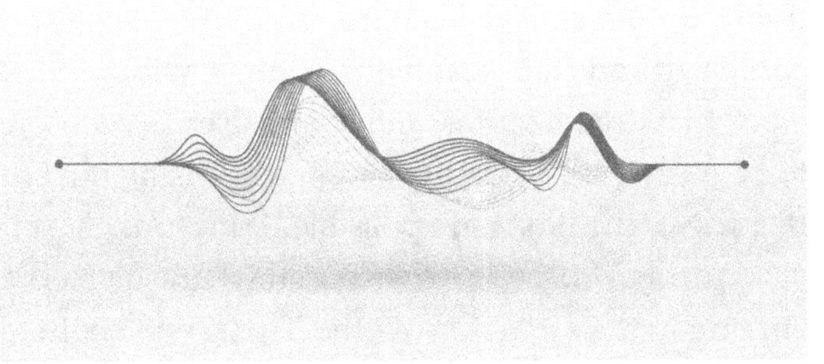

IN HER OFFICE AURORA SPEAKS briefly with Red Jergens at *The Banner*, alerting him about what's transpiring with the Engel Trust's assets. Before driving home she and her parents draft a press release, hoping to minimize community concerns, and then she drops it off to Red at his office. He plans to run the story in the paper the next day.

Once home she exits her Lincoln in her driveway and stretches her aching back and legs. "Oh no," is the only thing she can immediately think to say. "Oh no! Ben, where are you? I need you," she cries. She shakes her head in disbelief that something this horrible could happen to her and her family. "Twenty-five million dollars gone. My poor parents worked so hard to build a successful company and then wanted to share it with others! Now, that dream's gone, and my husband's nowhere to be found. Is he hiding somewhere? Is he hurt or dead? No, this just isn't possible." She sobs.

Aurora proceeds to her porch when she feels a stirring in the air and hears the Virtue bell begin to chime. "Oh, not now. I don't think I'm in the right frame of mind for any woo-woo magic stuff."

"*Protect*," she senses the bell to say. "*Protect!*"

"Protect what?" she protests. "Protect myself, protect my family, protect Ben? Protect the family trust? Protect what?" she screams out of frustration.

The bell chimes louder and its vibrations reach deeply inside her. She runs up the porch steps as if she can outrun the bell's vague message, but to no avail. Even once inside the carriage house, she can still hear the bell's nonverbal message. She looks out a window at the bell and sees that it is bathed in a light radiating from the house's tower room. "Oh no, not the magic book thing too! I'm too bloody exhausted for this!"

She sees her mother's Woody pull into the driveway, and she goes outside again to join them.

"It did it again!" she calls out to them. "The Virtue bell. It 'spoke' to me again, and that damn light from the tower room is in cahoots with it. It's a freakin' cosmic conspiracy!"

Delano and Caroline see the glow from the tower painting the bell in a golden light. They look at each other warily, and Caroline's one-word remark summarizes it all. "Shit!"

"What did the bell communicate to you?" Delano asks.

"It said *'Protect'* a couple of times. That's all … *'Protect!'*"

"Look, I'm exhausted, and I'm scared to death about Ben being missing, and every time I think of you two and the $25 million I just want to roll up into a ball on the floor and cry."

Delano and Caroline walk further into the yard to meet their daughter and wrap her in their arms. "Yeah, it's a real mess!" Caroline agrees. "C'mon, we'll get you tucked in like we used to do when you were little. A good night's sleep will do us all a world of good."

The threesome approach the bell which rings ever so lightly as they pass by. No excessive chimes. No major vibrations. No communications this time. It's like it wants a good night's sleep as well. The night air is quiet and the light from the tower room dissolves into nothingness. Aurora gets settled into bed and is soon asleep. Caroline and Delano walk hand in hand back to the house wondering about magic books and bells, a son-in-law they thought they knew, and a stolen $25 million that was meant to transform life in their hometown.

In a secluded basement room in a hotel, Ben Witt sits on the side of his bed with his face buried in his hands wondering how the hell his life has flown so tragically out of orbit. He reaches toward the telephone to call Aurora, but pulls his hand back knowing that to do so could potentially be a death warrant for her. He curses Wendell Grossman's name and his so-called handlers.

The phone rings, and he reluctantly answers it.

"Benjamin, it's time to finalize the last transfer of the assets to my account. If you do as you are told, then perhaps your life can become more, uh, pleasant."

"What do you need for me to do, you traitorous crook?!"

"Now, now, young Witt! Remember your manners! The last thing you want to do is really piss me off. Now, here's what I want you to do when we hang up." Wendell gives Ben specific instructions on who to call and what account numbers to use. "Do this now! No questions. No explanations. Just do it now!"

The line goes dead, and Ben does as he's been instructed. He calls the number the general gave him. A voice with an eastern-European-sounding accent comes on the line, and Ben tells him the instructions and account numbers. A few minutes later, the voice on the other end of the line says, "Done! Thank you! Have a nice day!"

Early the next morning, Delano receives a call from Conrad. "So, any good news?" Delano asks.

"Well, I've got news, but I don't think you're gonna like it."

"Tell me."

"The Irvin Financial firm that Ben chose for us to use with the trust is a very sophisticated company. Their people are working with the FBI to try to determine who the thieves are, how they directed the money away from our firm, and where it might be now."

"Yeah, go on," Delano replies.

"Early indications are that the main culprit is Benjamin. He made the calls and transfers. We're still trying to figure out where the money was transferred to. It may take a little bit of time, but we feel that we should be able to track it down before too long."

"Yeah, well, that's assuming the money will remain in just one location. My guess is that it'll be divided up into various accounts and then laundered."

"I understand, Delano. We're kinda flying blind here, but let's keep the faith. I'm also calling you because I don't want to be the bearer of bad new about Ben's involvement to Aurora."

"Neither do I, but I'll speak with her," Delano says softly. "Connie, please keep me informed of any progress, okay?" They hang up, and Delano immediately finds Caroline.

"We have a problem, sweetheart. I just got off the phone with Conrad, and he said that the forensic evidence collected by Irvin Financial and the FBI directly link Ben to the theft. We should go see Aurora now before she leaves for work."

"Of course. Oh Ben, why'd you have to go and stink everything up?!" she cries out in frustration. They head across the lawn toward the carriage house and see Aurora sitting on the porch steps with a cup of coffee reading the morning *Banner* newspaper.

"Have you seen the paper yet?" she asks somberly and then turns the front page of *The Banner* toward them so they can see the huge headline.

Engel Family Trust Target of Major Theft

"Whew! Well, I guess the you-know-what is about to hit the fan," Caroline speaks frankly.

"I need to get to the office and start fielding some phone calls. No doubt, we're going to have some very anxious representatives from charitable organizations wondering about their grant money."

"Before you go we need to talk about something else."

"Oh?"

"I spoke with Conrad a little bit ago, and he told me that all of the evidence so far is pointing directly at Ben being the perpetrator."

"I can't believe that,"Aurora replies. "I mean, why would he do that. It's not like we need the money, although $25 million is a boat load full of money."

"Did Ben say anything to you that would give you any clues as to why and where he might've transferred the cash?"

"None, I mean I'm as clueless about this as anyone. I just wish he'd call me so I know he's okay; that we're okay." Caroline hugs her daughter. "We'll get this figured out, sweetheart, there's got to be a logical answer."

As they are about to part company, a sudden rush of wind picks up and the clapper on the Virtue bell begins to sway rhythmically. Aurora stops dead in her tracks as she begins to feel the vibrations in a very visceral way. She looks at her parents oddly. "Can you feel that?" she asks them.

"Feel what, Aurora?" her mother asks.

"The bell. It's saying something. I can feel it."

Delano and Caroline stare at their daughter and are perplexed by what she's experiencing.

"I don't hear anything other than the bell ringing a little," Delano says.

"Me neither," Caroline concurs.

"It's getting louder and repeating the same thing to me. *"Protect … keep safe!"* And now it's gone. How's this even possible?"

"If it weren't for the fact that we've experienced similar, uh, magical communications in the past with the Book of Tamberg, I'd swear you're a little daft, but …"

"But," Delano continues, "We believe you, darling."

"How is it even possible that sounds from an old bell can create its own language? How can it 'talk' to me?"

"Our honest answer is that we don't know, Aurora, but I think I know someone who might be able to shed some light on that for us. I'll give him a call and see if he's willing to meet with you, okay?"

Aurora nods her agreement, and the Virtue bell chimes softly in approval.

Chapter 11

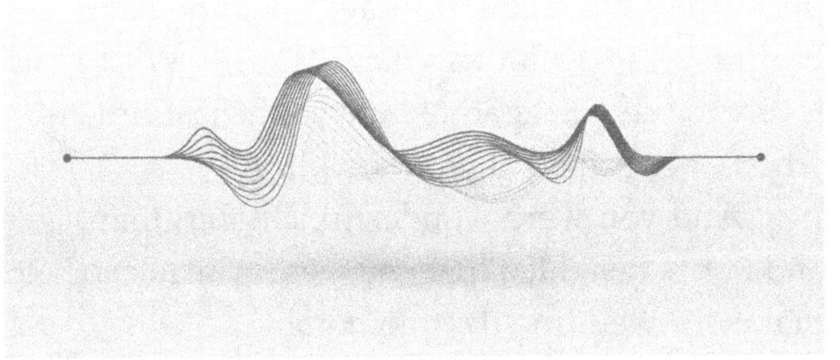

LATER THAT DAY AURORA WALKS onto the lovely campus of Asbury College and follows several students carrying their musical instruments into the Kissinger School of Music. She goes past the entrance to the Green Auditorium and comes to the school's main office. An affable woman named Clare greets her and asks how she can be of assistance.

"I have an appointment with Dr. Bergman. I may be a few minutes early. My name is Aurora Witt."

"Of course, Mrs. Witt, everyone knows who you are. I'll contact Enrique, I mean Dr. Bergman, and see if he's available to speak with you now." Aurora has a seat and looks at programs from past performances. A few minutes later she hears Dr. Bergman's mellifluous voice. "Aurora Witt! How lovely to see you again. I believe the last time was when I performed at your wedding."

"And you were wonderful, Dr. Bergman! Ben and I were delighted that you were available to help make our wedding day memorable."

"Of course! Please come with me. We can speak in my office."

They walk down the corridor and into his office. Each takes a chair in a cozy corner. Aurora looks around and is taken by how personally appointed his office is. It's clear that Dr. Bergman spends a lot of time here when he's not in class or in the auditorium. Aurora stands up to get a closer look at some of the framed items on the walls. A framed letter from Pablo Casals immediately catches her eye, and then she sees two others from Gregor Piatigorsky, and Mstislav Rostropovich. Enrique enjoys watching her glance at letters from fellow cellists he's come to admire.

"Pretty heady company, Dr. Bergman! Very impressive indeed!

She looks around his office a bit more. Visually, it exudes a warm glow. "Tiffany art glass lamp, Dr. Bergman?"

"It is. It was a gift from my parents when I graduated from Juilliard."

"Lovely, and I see that you have a rather extensive library." The leather book covers reveal years of affectionate use. She returns to her chair and eyes Professor Enrique Bergman closely. He's a man in his midfifties with graying hair at his temples and a very distinct one-inch band of whitish hair traveling the length of the right side of his otherwise dark brown hair. Very theatrical in effect. He wears a tweed sport coat with leather patches on his elbows and leather buttons on the front and cuffs. Quite professorial. It's not immediately visible, but from the aroma in the office and on Dr. Bergman's coat, it's clear that he enjoys smoking a pipe.

"So how may I help you, Mrs. Witt?"

"Please, Professor, it's Aurora."

"And you, my dear, please call me Enrique."

She looks him directly in the eye and remains quiet for a few seconds and then says, "I have some questions that I want to ask you, and they may appear very strange. My father seems to think that you may have some answers, and so here I am."

"I see. And, these strange questions, what are they regarding specifically?"

Before Aurora can censor herself, she blurts out, "An old bell that communicates with me!"

Without showing any emotion, Dr. Bergman reaches into his jacket pocket and pulls out his pipe and begins filling it with tobacco. "A bell that communicates, you say?"

Aurora watches the professor as he lights his pipe and takes a few puffs to get it going. "Can you please tell me more?"

"Only if you promise not to laugh at me."

"I may smile perhaps, but I promise not to laugh at you, my dear."

Aurora looks around the music professor's office and then directly at him again. "I want to know if it's possible for a bell to be sentient and have the ability to make its thoughts known through vibrations."

"I take it you're very serious about this."

"I am. I have an old bell that was recently given to Ben and me as a wedding gift. I swear that it produces vibrations in such a way that I feel, rather than hear, its thoughts. It's like they vibrate to my inner core, my skin, bones, and teeth, and I understand it. No words, just feelings."

"Can anyone else *feel* these communications?"

"No. My parents have been with me when I've experienced them, but they haven't felt them the way I can."

"Most curious, Aurora. Have you ever experienced anything like this before?"

"No, I haven't. The older gentleman who gave us the bell said that it had some 'unique characteristics,' but that was all that he shared."

Enrique gets up from his chair and walks over to his book shelves. He peruses one shelf and then another until he finds the old book that he's looking for. He takes it off the shelf and rejoins Aurora.

"*Revelations from the Music of the Spheres!* A true underappreciated classic if there ever was one!" he declares. "I take it, Aurora, that you're familiar with the concepts behind the 'music of the spheres,' yes?"

"Vaguely. I mean, I recall hearing the term in school, but it struck me as a bunch of antiquated mumbo jumbo."

"Uh huh, so please allow me to reeducate you on the subject. The Music of the Spheres, or Musica Universalis, or Harmony of the Spheres is a philosophical concept that regards proportions in the movements of celestial bodies—the sun, moon, and planets as a form of music." He flips the pages of the book until he finds the passages he's looking for. "The theory actually originated in ancient Greece with Pythagoras and was later developed by the sixteenth-century astronomer, Johannes Kepler. Kepler did not believe this 'music' to be audible, but felt that it could nevertheless be heard by the soul."

"That's all very interesting, Enrique, but I'm not sure what that has to do with what I've been experiencing."

"Please bear with me a little while yet, Aurora. It may have nothing to do with what you're experiencing, but hear me out, okay? Pythagoras proposed that the sun, moon, and planets all emit their own unique hum based on their orbital revolution, and that the quality of life on Earth reflects the tenor of celestial sounds which are physically imperceptible to the human ear."

"You'll have to excuse me, Professor, but I don't have the slightest clue what you're talking about."

"Yes, well, it's a rather obscure concept, one that went out of vogue by the end of the Renaissance. Regardless, I think there's a great deal to be said about the power of harmonics as a legitimate form of extrasensory communication. We're so accustomed to our brains working in certain ways, and yet most learned physicians and scientists would concur that we actually use very little of our brain's capacity. So, who are any of us to say that what you're experiencing with the bell isn't real? Certainly not me!"

Aurora stares at the professor wondering what the heck she's doing in his office listening to a bunch of pedantic palaver. She stands and says, "Well, I appreciate you taking the time to meet with me today, Professor Bergman, but I must say that I'm more than a little bit bewildered."

"I understand, Aurora, but since you're confused let me throw another concept at you. Pitch Psychoacoustics!"

"Oh boy," Aurora cynically thinks to herself. She takes her seat again and waits for the next volley of intellectual crap to get flung at her.

"Pitch is a major auditory attribute of musical tones, along with duration, loudness, and timbre. Pitch may be quantified as a frequency, but pitch is not a purely objective physical property; it's a subjective *psychoacoustical* attribute of sound."

"Okay, Professor Bergman, that's all well and good, but I don't see what this has to do with anything I'm experiencing."

He smiles at Aurora, and despite her protestations, he continues. "Psychoacoustics is the branch of psychophysics involving the scientific study of sound perception and audiology—how humans perceive various sounds. It's an interdisciplinary field of many areas, including psychology, acoustics, electronic engineering, physics, biology, and physiology."

For the first time Aurora is beginning to have a glimmer of an idea of what Enrique is getting at. "So then, you do think it's possible for a bell to communicate with me?"

"I've never experienced the sensation personally, but yes, I do."

Aurora stares at him curiously wondering if both of them have lost their marbles. "So, what do I do now?" she beseeches him.

"Darned if I know. I've never known anyone to ask about this before, but I do believe that you're very fortunate to have this kind of mystical connection. I would seriously encourage you to listen closely to your feelings when the bell *speaks* to you. Very closely indeed!"

Aurora slowly nods her head in agreement, but she's still having trouble processing all of this.

"You've been given a rare gift, Aurora, I encourage you to let the bell guide your way."

They say goodbye and promise to keep in touch. Aurora walks down the corridor past the Green Auditorium wondering what to make of the last thirty minutes. "Music of the Spheres. Psychoacoustics. A professor with way-out beliefs. "I sure don't understand it. All I know is that I have an old bell that was given to us by an old farmer who says it has unique characteristics … and I'm supposed to listen very closely."

"Oh, Ben, where are you when I need you, and why haven't you called me?"

Chapter 12

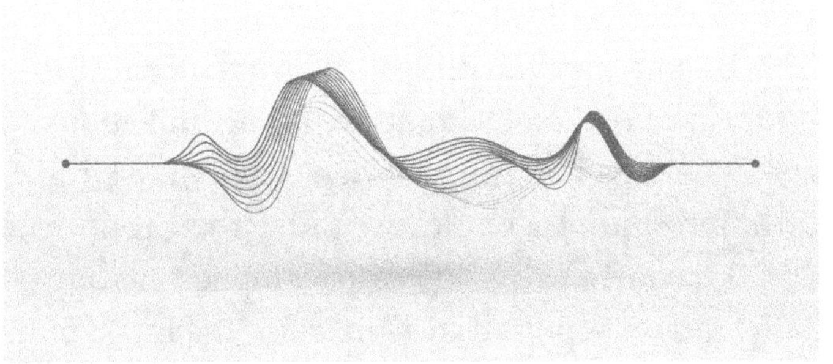

Wᴵᵀᴴ ᴀ ᴍɪʟʟɪᴏɴ ᴛʜᴏᴜɢʜᴛs swirling around her brain, she absently walks the four blocks back to her office and is surprised by the large throng of people who've congregated in front of the Engel Trust's main entrance. She sees the frustration and fear etched on some of the peoples' faces.

She seriously considers entering through the rear of their office building to avoid the hullaba-loo but decides to take the bull by the horns. She approaches the throng, and it separates as she moves through. She stops and turns to face the people. She recognizes several of them as leaders of local civic and charitable organizations. A Greencastle police officer approaches and asks her if she requires assistance. She declines.

"Aurora, can you please tell us if the Engel Trust will make good on its grants to our organizations?!" someone calls out. Another person shouts a similar question, and other voices vocalize their concerns.

"Of course, we will!" Aurora replies unequivocally. "As we reported in *The Banner*, the Engel family has made firm commitments to our community, and we will definitely honor them."

"Do you have any idea what happened to the trust's assets?" a voice shouts.

"That's something that the FBI and our investment firm is investigating. We will make their findings public once we have definitive information. In the meantime please know that our family will make good on everything we've agreed to."

"What about going forward? Several of our organizations have made serious financial commitments to expand our services, and we'll be in big trouble if we can't follow through."

"We understand, and we're as concerned as you are. As we've said, we plan to honor all of our commitments. That's all I can report to you right now." She turns to leave, and a voice from the rear of the throng yells, "What about Ben Witt? Word is that he's missing."

Aurora chokes up a bit, but stoically replies, "Ben is on assignment right now working with some of his clients. We expect him to return soon." She then turns again and enters the trust's front door. Once alone inside, her sadness overtakes her, and she cries. In the distance she hears the courthouse bell dolefully gong as if in sympathy. Aurora composes herself and then takes the elevator up to her office. The mood among the office staff is somber, and her assistant, BJ, shakes her head negatively when Aurora asks if they'd heard any word from Ben.

"No, but we're hearing plenty from a lot of other folks," BJ replies. "Here's a list of people who are asking you to contact them, and Red Jergens at *The Banner* wants to know if we have anything further for the paper to report. I told him you'd get back to him."

"Thanks, BJ, and I'm not surprised that the phone's been ringing off the hook. We're all anxious as hell, and I just came through a group of people at the entrance looking for any positive word. I swear, for a moment there I felt like the Frankenstein monster being pursued by villagers with flaming torches. Well, maybe that's a stretch, but people can do squirrelly things when their livelihoods are threatened." She goes into her office and begins returning phone calls. The first one is to Red Jergens.

"What's the good word?" Red asks hopefully.

"Nothing more than what we've already shared with you, Red."

"There's a rumor swirling around that Ben's missing in action. Any possibility that he's involved in the theft?"

Aurora bites her lip and says, "So, we haven't heard from him for a few days, and honestly, Red, we're not sure what to think, and to report anything implying that he's involved would be way too premature."

"I understand, Aurora, but I just want you to know that the rumor is out there."

"Thanks, Red, I'll keep you posted as soon as we know anything, okay?" They hang up, and Aurora looks at the list of messages that BJ had taken and begins prioritizing who to call next. By the end of the day she's repeated the same words to some twenty individuals regarding the status of the Engel Trust's grant-making capabilities. She's emotionally spent and sits at her desk wondering what the hell went so wrong. She hears the courthouse bell chime seven times, and she decides to seek another person's counsel.

With the sun dropping low in the western sky, she gets into her Lincoln and drives south on U.S. Route 231 through Cloverdale and hangs a left on S.R. 42. Ten minutes later she's greeted by a cacophony of ringing bells as she pulls into Max Kindred's gravel driveway.

Max hears a car approach his property and comes to the door. "Well, hello there, Aurora, this is a nice surprise. I was wondering who or what was causing all of that racket out there."

"Good evening, Max, I'm sorry to barge in on you unannounced, but I need to speak with you."

"No problem, young lady, it's always nice seeing you. C'mon up to the porch, and we'll sit a spell and talk." The sounds of the bells in Max's yard diminish until only one is left audibly swaying in the breeze.

"So, to what do I owe the pleasure of your company on this fine evening? Are you and Ben enjoying your bell?"

Aurora chooses not to say anything immediately about Ben's disappearance. "We love the bell, Max. It's a wonderful gift, and that's what I've come to speak with you about."

"Oh?"

"Yes, when you gave us the bell you mentioned that it had 'unique characteristics', but I wasn't sure what you meant by that."

Max looks at her knowingly. "I take it you've experienced something quite unusual about it, yes?"

She looks at him intently trying to plumb the depths of his cryptic reply. She pushes forward. "It communicates with me, Max! I don't know how or why, but it speaks to me without using words."

Max smiles at her. "Oh that!" he laughs. "I was wondering when you'd get around to asking me about that."

Aurora smiles at the old gent and says, "Max, both you and the Virtue bell are mysteries, my friend. So, what can you tell me about your experiences with the bell? When did you first learn of its, uh, 'unique characteristics'? And, how do you explain its powers?"

"I gave up trying to explain its powers a long time ago, but I noticed something unusual about it when my brother, John, and I went to that auction in Cloverdale where we purchased it. It spoke to me, not with words, mind you, but I understood its meaning ... clear as a bell, you might say. The curious thing is that it never communicated with John. For years he teased me about gettin' hit by lightnin' or something whenever I tried to tell him some kind of weird communication was going on between me and the bell. After a while I just quit tellin' him. But, I'll tell you this, Aurora, I learned to trust the Virtue bell whenever it *spoke* to me. Yep, I learned to listen to it, and when you and Ben and your folks first came here, the bell intimated to me that it should go home with you. No explanation why, but I didn't need one because like I said, it never steered me wrong. So, do you mind sharing with me what it says to you?"

"Protect. It says to protect and keep safe, but honestly I'm not sure who, or why, or what."

"Uh huh. Anyone else know about this?"

"Yes, my parents, but they can't hear its communications."

"And do they think you've been struck by lightnin'?"

"No. Actually they shared their own secret with me about a magical Book of Tamberg that had similar sentient powers. When I was an infant it gave them guidance by making words magically appear on its blank pages. My parents just told me that I was kidnapped when I was very young, and the book gave them the guidance they needed to get me back."

"Ya don't say! Seems to me that their Book of Tamberg and our Virtue bell are mystically related in some way."

"Yeah, sorta like first cousins!" And, they both laugh.

"Seriously though, Aurora, I don't know how much more I can tell you. Over the years I just learned to accept that I had a special bell that for whatever the reason chose me to be its confidante. My relationship with the ol' Virtue served me well, and now it's your turn."

The two of them chat for a few minutes longer. "Didn't I just read in *The Banner* that the money in that big charitable trust your family created has been stolen?"

Aurora squirms a little. "Yes, you did, Max, and we and the authorities are still trying to figure out what the hell happened. This is not for public consumption, but our fear is that my husband, Ben, is directly involved in the theft."

"Oh no, and he seems like such a fine young fellow."

"He's definitely a fine fellow, and that's why this is so painful. I keep trying to reach him, but he's not calling or showing his face. I just can't accept that he may not be as fine a fellow as I believed."

"Well, one thing that you and I and your parents have learned is that things aren't always as they seem. Try to keep the faith, and I encourage you to listen closely to the Virtue bell. And, if people think that you've been hit by lightnin', let 'em think it!"

Aurora gives Max a big hug and asks permission to drop by from time to time. As he walks her to her car, the bells in the yard begin pealing in a soft, soothing way. "Hear that!" he says as he winks and waves goodbye. "Kinda like the Music of the Spheres."

Chapter 13

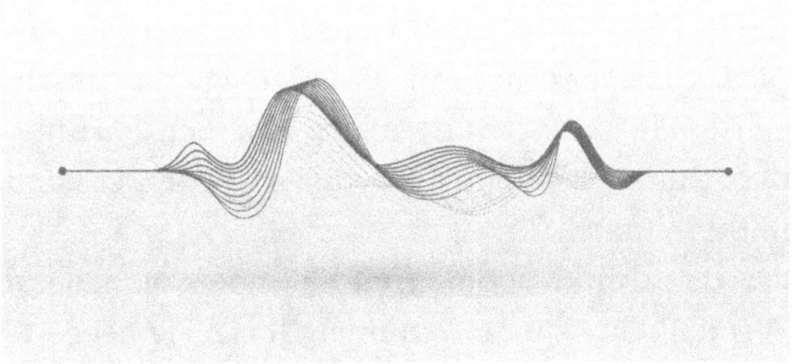

BEN AWAKES IN HIS DARK HOTEL room hoping beyond all hope that everything that's happened in the past forty-eight hours has only been a very bad dream. He knows better though. He stares at the ceiling and the very first words out of his mouth are: "Aurora must hate me. How can she not?! I hate myself! I've ruined everything."

He inhales and exhales slowly trying to get his equilibrium and think of a way out of this mess. He knows beyond a shadow of a doubt that General

Grossman will have him blown away if he doesn't comply with his wishes. In some ways that would be an easy way out for him, but he knows the ugliness wouldn't stop there. He shudders thinking what the Russians would do to Aurora and her parents, plus whatever other collateral damage they might cause. He closes his eyes and whispers, "Think, Ben, think … is there a way to get the upper hand in this situation?"

Ben thinks about what he knows of General Wendell Grossman. Extremely little. He needs to get answers to some questions: Where he lives? Is he married and does he have children? Where does he spend his time now that he's retired from NATO? What's his medical history? Where does he do his banking and which credit cards does he use? He lies there pondering how to get answers to those questions, and even if he had the answers, he wonders how he alone could tackle the general and a bunch of well-armed, well-funded, experienced, and motivated Russians. "I should just let 'em shoot me!"

After several minutes of self-pity and self-doubt, he turns on a table lamp and sits up at the side of the bed. He recalls his time working at NATO, and the germ of an idea comes to him, but it means going to his old stomping grounds in Brussels, Belgium.

He considers calling Aurora, but he knows better than to risk it. His heart is broken knowing that he's breaking hers. He believes Grossman when he says he and his handlers have access to telephone lines and sophisticated listening devices, not to mention plenty of armed thugs to do surveillance. No, this is something he has to do alone. It's a penance he has to pay for all of the turmoil he's caused.

"Maybe someday I can make it right by Aurora and her folks."

Using the cash that the general had given them as a wedding gift, Ben buys a one-way ticket to Brussels and lands eight hours later in a city that he'd gotten to know well in his previous life as a young diplomat. His first order of business is to find a hotel he's never used before and grab some shuteye before moving on to the next step of his questionable plan. He arises again the next morning in a dark room and hastily cleans up and grabs a quick breakfast in his hotel. Rested and energized, he sets out on foot to a place he reported to work for two years.

Formed at the end of WWII, the North Atlantic Treaty Organization (NATO) is headquartered in a modern complex in Haren. The staff at the headquarters is composed of national delegations of NATO member states and includes civilian and military liaison officers and diplomats of partner countries. From across the street, Ben spies the front entrance to the building and watches as staff and visitors are questioned and searched before given permission to enter.

From his wallet he attaches his old NATO ID card that he'd kept as a memento of his service, and takes a deep breath. He walks across the street, past concrete security barriers, and approaches the guard.

"G'morning, officer, I have an appointment in the personnel office."

"Is that you, Ben Witt?" the officer asks. "What's it been, three years since you left us?"

Ben doesn't immediately recognize the officer, but sees Smith on his name badge. He fakes it.

"Smitty, is that you?" he repeats. "I swear I barely recognized you looking all spiffy and official in your uniform. How the heck is life treating you?"

"Not bad, not bad at all. So, what brings you back?"

"Oh, I was in northern Europe and wanted to stop by the personnel office to discuss my health-care and education benefits. I don't have an appoint-ment, but I'm hoping someone can go over my per-sonnel file with me before I fly back to the states."

"Here, let me make a call for you to see who's available. You made quite a name for yourself in the brief time you worked here. I'm sure there'll be some folks that'll be very happy to see the golden boy return." Smith picks up his phone and dials the personnel office.

"Uh huh, uh huh," Ben hears the officer say. "Well, it appears you're in luck, but we do have one problem."

"Oh?!" Ben replies a little nervously.

"Yeah, there's no way you can enter the complex with that old name tag you're sportin'. You should've turned that in when you left our employment."

"I know, but my time here was special, and I wanted to have it as a keepsake."

"Well, as you can imagine, our security rules have gotten very strict. Give me that old employee badge and wear this visitor tag instead. I assume you remember the way to the office. A staffer will meet you there."

"Thanks, Smitty, great seeing you again," Ben feigns and walks inside the gleaming steel-and-glass building appointed with flags of the NATO member countries.

Ben walks down a marble corridor and wends his way past a number of offices until he sees a staffer waiting outside of the personnel department for him.

"Good morning, I'm Ben Witt," he says with a broad smile on his face. "I sincerely appreciate you folks agreeing to meet with me on such short notice."

"Mr. Witt, please come this way," Corporal Carter says politely. "I understand you used to be a NATO employee of some note."

"Well, I don't know about that, but it's good to see my old digs. I ran into Smitty at the front entrance, and it was nice seeing him again."

"We're a little short staffed today with employees either in training sessions or on holiday, but

Major Hunter is available to meet with you briefly." He leads Ben to a closed office door and knocks.

"Enter!" comes a basso voice from inside.

"Major, Mr. Witt is here to see you, sir." Ben enters the corner office, and the corporal recedes into the hallway.

"Good morning, Mr. Witt, it's nice to meet you. I was still stationed in Germany while you were employed here so I don't believe our paths ever crossed. I've glanced at your employment record, and it appears you made quite an impression on senior folks while you were here."

"Yes, sir, I don't think our paths ever did cross, but it's a pleasure to meet you, and I sincerely appreciate you taking the time to meet, especially without an appointment."

"So, what can I do for you today, Mr. Witt?"

"Well, I'm in Europe on business, and since I recently got married, I thought it might be good to go over my personnel file with you and add my wife's name as the contact person and the beneficiary of my estate in the event I croaked or something."

"I see, and what have you been doing since you left NATO employment?"

"I went to law school at Northwestern University, and now I'm residing in Greencastle, Indiana, with my new wife, Aurora, and I'm practicing law."

"I see. Sounds like you opted to have a quieter life rather than being on the front lines of the diplomatic service."

"Something like that, sir."

They spend a couple of minutes reviewing the contents of Ben's file, and he's surprised by how much detail is contained within, including test scores, promotions, family background, medical history, psychological profile, and financial records that he doesn't recall ever giving. It's quite complete, and given the sensitive nature of NATO's work and his specific assignments, he's not entirely surprised by the depth of information about him that the government had procured.

"Wow! You folks know more about me than I know!" he jests.

"Yes, we do take pride in being thorough." The major picks up the phone to request some new forms, including waivers of liability and retirement fund beneficiary designations. The phone rings several times, and Major Hunter gets irked that no one is answering.

"We're a little short staffed today, so I guess I'm going to have to get the paperwork myself. Please make yourself comfortable and look through your file. I had my assistant make a folder for you containing information that you're permitted to take with you. It may take me a few minutes to locate the new forms though, okay?"

"Yessir, my flight doesn't depart for another two hours, so I'm fine waiting."

Major Hunter exits the office, and Ben stands up ostensibly to look at the photographs and commendations mounted on the walls. He listens closely for the sounds of voices or footsteps in the corridor outside, and hearing none, he quickly moves over to a large row of filing cabinets containing personnel files. As he expected everything is very neatly organized in alphabetical order, and he begins flipping through drawers until he comes to the Gs ... Gabriel, Gaston, Gendell, Getz, Gibson, Gilhooley, Glotzbach, Gossage ... finally he sees the name he's looking for and pulls General Wendell Grossman's file from the drawer. He hears voices outside in the hallway and quickly closes the cabinet and stuffs the general's file into his own folder that Major Hunter had given him. The office door opens, and the major sees Ben admiring some of the photos on the wall.

"Impressive collection you have here, sir."

"Thanks, Mr. Witt, here are the forms we need you to complete."

They go over the forms together, and Ben fills in the salient information. "Sorry to rush off, Mr. Witt, but the colonel has asked me to see him ASAP."

"I understand, Major! Duty calls! Thank you very much again for seeing me on such short notice. I need to get to the airport anyway."

The major has his administrative assistant escort Ben down the polished corridor to the building's entrance. They say goodbye, and Ben notices that a new guard has taken over Smitty's post. Ben gives him a brisk salute as he passes him and then walks across the street, curious about what he'll discover in General Grossman's file. Thirty minutes later he checks out of his hotel and hails a taxi for Brussels' airport. Another hour after that the wheels of his plane are up for his flight back to the states. Ben sits alone in his row in the first-class section and waits for the cabin lights to be lowered for the overnight flight home. He pulls the file folder out and is intrigued by the extensive amount of personal information contained within.

"Okay, you son of a bitch! Let's see what I've got here!"

Chapter 14

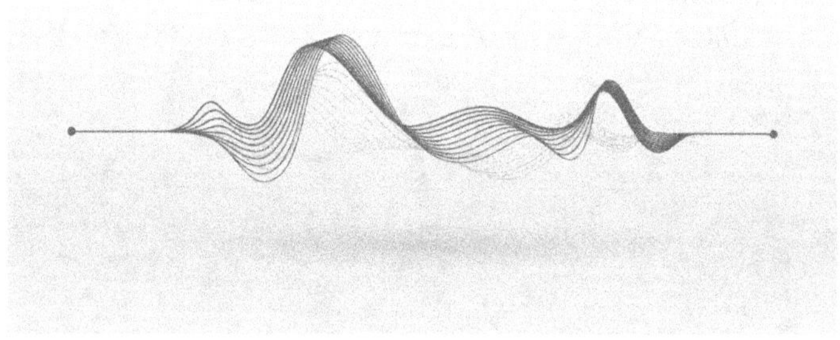

Some eight hours later, Ben's Douglas DC-4 lands at Idlewild Airport in New York, and he collects his belongings and steps onto the tarmac. During the flight he'd forced himself to memorize as many details about Grossman's life as he possibly could. It was a practice he'd cultivated as a first-year law school student, and he put it to good use on the plane. He cautiously surveys his surroundings knowing full well that the FBI is probably looking for him. He doesn't notice anything suspicious, but before heading to customs, he ditches Grossman's file in a large trash receptacle. "This is where your life belongs, you jerk!"

Ben gets into one of the queues for customs and tries to act as nonchalantly as possible. His turn comes and he composes himself as he hands his passport to the customs agent. On the inside he's a nervous wreck. The agent eyes him fully and looks at a list of names on a sheet of paper.

"Where are you coming from, Mr. Witt?"

"From Brussels, Belgium."

"Business or pleasure, Mr. Witt?"

"It was personal business. I used to work at NATO headquarters, and I needed to meet with people in the personnel office, plus I wanted to see some old colleagues."

Ben notices the agent nod to a security officer several feet away and figures that he's been identified.

"I see, Mr. Witt, would you please step over here. We have some more questions we'd like to ask you."

"Is there a problem, officer?"

"No, sir, this is standard procedure on international flights. If you would please step over to that agent, I'm sure we'll have you on your way in no time."

Ben knows that his goose is cooked. He takes a couple of steps in the direction the agent indicated, then turns on his heels and runs at full speed back toward the tarmac. Instantly, other agents take off after him, and he can hear their radios squawking. Ben hurries down a flight of stairs and exits the terminal. He casts a quick glance over his shoulder and sees two security agents running after him. He leaps over a baggage cart and accidentally knocks an employee to the ground. He's winded and scared but determined to outrun his pursuers. He notices another security guard bolt out of a terminal door to his left and decides to run straight at him. He bashes into the guard like a running back heading for the goal line and quickens his pace. That's when he hears the sound of a gun discharge and feels a swoosh of air as the bullet goes whizzing by. Recognizing that he's an easy target out in the open, Ben chooses to reenter the terminal, hoping to find anonymity among the mass of travelers.

Once inside, he rips off his jacket and ditches his hat hoping to change his appearance. "Well, that's one way to get around customs," he murmurs to himself. He slows his gait and moves with the pace of the crowd. He looks over his shoulder and sees guards entering the terminal, but it's obvious to him that his strategy is working. He moves with the group toward baggage claim but peels off from the group and quickly walks outside to ground transportation. He spies a line of taxis waiting for fares and jumps into the back seat of the first one and shouts to the driver: "There's a hundred bucks in it for you if you can get me into midtown Manhattan right away." The driver is more than happy to comply, and the cab moves swiftly away from the curb. Ben looks out the rear window and sees a half-dozen security guards looking in all directions for their suspect. He closes his eyes and exhales in relief.

"Any idea where the closest car rental agency is?" he asks the driver. The driver nods and replies to him in broken English. "Yes, there are a couple just a few miles ahead, but I thought you wanted to go to Manhattan."

"Change of plans." Ben sees a road sign for Hertz and tells the driver to go there. A few minutes later Ben tosses a C note to the driver and walks briskly into the rental agency. He patiently waits at the counter while a customer in front of him is served. Twenty minutes later he's sitting inside a Mercury sedan looking at a road map for the fastest route back toward Indianapolis and Greencastle. His goal is to drive for several hours, then find a roadside inn somewhere in Pennsylvania to hole up. As his adrenalin gets under control, Ben settles in for a long drive and keeps himself alert by recalling the detailed information he'd gleaned from General Grossman's NATO file.

Aurora sits on the porch steps of the carriage house thinking about the last twenty-four hours. She reflects on her strange but informative conversation with Professor Bergman, the crowd of frightened people outside the foundation's office, and the elucidating talk she had with Max Kindred. She closes her eyes in a combination of bewilderment, sadness, frustration, and anger thinking about Ben's abandonment and apparent theft.

"I never would've dreamed in a million years, Benjamin Witt, that you'd ever be capable of such betrayal!"

She sips from her coffee cup and looks at the Virtue bell. "So, everyone thinks that you're something special, and that I should listen to you. What do you have to say about that, Mr. Bell?"

As if on command, the bell's clapper begins to sway in the breezeless morning air. *"Listen … forgive,"* it intones to Aurora.

"And why should I do that? I can think of twenty-five million reasons not to forgive at this point."

"Loves you."

A tear rolls down Aurora's cheek. "Then, why doesn't Ben call me? I feel so alone without him."

"Not alone."

She looks across the yard to her parents' house and sees her father and mother coming to join her. She wipes the tear away and tries to put a smile on her face, but her sadness belies her brave attempt.

"Good morning, darling!" comes Caroline's greeting. "Getting ready to go into the office?"

"Yes, Mother. I just wanted to sit here for a few moments before going to work and fielding more calls from scared and frustrated grant applicants."

"How'd your conversation with Professor Bergman go?" Delano inquires hopefully.

"It was, uh, unusual to say the least. He talked to me about the Music of the Spheres and Psychoacoustics … pretty highbrow stuff. Basically, he concluded that it's possible for a bell to communicate with harmonics, and that I was lucky to have it as a confidante."

"Confusing, isn't it? Your father and I felt the same way about the Book of Tamberg. Still do, actually, but we came to acknowledge its sentience and the existence of another, unseen realm." Delano nods his head in agreement.

"And then after visiting with the professor, I decided to visit Max Kindred again to get more clarification of what he meant about the Virtue bell's 'unique characteristics.'"

"And?" Caroline asks.

"And, he acted as if it was perfectly normal to have a big ol' bell communicating with me. Said that originally he didn't know quite what to think about the bell's guidance, but that over time he just accepted it as a helpful friend. He also encouraged me to keep the faith about Ben." The Virtue bell sways again and lightly rings a pleasant tone.

"I need to get to the office so my staff doesn't feel overwhelmed with phones ringing off the hook and anxious people showing up unannounced."

"We'll meet you there and lend a brief hand, but your mom and I have a fairly full day too." In the distance they hear the bell in the courthouse clock gong eight times indicating the hour, and the three of them can't help but wonder if it's sentient too. While Aurora finishes her coffee, her folks walk across the lawn and get in Caroline's Woody.

Aurora lightly touches the bell's aged, patinated surface. "You won't abandon me, too, will you?"

She feels a soft but spirited vibration resonate deeply within her. *"Never."*

Somewhere in central Pennsylvania, Ben finally gives in to his weariness and pulls into the gravel driveway of a roadside inn. It's midafternoon, and he's hungry and exhausted. He's hoping to get a decent meal and at least a few hours of sleep before continuing his drive west. He rings a little bell at the front counter, and an elderly man shuffles into the room wiping soup from his chin.

"Help you, young fella?!"

"Yes, I need a room for a few hours, preferably one that's quiet."

"We're pretty full, but I think we can accommodate ya. A lot of folks here for the big football game. Got a room at the end with no little kiddies nearby. How's that sound?"

"Sounds fine. What do I owe you?"

They settle the bill, and Ben asks if their restaurant is still serving.

"Should be. We often shut the restaurant down this time of the afternoon, but my wife, Marvel, will be happy to fix you something. Plus, we got ourselves a new TV if you're interested in watching the news or the football game."

"Thanks! I appreciate the hospitality. A late lunch, a few hours of sleep, and then I need to hit the road again."

Ben takes his door key and walks next door to the diner. A small bell tinkles as he walks through the door. There's no one around, and he calls out, "Hello?!"

A moment later Marvel comes rushing from the kitchen, wiping her hands on a gingham apron and welcomes him. "Afternoon, sir, please have a seat wherever you wish."

Ben sits at a table in the corner and looks at the menu. Marvel approaches and asks him for his order.

"Are you still serving breakfast this time of day?"

"Yessir, I can fix you anything you want."

"How about an omelet with hash browns and sausage?"

"Of course! You want pancakes or toast with that too?"

"Wheat toast, please. No coffee, just water."

"Yessiree! It'll just be a few minutes, okay? Here, I'll turn the TV on for you while you wait." Marvel hustles back to the kitchen.

Ben idly watches the television set mounted on the wall. An advertisement for Ovaltine is on, followed by another ad for Ipana toothpaste featuring Bucky Beaver. Then, the news comes on, and a reporter announces, "I'm standing outside the international terminal at Idlewild airport with our continuing coverage of the shooting that occurred earlier this morning." Ben's ears perk up, and he's stunned to see a grainy photograph of him identified as a person-of-interest to the FBI. The reporter goes on to say that we've learned the individual's name is Benjamin Witt, and that he's suspected of orchestrating a major multimillion dollar fraud involving the Delano and Caroline Engel Charitable Trust in Indiana. Citizens are advised to report any sightings of this man who the FBI says may be armed and dangerous."

"Holy shit!" he says to himself. "Me?! Armed and dangerous?!"

A spokesman for airport security comes on and reports, "It was just business as usual at customs until one of our alert guards saw Mr. Witt's name match a name on our suspect list. When he was asked to come with our agents, he brutishly bashed into other travelers in an attempt to avoid detainment. He ran through those doors and onto the tarmac. An officer discharged his service revolver, but the suspect was able to get away. He remains on the loose, and law enforcement is asking for any information about this desperate man's where-abouts." The news transitions to another advertise-ment. This time for Ivory soap. "It Floats."

"Brutish … dangerous?!! Me?! What the hell?! Oh, I'm sure this will just make Delano and Caroline's day," he mumbles sarcastically, "not to mention the unbearable heartbreak my Aurora must be feeling."

A few minutes later Marvel returns carrying a steaming breakfast platter. "There you go! How's that look?"

"Looks great! Thank you. You know, I think I will have some coffee after all."

"Coming right up. I just brewed a fresh pot, and I'll bring you some of our local dairy cream too." Marvel returns in a jiffy, and the television is now back to covering the mayhem at Idlewild. Ben blanches in horror as he sees a grainy security photo of him fill the screen. Marvel places the coffee and cream on the table and glances up at the television.

"I've been watching that story all day. I swear to goodness, some people …" She looks away from the television and then at Ben. "Would be nice to get away with all of that money though," she laughs. Ben gives a nervous laugh in reply. "Ya know, you look a little like that feller the authorities are looking for."

"Yeah, people say I look like a lot of different people," Ben deflects. "Thanks for breakfast!"

Marvel stares at his picture on the TV and then back at Ben. "Well, I've got to tend to something in the kitchen. Just sing out if you need anything, okay?"

Ben dives into his omelet and hash browns. It's been hours since he's had a wholesome meal, and he knows he needs the energy if he's going to do what he hopes to do. He finishes his meal and leaves his payment on the table. He calls out to Marvel to say thanks, but doesn't hear a reply. He glances out the window and sees Marvel outside talking with a skinny police officer and pointing in his direction. The door flies open and a Barney-Fife-looking cop points his gun directly at him. His hand is shaking with anxiety.

"Freeze! I've got you covered and backup is on the way!"

Ben raises his hands in resignation.

"Get on the floor on your belly! And, no funny stuff!"

"No," comes Ben's reply.

"I said get on the floor now or I'll shoot your sorry ass!"

"No, I'm not getting on the floor, and you're not shooting me either!"

"I said 'now'!"

"And, I said 'no'! Go ahead and shoot me!"

"Turn around then so I can cuff you! I'm not playin' with you!"

Ben begins to turn around and quickly grabs his empty breakfast platter and smacks the officer in the face. The hapless officer falls groggily to the floor, and Ben kicks his revolver away and cuffs him to a table leg. He grabs the officer's radio and car keys and makes a beeline for his cruiser. He looks in the rearview mirror and sees Marvel goin' all apoplectic, jumping up and down in front of the diner. As he speeds away he hears chatter on the radio and sees two more police cars pull into the lot of the roadside inn.

"Seriously! First, the FBI and airport security … and now the Keystone cops! Thank God it wasn't Grossman and the bloody Russians!"

Chapter 15

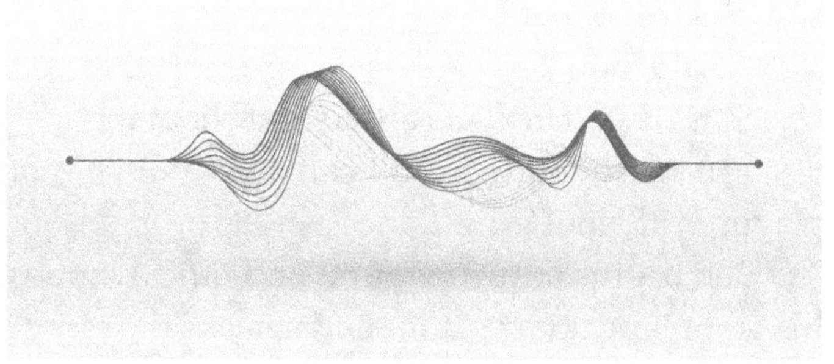

As Aurora arrives at her office, her assistant, BJ, says, "Red Jergens is on the phone for you. Do you want to take it, or do you want me to say you'll get back to him shortly?"

"Thanks, BJ, I'll take it in my office." She goes inside and drops her jacket and purse on a chair and picks up the receiver. "Red, sorry to keep you waiting. Just got into the office. I wish I had more to report to you, but I don't."

"Do you have a television in your office? If you do you might want to turn on the news. I'll hold while you do."

"Yeah, hang on a second, I'm turning it on." She changes channels and sees a graphic headline, *Turmoil at Idlewild.* Then, she sees her husband's face and has to steady herself against her desk. "My God … Oh, Ben …" she cries.

"I'm very sorry to be the bearer of bad news, Aurora. I'm very fond of Ben, and this makes no sense, at least not to this small-town newspaper editor."

"I know, Red, it makes no sense at all. Thanks for giving me a heads-up, and I promise to get back to you as I learn things, okay?"

They hang up and Aurora continues to use the desk to steady herself.

BJ appears again in her office doorway and says, "Linda Stanley and Kristi Donovan are here from the homeless shelter. They're hoping you have a few minutes to speak with them."

"Yeah, BJ, please give me two minutes and then show them in. Thanks." Aurora stares out her office window to the street below and sees her parents walking toward the entrance. They stop to talk with a few concerned citizens. The police officer on duty approaches them in case things get out of hand, but she sees her father politely wave him off.

BJ shows Linda and Kristi into her boss's office, and Aurora turns away from the window to greet them.

"Good morning, it's always great to see the folks who run our homeless shelter, but I'm sure this isn't a social call, is it?"

"We're very nervous, Aurora. You know, when you announced that we'd be getting $100,000 from the Engel Trust, we were all over the moon with joy. We went ahead and spent most of the money to expand our facilities and hire another staff member. Remember, just like we proposed in our grant application?"

"Yes, I remember, and there's no organization in our community that I respect more."

"Aurora, we're very close to running out of dough if we don't receive the grant money you've approved. If that happens I'm really afraid we're going to have to turn people away and lay off some staff. It's getting dire, and Kristi and I are here representing our board to see what we can do."

"I hear what you're saying, Linda, and I promise we'll honor our commitment to you."

Just then Delano pokes his dead in her office door to say hello. "Hi ladies, it's nice to see you."

"Dad, the homeless shelter is close to running out of money. Linda and Kristi are here to see what we can do."

"Whew! That's not good. Let's see what we can do about that." Delano picks up Aurora's phone and calls Conrad Zyer in Chicago. They listen as he says, "Connie, you'll recall that the Engel Trust has made a commitment of $100,000 to the Putnam County Homeless Shelter."

They hear Conrad's voice acknowledge that on the other end. "I need you to move $100,000 from the Engel Air charitable account to the shelter as soon as you can, okay?"

They hear Mr. Zyer's voice again. "I understand that, Connie, but find the dough somewhere and direct it to our charitable account and then pay them, okay?"

Again, they hear Conrad's voice on the other end. "Yes, Connie, I know we'll go over the amount that the company has budgeted for charitable contributions, but this is something that we really need to do." Again, more talk from the other end. Then, "Thanks, Connie, you're a prince!" They hang up.

"I've worked with Conrad Zyer for some thirty years. He's the best, but I'm sure he thinks I'm a royal pain in the ass sometimes." He winks at Linda and Kristi. "You'll have the dough within forty-eight hours."

"We can't thank you enough, Delano. You and your family have been a lifeline for a lot of people."

"Well, the last thing we'll ever do is let the homeless shelter go down the tubes. I can't think of anything more important than looking after our neighbors in need." Aurora beams at her father with pride, and the ladies from the shelter hug them both in gratitude.

Kristi and Linda leave Aurora's office, and Delano closes the door. "Any word from Ben?"

Aurora shakes her head negatively. "It's been four days now. Red Jergens phoned me a few minutes ago and had me turn on the television news.

Apparently, Ben had been to Belgium for some reason, and the customs people at Idlewild tried to apprehend him when he returned to New York. He bolted, and they shot at him, but he got away. He's on the run."

Delano hugs his daughter. "We'll get this figured out one way or the other, sweetheart. I promise you. I've got to get to the office right now to go over some aircraft engineering specs, and your mother has a meeting with some civic volunteers on the square. Let's have dinner this evening and see where we stand at the end of the day, okay?"

"Okay … and dad, thanks for talking care of the homeless shelter."

Ben drives his purloined police cruiser along country roads and eventually comes to Punxsutawney, Pennsylvania. A large sculpture of a groundhog named Phil greets him as he enters the city limits.

He ruminates aloud, "I've got to dump this car before a local cop hails me down for some reason. There's got to be an APB out for me. Then, I need to figure out a way back to Greencastle."

He drives through the downtown area and finds the local Greyhound station and decides to take his chances finding a bus heading west through Ohio and Indiana. He scopes out a secluded place a few blocks away and ditches the cruiser. Ben approaches the station's ticket window, and luck is with him. There's a Greyhound bus leaving for Indianapolis in an hour which gives him enough time to wash up in the bathroom. He buys a ticket with cash and a ball cap with a picture of a groundhog on it to help conceal his features. Like clockwork a Greyhound arrives on time and is promptly refueled. Several minutes later his bus departs the station, and once he feels secure in his anonymity, he closes his eyes and the rhythmic sounds of tires on the pavement lull him into a deep sleep … and he dreams …

In his dream Ben soars above the landscape like a red-tailed hawk windsurfing a cerulean sky. He rises on the warm thermals and lets the wind carry him where it will. He banks his wings and veers toward the dawn sun … Aurora rising. Below he spies a creature in flight, another bird rising on the thermals as well. He angles down to get a better look and glimpses another red-tailed.

Ben's dream morphs into a classroom setting. He's in law school at Northwestern attending an estate planning lecture, and he notices an intriguing-looking woman seated a few rows in front of him. He doesn't recall ever seeing her before, but he's not likely to forget her now. After the class Ben approaches his appealing classmate and asks if she would like to soar with him. She agrees and their time together takes flight.

The dream shifts to his new life as a married man living in the small town of Greencastle, Indiana. It's an idyllic existence, with a loving wife, happy and supportive in-laws, a fulfilling law practice, and involvement in major civic and charitable projects. But, the brightness of the mood descends into a dark abyss of ugly threats. Angry, taunting faces of General Grossman and Russian henchmen swirl around in his mind, and lightning and thunder dominate the scene like a circle out of Dante's hell. As if from an unseen realm, Ben hears the resonant peal of a great bell in the distance and awakens, sitting on the bus, a little rested, though very much alone.

He stares out the bus window at the landscape rushing by and sees a road sign indicating that Dayton, Ohio, is three miles ahead. He figures he's got a few more hours before reaching Indy, and he decides to put his time to good use by focusing again on the details of Grossman's NATO personnel file. He knows where the general lives. He knows where he likes to dine. He knows where he banks and where his retirement account is managed. And, he's aware of that small resort town near Puerto Vallarta, Mexico, where he's spent numerous vacations. By the time he arrives in Indianapolis, Ben's road weary but ready to try to restore his life. The Greyhound pulls into the bus station, and he purchases a ticket for the interurban railway back to Greencastle, back to an uncertain future.

It's dark when Ben finally returns to Greencastle, and he pulls his groundhog cap low over his brows to conceal his identity more. He grabs his meager belongings and trots off into the night heading for the courthouse square. Along the way he sees that the Mexican cantina is still open, and he quickly places a large carryout order and drifts away.

Despite Greencastle's emergence as a trendy town, there are very few people out wandering the streets at this hour midweek. Ben walks to an alley a block north of the square and stays in the shadows as he approaches the rear entrance to his law office building. He looks both ways and jimmies the door lock, then leans his shoulder against the door frame to gain entrance. He leaves the lights off and walks stealthily to his office, and once there, he drops into his desk chair, exhausted from hours of stress and travel. Sleeping on the bus only refreshed him so much. At least now he can spend some quiet time figuring out his next steps.

Chapter 16

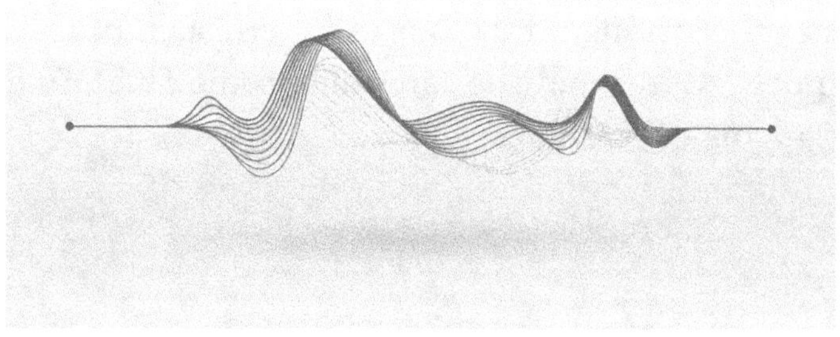

WHEN AURORA ARRIVES AT the carriage house that evening, she sees that her parents are already home. Her work day was filled with calls from the FBI, with Tyler Irvin, and various others ranging from media people looking for a story, and of course, local folks wanting to know the status of their grant applications. About the only person she did not hear from was Ben. At one point during the day she closed her office door and just stared out the window in abject sadness. Now that she's away from her office, she feels less immediate stress, but the sadness clings to her like a funeral shroud.

Before walking up to her parents' house, she sits on the porch steps by the Virtue bell and whispers, "I think it's about time that you and I got to know each other much better, Mr. Bell. If you're as wise as others seem to think you are, I'd sure appreciate your sending some of that sage wisdom my way."

The bell's clapper quivers, and she feels an unmistakable sensation in her core, *"I am here for you."*

Aurora lightly lays her hands on the bell's curvature and weeps softly. "Thank you. I need you. I miss Ben so much."

She's shocked when the sensation she feels becomes even more vibrant. *"He misses you too ..."*

"But where is he, and why hasn't he called?"

"He is not far away, but he needs to protect."

"But, why can't he just contact me?" Aurora awaits the bell's reply, *"When the time is right."* She waits for more details, but there are none, and after a few moments of silence, she turns in the direction of the house and walks away.

"Hello, darling," Caroline says brightly as her daughter walks into the kitchen. "Any good news to report?"

"No, not really. The authorities are still trying to figure out a paper trail for the money, and I've not heard a peep from Ben. I guess the only good news is that the Virtue bell communicated with me that Ben misses me and is not far away, but I'll believe it when I see it at this point."

Delano enters the kitchen and listens as Aurora expresses her frustration and sadness. He gently puts his arms around her.

"So, are you willing to tell me more about your experience with the Book of Tamberg?"

Caroline looks at Delano. "Well, I think we've told you most of it, sweetheart, but it's not just the book that has special powers. In some ways, it's also this house and your carriage house too."

Delano nods his head in agreement. "When Christopher and Elizabeth Wright originally built this home in the 1880s, something inexplicably transformative occurred as well."

"Like what? And, what happened to the Wrights?"

"Great questions, and trust me when I say that we've spent our adult years trying to figure it out. But, it was like Max Kindred said to you, after a while you just stop trying to figure it out and just accept it."

"But, did you ever learn what happened to the Wrights and their worldly possessions?"

"No," Caroline confesses. "The only time we ever had any direct connection with them was when we safely got you back from the kidnappers, and they briefly appeared to us in a vision in your carriage house, waving at us and looking happy."

"That is just so weird," Aurora replies. "And now, we've got the Virtue bell. Do you think the Book of Tamberg will ever reveal itself again?"

Delano shrugs. "We don't have a clue, but it wouldn't come as a complete surprise if it did. It's like your mother and I shared with you earlier, we're convinced there's an unseen realm out there beyond our comprehension that connects with us from time to time, but we have no clear understanding of it."

There's not much more they can discuss about the bell, the book and the *unseen realm*. It is what it is … a surreal mystery, and after a quiet dinner,

Aurora tells her parents that she wants to turn in early. They say goodnight, and Aurora slowly walks across the yard. At one point she stops and glances up at the house's tower room. She sees a soft golden light radiating from the attic window casting a glow all the way to the Virtue bell. She walks the rest of the way to the carriage house and stops again by the Virtue bell.

"You look all lit up with that glowing light from the tower room. I don't suppose you have anything further you want to convey to me."

"I do," comes the visceral resonance. *"With you … beside you, in you. You are not alone."*

"Well, that's a relief," Aurora says rather sarcastically. "I don't suppose you know where Ben is?"

"Near." And, then there is silence, and the light from the tower room fades away. Aurora waits a few moments longer hoping that the bell will comment more about Ben's location. She touches the bell briefly and then goes inside to get ready for bed.

A few hours pass during which Aurora sleeps fitfully. She can't get the thought of an unseen realm out of her mind, especially knowing that her parents corroborated their own mysterious connections when she was an infant. Then, she keeps thinking about the bell communicating that Ben is near. How near? Where? She manages to fall back asleep again until she hears and feels the Virtue bell's animated peal followed by the sound of what she thinks are tree branches scratching at the window's screen. She lies awake listening and wondering until she hears a flower vase fall from the window sill and crash on to the floor.

"What the?!" she blurts out as she reaches into her night stand and pulls out a Smith & Wesson handgun. She sees a shadow darken the window, and she scurries to the floor on the other side of the bed. She hunkers down with her pistol pointed at the window waiting to see if an intruder is trying to gain entry.

The next thing she hears is the sound of the screen being pushed aside and the window pane being opened. "That's far enough!" her quivering voice commands. "I have a gun, and I know how to use it!" She sees a figure fall through the window and land with an audible thud on the floor.

"Don't shoot, Aurora!" she hears Ben's voice implore. "Don't shoot and don't turn on any lights!"

"Oh Ben! My God, it's you!" She rushes over to join him and is overwhelmed by shock and joy. "Where the hell have you been?" He manages to get into a sitting position, and the two of them hold each other tightly for a long several moments. "I don't know whether to shoot you or smother with kisses!"

"I prefer the latter, darling, but I understand your feeling perplexed. I would, too, if the circumstances were turned around."

They embrace some more, and Aurora says, "Now, before I ask you what the hell happened to my family's money, tell me where the hell you've been and why I hadn't heard from you." She punches his chest hard and chastises him, "That's what you get for scaring the bejesus out of me. Why didn't you call me?!"

Ben massages his chest where she hit him. "It's a very long and unpleasant story, my love, but if you'll give me a few moments. I'll try to explain."

The young couple sit on the floor in the dark room, and Ben begins telling her about General Wendell Grossman and the menacing Russians. Aurora's eyes go wide in shock and terror.

"I only met General Grossman briefly when I was on assignment at NATO before you and I met in law school. We never worked together, but apparently his interest in me grew when he learned about my marrying Delano Engel's daughter. The Russians apparently had some very incriminating stuff on the general, and they leaned on him to see if he could turn me into an asset so they could not only steal a lot of money, but also get their hands on trade secrets from Engel Air Corporation."

"But, why didn't you just tell us or go to the authorities, darling?"

"You don't know these people, Aurora. Grossman told me that if I breathed one word about this to anyone that they'd kill you, your parents, all of the employees at Engel Air and the Engel Trust, and anyone else that we cared about. Grossman was crystal clear about the certainty of these threats, and so I had no choice to do anything but follow his commands. That meant transferring the money from the Engel Charitable Trust to a foreign account in the general's name. It was the most painful decision I've ever made because I knew that I'd never be able to look you and your parents in the eye ever again." A tear rolls down his face as he expresses how sorry he is for violating the trust of the people he cares about the most.

"The only thing I could think to do was … *protect!*" At the mention of that last word, Aurora hears the Virtue bell peal outside, and she now understands what the bell had meant with its earlier communications with her.

"Oh, Ben, darling! I'm so sorry you had to go through all of that alone. I love you so much, and I just didn't know what your silence and the theft of the money had meant." They hold each other for a very long time. "So, what do we do now?" she asks anxiously.

Ben exhales audibly. "For now we have to continue maintaining silence about this. As hard as this will be for us, you can't tell anyone that we've spoken, and that includes your parents. I have some thoughts about how to get to Grossman, but for now we need to act as if nothing has changed. Please trust me, darling, because to do otherwise would prompt very ugly retaliation by the general and the Russians."

They talk for another thirty minutes or so, and Ben tells Aurora about traveling to the NATO headquarters in Brussels and stealing Grossman's personnel file; then getting shot at as he attempted to return to the states.

"What can I do to help, Ben?"

"Please don't ever lose faith in me, in us. I'm so sorry I didn't contact you, but I couldn't risk it. I'd love to stay with you here, but I don't know if that's safe. The general and Russians have lots of eyes and ears. I was thinking of hiding in my office, but I don't think it's safe there either."

"Why don't you get cleaned up and bunk upstairs in the loft? No one will know you're here, and I can bring food to you, and you can use my work telephone."

"Darling, I'm so tired of being on the run, and I've missed you so much. Honestly, I have no idea where else I can go, so I'm willing to give that a try." They hug and kiss more.

"It'll be light soon, and Mom and Dad are early risers, so let's get you cleaned up and stashed away upstairs. I need to leave for the office around eight, and my parents generally leave for the day around then too. You can get some sleep and a change of clothes. You'll be alone but safe."

Chapter 17

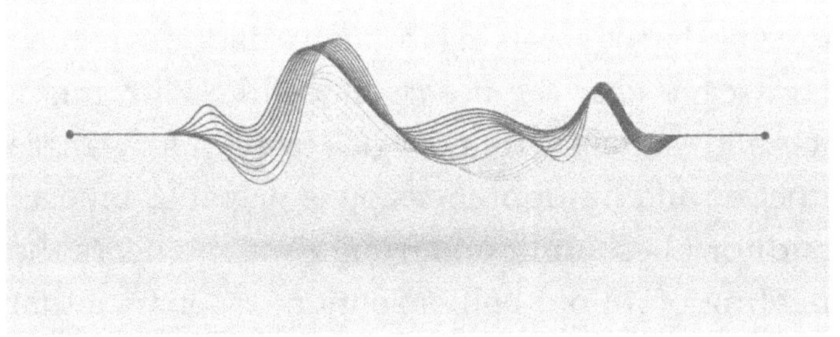

AFTER AURORA LEAVES FOR the office, Ben finishes washing up, puts on some fresh underwear, and eats a little breakfast. From his window in the loft, he watches Delano and Caroline climb into the Ford Woody and drive away. He feels an enormous pang of guilt knowing how warmly his in-laws have welcomed him into the family, and then how he'd trashed their faith in him and their dreams for Aurora and Greencastle.

"Now what?" Ben asks himself. He lies down on the spare bed in the loft and stares upwardly watching the ceiling fan make silent rotations. "What goes around, comes around, general," he says softly.

Shortly thereafter he falls into a deep sleep. He dreams that he's walking through a darkly shrouded landscape near the ocean, moor-like with misty fog and vague surroundings. His path forward is unclear and his apprehension is palpable. Like an auditory beacon upon a rough sea, he hears the pealing of an old bell, a sentient resonance that leads him to it. Ben moves in that direction, seeing and feeling a conveyance of reassurance, and then he wakes. He lies staring at the ceiling, his recollection of the dream still reasonably vivid to him. He closes his eyes, shakes his head, and softly says, "I've gotta make this work."

He finishes dressing and decides to make a bold move. He picks up Aurora's home telephone extension for the Engel Charitable Trust and calls an old friend, Tyler Irvin.

"Irvin Financial Group. Where may I direct your call?" comes the melodious voice on the other end of the line.

"Yes, I'm calling Tyler Irvin. Please just tell him that it's an old friend."

A few moments later Ben hears a familiar voice. "This is Ty. Which one of my old friends is calling? Hopefully somebody who owes me a lot of money," he gibes.

"Ty, it's me … Ben."

"Ben, holy shit! Where are you? Do you have any idea how much trouble you're in?!"

"If you mean having the FBI after me and dodging bullets at Idlewild, yeah, I've got a pretty good idea, Ty. Listen, I know I'm putting you in a very awkward position, but I need your help."

"What you need to do is turn yourself in and get a really good attorney, my friend!"

"I can't do that right now, Ty, and I'll explain why if you just give me a few minutes, okay? I really need your help, and I'm counting on you believing that I'm still the same upstanding guy you've always known."

"Okay, I'm listening, but this better be good because the last thing I'll do is go to jail and ruin the reputation of my company for an old buddy who stole $25 million from one of the most respected industrialists in the country. Right?!"

"Right," Ben concedes. Over the next two minutes Ty listens patiently as Ben tells him about the threats from General Wendell Grossman and the Russians. "Obviously, they wanted to steal the money, but they're also after as much aircraft and munitions intelligence as they can get their hands on. I'm talking about really sensitive stuff."

Ty remarks, "I still think you need to go to the authorities instead of trying to do anything further on your own. Ben, I'm telling you this as a friend."

"These people will kill everyone I care about, Ty, and then they'll go after Delano and Caroline's employees and staff. The collateral damage could be grisly. And, I don't think they'd stop there. You and Conrad Zyer could also be in the crosshairs because of your roles with the money. 'Dead men tell no tales,' as the saying goes."

"Jesus, Ben! I had no idea, and you don't think you can trust the authorities with this information?"

"No, I think the fewer people that know, the better. I told Aurora last night, and aside from the two of you no one else knows, and I'm asking you to keep it that way … please."

"I don't know, Ben, every cop in the country is looking for you. I sure don't want to get busted as an accessory or for obstructing justice."

"I understand, Ty, but I think I have a plan that might help us get all of the Engel Trust's money back. The fact that they think of me as a turned asset is to our advantage. I can let them think that and see if I can control the narrative; perhaps use that as a diversion to our getting the money returned through a back door. I simply can't do it alone, and you and your company have great forensic financial skills. That's one of the reasons why we hired your firm in the first place. I'm just asking you for thirty-six hours, then you can do as you wish."

There's a lengthy pause on the other end, then Ty says, "All right, Ben, what do you need me to do?"

"First of all, tell me what you and Conrad Zyer and the feds have been able to find out about the transfer of the $25 million. Where the money went after I transferred the bulk of it to Grossman's offshore account. There's got to be a trail we can follow. One that I can exploit."

General Wendell Grossman, Retired, is the happiest he's been in years. After his spit-and-polish life in the U.S. military for over forty years, he's very content sitting on a beach chair in front of his oceanfront home near Sayulita, Mexico. He smiles as he looks at the sand on his feet, knowing that his days of keeping a sharp uniform and highly polished shoes are in his past. He gazes out over the Pacific Ocean and casually sips from his second margarita of the early afternoon.

"Yessir," he slurs, "I think I pulled the ol' rabbit out of the hat this time. My dear, departed wife's been gone a long time now, but I've got me a cozy place to hide out, with a pretty señora looking after me, and enough dough to keep me living like a king for the rest of my days. I gave the Russians enough of the money I stole from the Engels to keep them off my back for a while, and I've got ironclad plans to get that kid, Ben Witt, to supply me with Engel Air's secret aircraft designs. Yessir, the Russians may have turned me into a corrupt spy because of my past indiscretions, but I think I've got life pretty well licked at this point!" He closes his eyes with a self-assured smirk on his face and drifts into a well-earned siesta.

An hour later the general is aroused from his alcohol-induced nap by his housekeeper, Lucinda. "Señor Wendell, wake up. You have a telephone call."

Grossman mumbles something unintelligible as he tries to regain his lucidity. Finally. "What do you want, woman?!"

"Senor Wendell, it's someone from el banco. They say they need to speak with you right away."

"Are they still on the line?"

"No, señor, they hung up but asked that you come to town to see them pronto."

"Now what?!" Grossman grumps as he struggles to get out of the beach chair. "Get my car keys, will ya, Lucinda, and my wallet and hat too!"

Twenty minutes later Wendell Grossman parks his Toyota Land Cruiser in Sayulita's town square and ambles into the bank and barges into the manager's office. "We got a problem, Ricardo? I don't appreciate being distracted from my important business!"

"Si, señor, it appears we do have a bit of a problem. The money you deposited here in our bank, well, it seems to have disappeared."

"What the hell are you talking about?" the general rages. "I deposited $5 million here and sent the rest of it to other accounts. You better not be trying to steal my dough, you little douche bag!"

"No no, of course not, senor, but your dinero is gone!"

"Well, get it the hell back or I swear you'll be sorry!"

"Si si, senor, we've tried but it seems to be gone. It appears that it went to a shell account back in the states."

"What about my other money that I sent to my accounts in Switzerland and Russia?"

"We don't know the status of those accounts, sir. Once you instructed us to transfer those dollars, they were no longer on deposit with us. I presume they went exactly where you instructed."

"So, how much money do I have left on deposit in your bank?"

Ricardo looks at a sheet of paper in front of him and says, "$8,457 ... and change, sir."

Grossman blanches in horror. "You mean to tell me that MY $5 million that I deposited into the safety of your stupid-ass bank is gone?"

"Si, senor, it would appear so."

Grossman rages some more and kicks over a yucca plant as he stomps out of the bank manager's office, mumbling and cursing, all the way back to his Land Cruiser.

"Sonovabitch! Well, at least I still have the $10 million I transferred to my Swiss account, but I'm going to get to the bottom of this crap ASAP!"

He sits in his car thinking, wondering how this theft could happen, and then a scowl of realization comes to his face. "It was that little weasel, Ben Witt! I'd stake my stars on it. Okay, young Witt, you want to play games with General Wendell Grossman? Well, it's time to lock and load because I'm coming for ya! Yessir, ya little weasel!"

When he arrives back at his hacienda, he picks up the phone and calls his old friend in Moscow, Yuri Tabeshenko. "Buenas dias, comrade, it's Wendell. I got a little problem I need your, uh, help with." He holds the phone away from his ear as the Russian barks a reply back at him. "Yeah, yeah, I know you still want Engel Air Corp.'s design plans, and I'm working on that, but I need you to do something for me first." Again Grossman holds the phone away from his ear as Yuri barks more. "Yeah, yeah, I know you're the one running the show, comrade, but we need to iron out a little wrinkle first."

Chapter 18

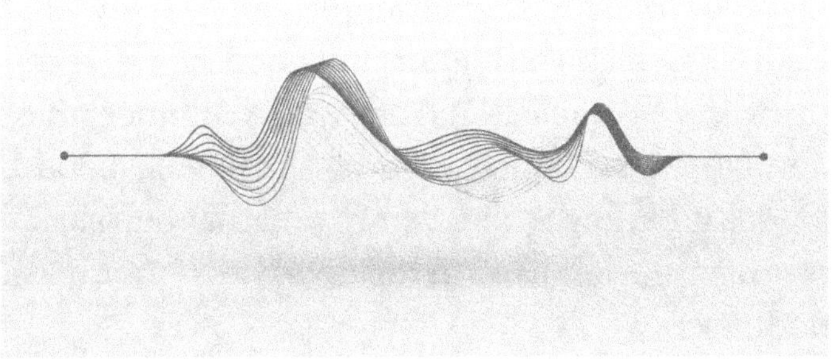

WHEN AURORA ARRIVES IN the office, her assistant, BJ, can't help but notice she has a little extra zip in her gait. "My, my! It appears that someone's feeling a little less stressed today," she exclaims.

"Good morning, BJ! Yes, I guess I just got a good night's sleep and feel a little better about things. So, any more news from Mr. Zyer or Tyler Irvin about tracing the money?"

"Nothing so far today, but it's early. We're bound to catch a break at some point."

"I agree, BJ, I just wish it would happen sooner rather than later. We need to offer more encouragement for folks in the community, and I know that Red Jergens is waiting for any good news he can print in *The Banner.*" Aurora walks into her office and closes the door. "Whew," she exhales aloud. "At least I know where Ben is, and that he's safe."

BJ sticks her head in the doorway. "Your dad's on line one."

"G'morning, Dad, what's the good word?"

"I was about to ask you the same thing."

"Nothing more to report right now."

"Your mother and I are going to be pretty busy at my office today, but I'm hoping we can all have dinner at home tonight. Are you free?"

"Yeah, sure, what're you working on?"

"Our tech guys have made some major breakthroughs on jet propulsion for commercial aircraft, and we're trying to get the patent work finalized. Our competitors and our enemies would love to get their hands on our hard work, and we need to protect our intellectual property."

"I get it. What's Mom up to today?"

"She and a couple of her fellow volunteers are working at the animal shelter today. She feels that we're very close to making the shelter a no-kill facility. Losing their grant money obviously puts a boulder in the path, but we'll figure it out. We have to. Why don't we meet at home say around 7:00 PM?"

"Sounds good, I'll see you then. Love you, Dad!" They hang up.

Just then BJ steps into Aurora's office doorway again. "It's Conrad Zyer on line two. Can you take his call?"

"Sure!" She picks up the phone. "Connie, what's going on?"

"Aurora, you're not going to believe this, but $5 million of the Engel Charitable Trust money is now back where it's supposed to be!"

"You're kidding. How'd you pull that off?"

"Darned if I know. Ty Irvin and I spotted it back in the account first thing this morning. It appears that someone reversed the deposit that went to an account in Sayulita, Mexico. We're trying to pin down who made the transfer, but it's pretty well concealed. At this point, I'm just thrilled to see something positive happen for our team."

"Ditto that!" Aurora replies. "Please keep us posted of any other windfalls that come our way, okay?"

"Will do!" They hang up, and Aurora steps to her office window and gazes heavenward. In the distance she hears a gentle peal coming from the courthouse bell. "Finally, it looks like we've got some things going our way. I can't help but think that Ben has his hands in this."

It's everything that Aurora can do to stay focused on work the rest of the day. All she wants to do is go home and be with Ben, but she knows she has work to do, and she needs to maintain appearances so no one suspects anything out of the ordinary. She looks at her watch. A couple more hours, and then she can head home.

Delano and Caroline finish up the paperwork for their patents on Engel Air Corp.'s new jet aircraft designs, plus some very high-tech missiles they've been developing for the military. World War II is over, but the specter of open warfare on the Korean peninsula continues to threaten world peace, and the Russians are rattling their sabres as well. It's no time for America to be lax about its defense, and the Engels stand to continue to make a fortune by keeping the country's defense capabilities second to none. They pack up their papers and head back to Carriage House Lane.

"I'm bushed," Caroline states as they enter the house. "All I want to do is kick my shoes off, put on some music, and have a glass of wine. How about you, Del?"

"Sounds good to me, darlin'! Why don't you pop a cork while I stow these papers in my desk. I told Aurora that we'd probably eat around seven, so we've got some time to kick back a little until she arrives home."

Caroline puts a Glenn Miller record on the turntable, and the two of them sway in their chairs listening to "In the Mood." A few moments later they hear a car on the gravel driveway followed by the sound of their kitchen door closing.

"We're in the study, Aurora. C'mon in and join us with a glass of cabernet before we fix dinner."

The next sight they see sends chills down their spines as two large, serious-looking men dressed in black leather coats enter the study pointing handguns in their direction.

Caroline drops her wine glass on the table, and Delano stands to protest their intrusion. "Who the hell are you, and what're you doing in our home?"

One of the men offers them a frosty grin, and with an eastern European accent calmly says, "Get up. Get up now. You're coming with us!"

"The hell we are!" Delano shouts as he reaches for the telephone on his desk. The next thing he hears is a loud gunshot causing plaster from the ceiling to flurry down upon them. The other man grabs the telephone cord and rips it out of the wall.

"What do you want?" Delano commands. "If you're after money, we don't keep anything of much value here."

One of the Russian thugs taunts him. "We already have a lot of your money. Now, we want you. Get up! I'm not going to ask you politely again."

Caroline and Delano stare at each other and reluctantly stand. While one man keeps his handgun pointed at the Engels, the other wrenches their hands behind their backs and slips restraints over their wrists. They then gag them and push them roughly toward the kitchen door.

From his hiding place inside the loft in the carriage house, Ben had seen the large black sedan pull up to the Engels' home and subsequently heard the discharge of the gun. Since he has no weapon, he's hardly in a position to intervene as he helplessly watches the two brutes push his in-laws out of their house and into the dark sedan, then swiftly drive away.

"Grossman, you bastard!" he screams. He runs downstairs and onto the carriage house's porch trying to figure out what to do next. He paces back and forth and can't think of what he's going to tell Aurora. First, the family's money is stolen; next he becomes persona non grata to the entire world, and now his wife's parents are abducted by very big ugly characters. He plops down on a step and holds his quivering face in his shaking hands. "Holy Mother of God! What do we do now?"

Ben sees Aurora's Lincoln pull into the driveway, and he steels himself to be the bearer of horrible news. As she exits the car, he hears the Virtue bell begin to ring, and he peers at it expectantly. She approaches her husband with a warm smile on her face which quickly dissolves when she sees Ben's pained expression.

"What's wrong, Ben, and why are you sitting out here where you can be seen?"

He runs to his wife and holds her closely. "The Russians have your parents. They barged into their house a few minutes ago, tied and gagged them, and just drove off. Grossman must've sent them after I stole a portion of the money back."

Aurora sinks to the ground in total shock, and Ben drops next to her. "I'm so sorry," he says. "I wish I were dead." She's in so much shock she can't muster any words in reply. Despite firmly shutting her eyes, tears stream down her face, and she slumps against Ben.

He lifts Aurora off the ground, and helps her into the carriage house where she collapses onto a chair and sobs inconsolably.

Even from inside, they hear the Virtue bell begin to loudly ring, first with a vague dolorous peal, and then as it changes its resonance and tone to something much more forceful and defiant. They feel it deeply within their cores. *"We are not victims! Now, we get them back!"*

Chapter 19

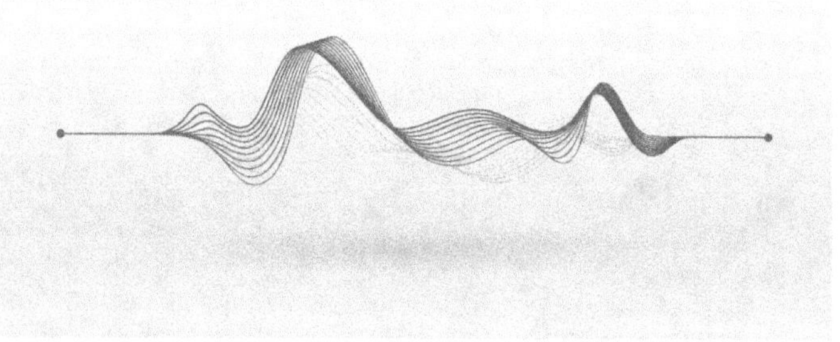

THE LARGE BLACK SEDAN wends its way through the heart of Greencastle. The strident sound of an atonal bell reverberates as they drive past the courthouse, but no one is the wiser. The Russian driver assiduously maintains the speed limit and heads north on U.S. 231. No one talks, and Delano knows it's fruitless to scream out, especially since they're gagged and have guns pointed at them.

As they drive past *The Banner's* printing offices, Delano sees Red Jergens standing on the sidewalk interviewing volunteers working on a beautification project. Delano hopes to make eye contact with him, but the car's darkly tinted windows negate that. They continue to drive north, and the abductors remove their gags. Delano asks, "Where are you taking us, and who's behind this?"

"People who are very interested in making your acquaintances."

"And, do these *people* have names?" Caroline challenges.

"Yes, of course, but the Russian pronunciations might present a challenge for you," the lead Russian guffaws. "We'll be where we're going soon enough, and then you'll make, uh, new friends. Won't that be nice?"

"Swell!" comes Caroline's sarcastic reply.

They continue driving north passing Somerset and Short-cut Road until turning west on SR 236. "Pull in here," the lead Russian directs the driver.

"Here? There's nothing here but a grassy field and a wind sock."

"Do as I say."

The driver goes another quarter mile and comes to a stop alongside a plane without any markings.

"Welcome to the Russellville International Airport!" the lead Russian chortles. "We hope you have a smooth flight and remember to stow any of your belongings under your seat or in the overhead bin!" he laughs again.

"I didn't know that Russellville had an airport," Caroline says to Delano.

"It doesn't. It's just an airstrip for crop-dusters and the occasional amateur pilot."

"Okey dokey, it's time for us to part company, Mr. and Mrs. Engel. Comrade Tabeshenko will be your friendly tour guide on the next leg of your journey."

Delano and Caroline are led from the black sedan and jostled onto the plane where they are roughly deposited into their seats.

"Ah, and now it's time for your cocktails!" A female flight attendant surreptiously comes up beside Caroline and jabs a needle into her arm.

"Ouch, dammit! That hurt!" She barely finishes her sentence when her head slumps forward from the sedation in the syringe.

"What'd you give her?!" Delano angrily snaps.

"Just a little sleep-aid," the attendant replies. Two of the Russians hold Delano in place as the attendant jabs another syringe into Delano's arm. He feels his head grow woozy and a moment later he joins Caroline in unconsciousness. Another minute after that the plane's wheels lift off the grass airstrip and depart the serene solitude of Russellville International Airport.

Once airborne, the plane flies in a southerly direction and stays well below the radar. Several hours later they enter Mexican airspace and land at a prearranged, secluded location to refuel. The Engels are still out cold from the drugs they'd received, and as the sun begins to dip in the western sky, the Russians' plane lands at a private airfield just outside of Puerto Vallarta, Mexico.

"Time to wake up, sleepyheads!" Delano vaguely hears an eastern European accent declare. Yuri Tabeshenko raps Delano's cheek to arouse him further into full consciousness. He does the same with Caroline. "Ah! There you are. I hope you both enjoyed your naps!"

"Where are we?" Delano demands. He looks out the plane's window and sees long shadows cast from palm trees across the small tarmac. "Are we in Florida?"

"No, Mr. Engel, you and your wife are now our guests in sunny Mexico."

"Mexico?!" Caroline questions, "And, I forgot to bring my sunscreen!" she ad libs sarcastically. "We'll need to return to Indiana!"

"That's very funny!" Yuri replies, "But, no can do, señora! Perhaps, if you and your husband cooperate, but then again, perhaps not!"

Caroline and Delano are lifted out of their seats and are half-walked, half-dragged through the aisle and down the steps to the tarmac where another large dark sedan with tinted windows is waiting for them.

A huge, serious-looking guard opens the rear passenger door and guides the Engels and Yuri Tabeshenko inside where they see another man dressed in casual attire.

"Hello, Mr. and Mrs. Engel, my name is Wendell Grossman, formerly General Wendell Grossman of the United States Army, now happily retired. Welcome to Mexico."

"Well, thank goodness, we have an American general here to protect us!" Caroline opines.

"Alas, Mrs. Engel, you misunderstand. Comrade Tabeshenko and I are now, uh, colleagues … joined together by the wallet as it were."

"You mean you're a damned traitor and a criminal!" Delano hurls.

"Sticks and stones, Mr. Engel, but before my Russian friends are finished with the two of you, you'll probably come up with even more colorful language."

Aurora finally composes herself and says, "I've got to contact the FBI about Mom and Dad. Do you recall any other details about the abductors?"

"The only thing I know for certain is that two big thugs restrained them and took them away in a dark sedan, but you should urge the feds to look into General Wendell Grossman's whereabouts. I know he spends a lot of time in Sayulita, Mexico, so maybe the CIA should be involved, too, but the FBI can determine that. This wouldn't have happened without Grossman's knowledge and collusion."

"And, how do I explain to them to track Grossman without getting you involved?"

"You might tell them that you recall his showing up uninvited at our wedding, and that I'd mentioned to you that he'd tried to bribe and pressure us into getting sensitive trade secrets from Engel Air Corporation for the Russians. That, plus the fact that $5 million had been transferred back to the Engel Charitable Trust from Grossman's personal account in Mexico. No doubt that Grossman's pretty ticked off about that!"

"That's not much for them to go on, but I'll do it." She picks up the phone and calls the Indianapolis field office and speaks with Special Agent Linton Loudermilk.

"That's frightening news!" agent Loudermilk says. "I wish we had more to go on. At this point they could be anywhere. We'll see about paying General Grossman a little visit."

Aurora then calls Conrad Zyer to tell him about the kidnapping and asks him to relay that information to Tyler Irvin as well.

"Connie, I think it would be wise for you and Ty to keep a watchful eye out for anything unusual, and to double whatever security measures you have personally and for your companies. We obviously were too lax in protecting Mom and Dad. I just pray we can get a lead on this before it's too late."

Aurora hangs up, and she and Ben go outside to the porch and sit on the top step near the Virtue bell. The evening air is warm with a slight breeze coming out of the southwest. They hold hands and stare vacantly into space, neither one able to adequately express words describing their sadness and fear. As the sun drops lower in the sky and their world becomes enveloped in purple shadows, they notice a warm bright light emanating from the house's secret attic room, glowing across the yard and shining its countenance on the Virtue bell.

"I don't remember ever seeing that light before," Ben says. "I sure wish it were a sign for us."

Aurora follows the radiant beam from the tower room to the Virtue bell. She squeezes Ben's hand and replies, "I prefer to think that it may be."

"What do you mean?"

"There are some things that I've learned recently that I haven't had a chance to share with you yet."

Ben shifts his position to face his wife, and the bell begins to softly ring. "What sort of things?"

"It's a bit of a long story, one that actually goes back many years ago. You're probably going to think I'm nuts, especially in light of Mom and Dad being abducted, but hear me out, okay?" The beam of light glows even brighter on the Virtue bell, and it peals a telling tone.

"I've been noticing some very unusual sentient communications from our bell here, and when I risked sharing that with my parents, they led me upstairs to their attic and showed me a secret room behind one of the cedar closets that contained a very old book sitting alone on an old rolltop desk."

Ben's eyebrows go up in surprise, but he remains silent and listens as Aurora continues.

"Apparently, the old tome was the Book of Tamberg which was the sum of the knowledge of the Tamberg Magical Dynasty. The Tambergs were a six-generation Dutch family that practiced magical arts going back to the seventeenth century. For many years they were the court magicians for the Dutch royal family."

"So, your parents found an old book?"

"Yes, but the Book of Tamberg was/is sentient, and it had the ability to communicate guidance by having words magically appear on its blank pages." She glances at Ben and sees that he's more than a little skeptical.

"Yeah, I know it sounds nuts. They then told me that when I was an infant that I'd been kidnapped by some nefarious local people, and it was the Book of Tamberg that guided my folks in getting me safely back."

"You're kidding! What happened to the book, and what does that have to do with the Virtue bell?"

"My parents say that the book disappeared twenty-five years ago, and they haven't see it since. Then, they noticed the golden glow from the attic room shining on the Virtue bell the way it is now, and they realized that some inexplicable power from an unseen realm was still around. It seems that the magic from the book can now be felt through the resonance of the bell."

"You're kidding me, aren't you?"

"No, I'm not, although that was my reaction when my parents told me their story."

"Darling, we've both been through hell these last several days, and it's no wonder that we're both feeling bewildered, but this story is way off the charts."

"I know, but wait, there's more. Dad suggested that I visit with Dr. Enrique Bergman at the college's school of music which I reluctantly did."

"And?"

I asked Dr. Bergman if it's possible for sound, like the reverberations from a bell, to be capable of communicating with humans. I told him about how when I asked the bell about your recent actions that it conveyed a word deep within me, *protect*. At the time I had no idea what *protect* meant until you returned and told me that was the reason you transferred our trust money and fled. He further surprised me when he told me of the Music of the Spheres and Psycho-acoustics, and that he thought it was, indeed, possible for sound to communicate through vibrations."

"An unseen realm ..." Ben says softly.

"I was so shocked by Dr. Bergman's theories that I paid Max Kindred a visit. Do you remember when Max gave us the Virtue bell as a wedding gift, he said he believed that the bell has 'unique characteristics'?"

"Yeah, I remember that now, but I figured he was an old, sentimental farmer who'd been living alone in the middle of nowhere for too long."

"Me, too, but when I told him about the Virtue bell communicating with me, he just laughed and said that he'd been well aware of the bell's special abilities and gave up trying to explain it years ago. In fact, he said the reason he gave us the gift was because the Virtue bell had communicated with him that it was the right thing to do."

They sit silently for a few moments while Aurora's revelations sink in. "So, when we were inside, I heard and felt the bell communicate deeply within me that, *"We are not victims! Now, we get them back!"*

"Yeah, me, too, so now the Virtue bell has apparently chosen to communicate with both of us which is great news to me, so I don't feel like the members of the Engel family are the only nutty ones around."

Ben offers her a wan smile. "So, Mr. Virtue, where do we go from here?" The golden light brightens on the bell, and its clapper begins to clang against its sides ... *"Puerto Vallarta, Mexico, but you must move quickly."*

"But, how will we know where to go once we get there?" Aurora questions.

"Listen and feel ... Another special bell will help guide your way."

Chapter 20

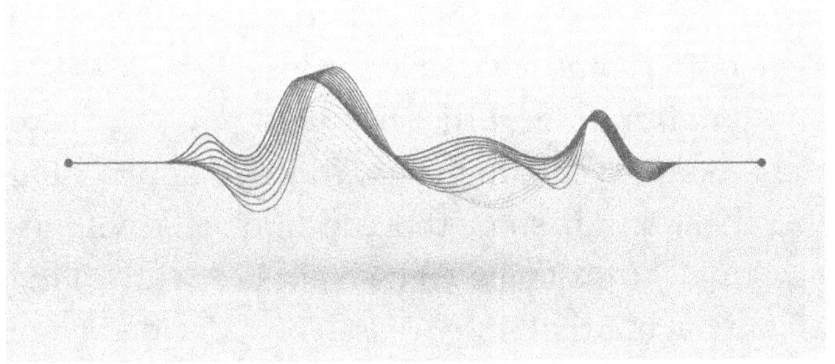

THE BLACK SEDAN CONTAINING the Engels, Yuri Tabeshenko, and Wendell Grossman pulls away from the private airstrip a few miles outside of Puerto Vallarta and is driven toward a warehouse near the center of town. The drive takes just a few minutes during which time very little is said.

Finally, Delano breaks the silence. "So, what is it exactly that you hope to achieve by abducting us, General?"

"Well, we've already received, I mean stole, $25 million of yours, some of which will come in handy for our Russian friends to rebuild their country after the war, and a hefty chunk is now mine. But, we know that your company has been developing some very advanced weapons systems and jet aircraft, and that technology would take the Russkies years to match, so we're hoping that you'll like to, uh, share those technologies with us. I originally threatened your son-in-law with killing all of you, but that little weasel, Ben, decided to go rogue on me, so I figured why not just take you instead and eliminate the middle man."

Delano and Caroline look at each other with some relief. "So, you're telling us that Ben didn't take our money of his own free will. Is that correct?"

"Yeah, that's correct. I made it very clear what would happen to him, your daughter, the two of you, and a bunch of your employees if he didn't do precisely as I instructed him."

"Gee, General, you're a real prince of a human being, and you're freakin' nuts if you think I'm gonna give up our company's trade secrets."

Yuri pulls his handgun out and points it directly at Caroline's temple. "Perhaps you don't understand that it's you we need to cooperate. Your lovely wife's presence is actually quite superfluous." Yuri cocks the gun, and Delano tries to knock it away, but he's met with a savage blow by the Russian.

"Screw you people!" Caroline snarls. "Don't do it, Del, they'll never let us out of here alive anyway."

"Your wife is a brave lady who also happens to have a very big mouth, Mr. Engel. I suggest that neither of you test our resolve because we're going to get the information out of you one way or another." At that, Yuri pulls two more syringes out of a leather holder and jabs both the Engels into unconsciousness.

"You Russians sure like your drugs, Yuri. Just don't give him so much of that stuff that it addles his brains to the point where he's useless to us."

"Shut up, Wendell, I don't need advice from some traitor to his own country."

The Russian driver pulls the sedan into the large warehouse and kills the engine. The driver and two other thugs lift the Engels out of the car and drag them to a private office that's outfitted with a couple of cots and a bathroom. They dump the unconscious Engels on the cots, remove their restraints, and post two guards outside the door.

From the carriage house, Aurora picks up the phone and calls their airport manager, Bryan Hilton. He answers on the third ring.

"Yes, ma'am, what's up?!"

"Is Dad's Spartan Executive fueled up?"

"Of course, you know I always keep our aircraft ready to take off at a moment's notice."

"Great! I'll be at the airport in about twenty minutes with another passenger. We need your help flying us somewhere, Bryan. I'll let you know where we're going when we get there, okay?"

"Okay, Aurora, we can have wheels-up shortly after you arrive."

"Ben, let's quickly pack some bags with extra clothes and toiletries. No telling how long we'll be gone." They immediately scoot around collecting items and throwing them into duffel bags.

"Ready when you are, Mrs. Witt!" he says to his wife. They step outside onto the porch, and the Virtue bell rings at them, *"Listen and feel and bring them back."*

Ben and Aurora pat the bell's curvature and nod affirmatively. "We'll do our best!" Aurora's Lincoln sprays gravel as they speed away from the carriage house.

When they arrive at the Putnam County Airport, Bryan is seated in the Spartan's cockpit with the engines running. Aurora enters the plane's cabin first followed by Ben.

"Well, saints preserve me! Where'd you come up with this international criminal?" he laughs when he sees his good friend, Ben.

"It's a long story," Aurora replies, "but since we're flying to Puerto Vallarta, Mexico, we'll have plenty of time to explain things to you. A bunch of Russians and a traitorous American general have kidnapped Mom and Dad to get our trade secrets, and we need to get them back."

"The hell you say! Have you contacted the FBI?"

"Not yet. I'll give Agent Loudermilk a call in a few minutes. Ben and I believe time is really precious to our getting my folks back, so we wanted to get in the air. If the Russians fly them to Moscow, we may never see them again."

"I understand. The feds should have ample assets in Mexico to help turn the country upside down to find your parents, but how do we find where the thugs took them once we get to Mexico?"

"I'm not sure you'd believe me if I told you, Bryan. Let's just say that we're going there on a wing and a prayer."

A minute later everyone is strapped in, and Bryan goes full throttle. It's roughly eleven hundred miles from Greencastle to San Antonio, Texas, and Aurora and Ben lean on each other as their pilot handles the controls. Bryan radios ahead to a private airfield in San Antonio and then settles in for the four-hour flight.

"So, am I breaking the law by aiding and abetting a fugitive from justice?" Bryan asks with humorous sarcasm in his voice.

"As an attorney, I can tell you that you definitely are!" Ben replies.

"But that's only until we can clear his name," Aurora adds.

"Nonetheless, if you were my client, I'd strongly advise against it, but you're not, and I'm in deep shit, so I vote that you go for the 'aiding and abetting' thing!"

"You say that Russian agents are in cahoots with a rogue American general, right? Are they likely to be well armed?"

"Yes and yes," Ben admits.

"And, what weapons do we have to beat these people? I mean, aside from the test rockets that this plane has."

"Uh, how about our resolve and a little luck?"

"Gee, now there's a winning combination. Do you honestly think we can pull this off?"

"I guess we're about to find out. Why don't you wake us when we get to San Antonio to refuel? Then, I'll take the controls while you grab some shut-eye. From San Antonio I reckon we'll have another thousand miles to fly to Puerto Vallarta. I just pray that we're not too late."

The remainder of the flight to San Antonio is uneventful, and with the steady drone of the Spartan's engine, Aurora and Ben manage to get some restful sleep.

"Okay, guys, time to prepare for landing. San Antonio is just ahead." Ben and Aurora return their seats to an upright position and stare out the windows at a small, well-lit airfield below.

"Why don't you two stay put in the cabin while I take care of the fuel and file a final flight plan. We don't need anyone suddenly recognizing Ben and getting all heroic on us."

Thirty minutes later the Spartan Executive is refueled and ready for take off. Aurora settles into the pilot's seat, and Ben sits next to her. Bryan gives Aurora a few reminder tips about the plane because it's been a while since she's flown it, but she's pretty familiar with the aircraft and soon has it in the air.

"Nighty night, folks!" Bryan says from the rear cabin. "Holler if you need me. Just maintain your current heading, and we should be fine."

Air traffic at this time of night is light, and Ben shares more details about his theft of the Engel Trust's assets and fleeing from the cops. He also tells her about his conversation with Ty Irvin, and how Ty will keep him appraised of any new information about the flow of money.

"So, Ben, where do you think the general and Russians transferred our money?"

"I know that the general transferred at least $10 million to a Swiss account in Geneva. What he doesn't know is that I've been able to track the account number. As for the Russians. it's been more of a challenge coming up with the exact location of their transfers, but they like to brag, so I've an idea of which financial institution in Moscow they made transfers to, but I'm going to need some more help coming up with the actual account numbers. Perhaps you can finagle that information out of the Feds and Ty Irvin. It's your family's money, after all."

"Good point." She places a radio call to Special Agent Loudermilk who initially is annoyed because of the late hour of her call, but he relents and gives her all of the account numbers that he and Ty are aware of.

"It's your dough, Mrs. Witt, but I strongly urge you to let us handle this case. Are we clear on that?"

"Of course we are, sir. I wouldn't have it any other way! But, you also need to know that Russian agents and a retired American general named

Wendell Grossman abducted my parents about four hours ago and are after Engel Air Corp.'s design plans."

"What?!" Loudermilk shouts. "They've got your parents?! Why didn't you tell me earlier? This puts a whole new level of seriousness on everything."

"Well, now you know, and I suggest you start making calls to some of your colleagues around Puerto Vallarta, Mexico, if we want to save my folks and keep the bloody Russians from gaining military equality with us. I'm on my way down there now to look for them."

"Mrs. Witt, I'm truly sorry about your parents, but I want to urge you again to please let us handle this. This is what we and the CIA do!"

"Thank you, sir, I'll take your suggestion under advisement, but these are my parents we're talking about. I'm not about to lose my husband and my parents over this, so I look forward to working with whoever you have in place in PV, Mexico. I've gotta go!" She hangs up, and Agent Linton Loudermilk stares at his telephone receiver in frustration.

As the evening wears on, their flight to the Pacific coast of Mexico is quiet with the exception of the engine's steady drone and an occasional snore and snort coming from Bryan in the back seat. An hour later Aurora radios the tower of a private airfield north of Puerto Vallarta and receives instructions for landing. They wake Bryan, and he takes over the Spartan's controls from Aurora for their final descent.

Chapter 21

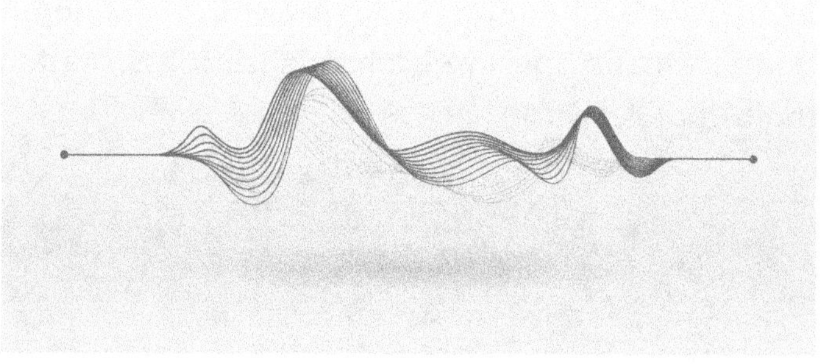

Puerto Vallarta is a resort town on Mexico's Pacific coast in Jalisco state. It's known for its beaches, water sports, and nightlife scene. Tourists from all over the world travel here to enjoy the area's charm ... and its privacy. Its cobblestone center is home to the ornate Nuestra Señora de Guadalupe church.

Upon landing Aurora rents a sturdy Jeep and gets maps of the area. Bryan is very reluctant to leave the Spartan in the hands of strangers in a strange land, so he bribes his way into refueling and staying with their aircraft. Ben and Aurora keep one radio and Bryan has the other.

"Listen," Bryan warns. "We have no idea what we're running into down here, except that the people we're trailing are stone-cold killers who won't hesitate to blow us away. Aurora, are you sure you don't want to simply let the FBI and CIA do the heavy lifting here?"

"Of course, I want them to do the heavy lifting, but no one yet has a clue on where to find my parents, so the more of us in the hunt, the better. Bryan, please keep your eyes on our plane. Ben and I are gonna drive into town and to see what we can see. C'mon, Ben."

Ben gives a casual salute to Bryan and says, "I'm with her." They climb into the Jeep and head for the center of town.

After they leave Bryan purchases fuel for the Spartan and checks out the wings, flaps, and instruments after their long flight. The Mexican airfield employees have never seen a Spartan Executive before, but understand that it's an aircraft for the very wealthy. After refueling Bryan slips the two local employees twenty bucks each. He points his finger from his eye to the Spartan indicating he wants the two Mexicans to help keep watch over the plane.

"Ah! Si, si, senor. Con mucho gusto!"

Bryan returns inside the Spartan and rummages around the interior cabinets looking for any sort of weapon. He grabs a heavy wrench but tosses it aside. "I don't think that would stop a bullet." He finds a large needle-nosed pliers, but knows that'll offer very little protection. Finally, he looks under a rear seat and sees a flare gun and a dozen or so flares. They come equipped with a canvas belt, holster, and pouch.

"They say you should never bring a knife to a gunfight, but maybe a flare gun will up my odds a bit."

He straps it on and plops down in a passenger seat to read the manual for the test rockets attached under the Spartan's wings. They're prototypes of the highly advanced military payloads that the Engel Air Corporation is developing for the government.

"Dang!" he mutters aloud. "I wouldn't want to be on the receiving end of one of these bad boys!" He looks out a window hoping to see the Witts, but he assumes they're still in town. He only sees his two new Mexican buddies sitting on a low wall playing cards and smoking cigarettes.

"I sure hope that Ben and Aurora know what they're doing, and I pray they don't wander too far out of radio range."

Meanwhile, Aurora and Ben have driven to a secluded street in the middle of Viejo Vallarta just north of Rio Cuale. They exit their rented Jeep and set out on foot toward the tallest landmark around, Nuestra Señora de Guadalupe, which is just a few blocks away. As they approach it, they're enthralled by the majestic stature of the cathedral. Standing proudly over the city's oceanside central plaza, Our Lady of Guadalupe Church, with its famous crown and bell tower, is the focal point of the Vallarta skyline.

"I never knew this city even existed," Aurora confesses, "but I certainly understand why someone would choose to make this lovely part of the world their home."

"Yeah, from Grossman's personnel file that I swiped at NATO headquarters, the general's apparently been coming to this area for a number of years. His hacienda is about an hour north of here in Sayulita. It's definitely a place that the FBI and CIA should search, but I seriously doubt that he and the Russians would have your folks stashed away in his living room. It's only a guess, but I believe that we're not that far away from them."

They enter the grand cathedral and feel humbled by the serenity of its interior. They sit in a pew at the rear of the nave and watch as the faithful come and pay homage to their savior.

"So, now what?" Ben asks. "Do we just sit here until we're moved by divine inspiration? If so, we could be here a long time," he offers cynically.

Roughly fifteen minutes pass, and the church's bell tower rings on the hour. Worshippers file out of the nave, and Ben and Aurora are soon alone, bathed in the colorful lights streaming through the magnificent stained glass windows.

"This is just so peaceful," Aurora whispers. "I haven't been in a church for a while now, but I can't help but feel connected with something very spiritual." She takes Ben's hand and leans against his shoulder. "I'm so glad we're together again, Ben. I felt so lost without you."

"I know, sweetheart, me too. And, I'm so sorry I've put you and your family through so much turmoil. I know I keep saying that, but I hope we can heal together again as a family."

"We will, but first things first. Let's get Mom and Dad back and then fly our butts back home!"

They stand to leave when they feel a stirring in the air and hear the church's bell begin to peal again. They look at each other expectantly and sit down again.

"Did you feel that?" Aurora asks.

"I felt something, but I'm not sure what it was," Ben replies. "Maybe it was communicating in Spanish."

Aurora rolls her eyes at him, and a moment later the bell continues to peal in soft resonant vibrations. *"They are very near … listen and feel."*

"Now, I feel it," Ben confirms. "I presume you did too. Let's step outside and listen for more guidance, maybe a direction to go, okay?"

"Yes, I felt it as well. It's almost unfathomable to believe that our Virtue bell and this church bell two thousand miles away could be on the same wavelength with us. I imagine both Enrique Bergman and Max Kindred would just smile and shrug as if to say, 'of course they are'!"

"Yeah, I agree, but it's like Max said to you, after a while you stop questioning and just accept the mystery of it all."

They walk outside into the plaza and shield their eyes from the bright sunlight. They glance in different directions and wait and listen. The church bell rings once marking the quarter hour, then ceases. They radio Bryan to make certain that they're still within range, and he answers quickly. "Yeah, I can hear you fine. I'm just camped out here with my Mexican buddies, and I'm familiarizing myself with the missile manual. Where're you?"

"We're in the plaza outside the big cathedral. You should be able to see the crown on top of the bell tower from your position."

"Yeah, I see it. What do you want me to do?"

"Just sit tight for now and keep a close eye on the Spartan. We may need to get out of here on a moment's notice."

"Right! Let me know if you run into any trouble, okay?" They sign off, and Ben and Aurora begin slowly moving away from the plaza when they hear and viscerally feel the church bell ring again.

"North ... warehouse ... careful."

They look at each other as if to confirm that they understand the bell's message. "Do you think we should contact Agent Loudermilk and let them and the Mexican authorities take over?" Aurora asks.

"Probably, but my guess is that Grossman and the Russians already have assets inside the Mexican police, and I don't think we want to risk tipping our hand to them. We're unarmed after all, and surprise is likely our best weapon. I say we do as the bell instructs and see if we can carefully find the warehouse where they're holding them."

Aurora nods her head in agreement, and they quickly buy hats and serapes from a street vendor to help conceal their identities. They take another glance at the bell tower and then join up with an inebriated mariachi band as they walk north.

"Mr. Engel, wake up!" Warren Grossman shakes Delano's shoulder as he lies on the cot next to Caroline's. "Wake up! We need to talk."

Delano tries to shake off the effects of whatever sedatives Yuri Tabeshenko injected into him and Caroline. He slowly gets his wits about him and stares at the disgraced general.

"I need some water and a promise from you that no harm will come to my wife."

Grossman goes into the bathroom and returns with a glass of water which Delano greedily drinks.

"As for the safety of your lovely wife, I would be willing to offer you that guarantee, but the Russians, well, they're another story all together," he laments. "The specs for the jet aircraft and the rockets, Mr. Engel, I need them, and you need to give them to me before things turn ugly."

"Even if I gave you the plans, Grossman, it would take the Russians months to replicate what we've done, and then even more months before they could produce the actual planes and missiles. You're a damn general, or you used to be, and you know how long things can take."

"Let me be very clear with you, Mr. Engel, as long as these thugs think I'll do whatever they tell me to do, I stay alive. The moment I don't, I'm a goner. And, come to think of it, since they have you and your wife, they really don't need me anymore. Perhaps the only thing keeping me alive is the money that they know I stole from you." Grossman winces at that sober realization.

"All the more reason you should helps us escape, because if they put us on a plane back to Mother Russia, we're all screwed."

Grossman considers his captive's words. He knows that what Delano is saying to him is accurate, but he's being held on a very tight rein.

"You know that I'm a very wealthy man. Why not help us and just give them the damn money you took from me. If you get us out of here, I'll pay you back, guaranteed! I'm hoping that somewhere in that heart of yours there's still a patriot who spent a lifetime defending his country from people like the ones you're now a slave too."

Delano's words strike a deep chord with the general. Their eyes meet, and then the door swings open, and Yuri strides in.

"Oh, I see our guest of honor has awakened. I hope you had a refreshing nap. Is he in a talkative mood yet, General?"

"I'm not saying anything until I revive my wife and you geniuses get us something to eat and drink. How's that sound, comrade?"

"I think that sounds splendid, Mr. Engel," he replies frostily. "I hope you enjoy Mexican food because if you don't cooperate afterward, well, you might just consider it your 'last supper.'" He laughs at his own joke, then steps outside to instruct his men to bring some food and drinks.

Delano sees Caroline begin to stir and then sits beside her, stroking her hair, trying to gently bring her back into full lucidity. The general watches.

"We didn't get a chance to finish our conversation, Grossman. To reiterate, I'll give you the money if you help us, and I'm willing to speak on your behalf with the authorities if you do."

"Very tempting, Mr. Engel. Very tempting, indeed, but I believe I've crossed the Rubicon, as it were. It would be damned hard for me to enjoy whatever money you gave me from a jail cell, and no matter how well respected you are, I've broken more laws than I can count, and even your best support wouldn't keep me from spending the rest of my days in prison."

"Yes, I agree, but at least you'd be alive."

Chapter 22

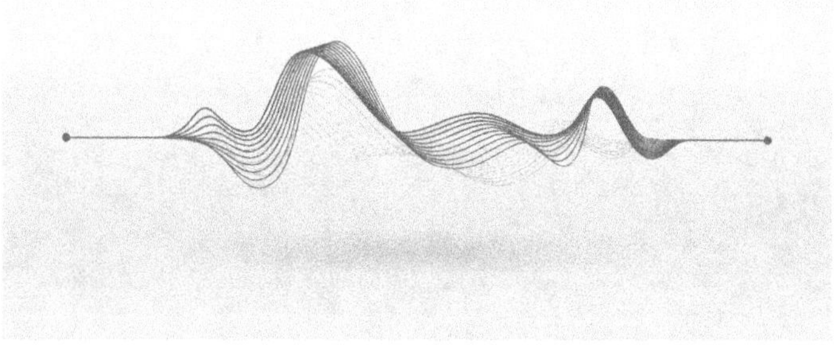

BEN AND AURORA WAVE adios to the mariachi band and stay to the shadows as they veer stealthily down a secluded side street. They notice a couple of older factory buildings up ahead and slow their approach to an adobe warehouse with a corrugated steel roof. In the distance they hear the cathedral's bell toll affirmatively. The Witts glance and nod at each other signifying that they both felt the same message. As they sneak closer they see a dark sedan with tinted windows at the rear of the warehouse with a very large individual standing guard.

"Wow, he's a big guy," Ben states the obvious. He picks up a brick and hefts it in his hand.

"I don't think we should tangle with this dude alone, Aurora. Let's radio Bryan and have him join us."

They duck down behind a wooden shed, and Aurora contacts Bryan. "Uh, we could use your help. We're looking at a rather huge hombre. Head over this way, will ya? Ben will meet you halfway and bring you here. We think Mom and Dad are inside a building that we're looking at." They hang up, and Ben sneaks off to meet Bryan. Five minutes later the threesome are behind the shed looking at the solitary guard.

"So, why do you think your parents are inside that warehouse?" Bryan asks.

"Let's just call it a hunch," Aurora says. "Things just look very suspicious with this mountain of a man standing guard next to an expensive-looking car."

"Well, hell, down here in Mexico that could mean anything … drugs, import-export, human trafficking. I hope your intuition is spot on."

"Let me handle this!" And, before the guys can say, *"No way, Jose!"* she takes off her serape and unbuttons the top two buttons of her blouse.

"What're you doing?" Bryan asks nervously.

"Watch and learn, darling!" She steps from behind the shed and begins walking toward the Russian guard.

"Sir!" she calls out. "Sir, can you please help me? I'm lost."

The Russian doesn't understand much English, but he does understand the sight of a very pretty woman.

"What is problem?" he asks in broken English.

"I'm lost, sir, and I'm very tired. Won't you help me please? I have no money, but I would be most grateful for your assistance." She steps past him so his back is now turned toward Ben and Bryan. She unbuttons a third button of her blouse. "Please! You look so big and strong, and I need your help."

The Russian looks at the warehouse and everything seems to be in order, so he approaches the woman and eyes her greedily. "Come here, little one," he says with a salacious grin.

Aurora walks slowly forward, and Ben rushes the guard and whacks him on the head with the brick. It seems to barely faze the big Russian who turns to fight his assailant. He hurls some colorful Russian obscenity at Ben and takes a swing at him. Ben sidesteps his meaty fist and kicks him in the groin. The big man goes down on one knee, gasping for breath and hurling more obscenities. Bryan leaps forward from behind the shed and savagely punches the man in the face. He goes down on both knees now, and Aurora grabs another adobe brick and crushes it on the back of his head. It's lights out for Moscow-man!

Ben and Bryan grab the unconscious fella by his feet and drag him behind the shed. Aurora looks inside the sedan and sees the car keys in the ignition. She leaves them there.

"C'mon! Let's get my parents and then vamoose!"

The three of them open the rear door to the warehouse and hear voices up ahead, but no one is guarding the back door. They see that the warehouse is packed with paper products and cardboard boxes. They walk down a narrow hallway and see another guard standing by an office door.

"Shall we try it again?" Aurora asks her partners in crime.

Before Ben and Brian can say no she approaches the guard asking for help.

"What are you doing in here? You're not allowed in here!"

"But, sir," she pleads. "I was told to meet my friend here."

"What friend? This is private here. Go away!"

Then, Bryan and Ben appear, and Bryan points the flare gun at the Russian. The guard raises his hands in surrender, and Ben quickly grabs his gun and motions him inside the office. Delano and Caroline are stunned to see their daughter, Bryan, and their fugitive son-in-law.

"Quickly!" Ben says. "We've got to move fast!"

No one needs to be told twice, and the five of them scurry out the back door and run for the sedan. Ben gets behind the wheel, and as the others are getting settled inside the car, Yuri appears at the backdoor in a rage. He shouts for assistance and pulls out his handgun and begins firing at the car.

Grossman appears next to him and screams, "Don't hit Engel. We need him alive!" Yuri tries to shoot the tires out, but Ben crams the car in gear and sprays gravel as the tires gain traction. While Yuri shoves another clip in his gun, Bryan lowers his window and shoots a flare at the Russian hitting him in the upper thigh and groin with a fiery burst. He fires another flare into the warehouse's opened backdoor, and the paper products instantly erupt in a huge conflagration. The other Russians try to get past the flames to assist their comrades, but the heat and flames are too much to get past.

Ben speeds away while the others stare in disbelief at the enflamed scene behind them. Two minutes later they're back at the Spartan Executive, and everyone scampers inside. Unaware that their pal, Bryan, started the fire, the two Mexicans point at the dense black smoke coming from a building four blocks away.

"Dios mio!" one exclaims.

"Thanks for your help, guys!" Bryan hollers to them from the open pilot's window. "Hasta luego, amigos! We've gotta go!" He pushes the Spartan's throttle forward and very soon afterward the plane rumbles down the runway and takes flight leaving

Puerto Vallarta and the church bell from Our Lady of Guadalupe behind.

At first everyone on board is quiet as they catch their breath and reflect on their successful escape, then everyone smiles and starts talking all at once.

"Holy guacamole!" Bryan gushes. "We actually pulled it off!"

"But how did you know where we were?" Delano asks. "I mean, we could've been anywhere on the planet, and you found us." He glares at Ben. "And, speaking of 'you,' I don't know whether to hug you, young man, or punch your bloody lights out. You've got a lot of explaining to do, despite the fact that Grossman admitted you were coerced into stealing our money and putting us all at serious risk."

"I know, sir, and I'm sincerely very sorry ..."

Aurora interrupts her husband on his behalf. "He didn't have much of a choice, Father, plus he managed to get $5 million of the money back from Grossman's Mexican account."

"That's a good start. Now, all we need is $20 million more," Delano declares. "But seriously, how did you know where to find us?"

"Let's just say that the answer to your question was clear as a bell to Ben and me."

Bryan looks at her as if she's had too many margaritas, but Delano, Caroline, and Ben understand her subtle reference to the sentient bells. Over the next thousand miles to San Antonio, Ben directs the conversation away from the magical bells and shares all of the details about his theft from the Engel Trust, his travels to Brussels to get intel on General Grossman, his odyssey back to Greencastle, and his reconnecting with Aurora at the carriage house.

"What now?!" Caroline asks. "Is it safe to go home considering that these thugs already got to us once?"

"No doubt that Grossman and the Russians are beyond livid that they got outsmarted," Aurora says. She picks up the radio and contacts Agent Loudermilk. "We got my parents back, and we're all flying to San Antonio to refuel the Spartan and then fly back to Putnam County Airport. We're all safe, but you should also know that Ben is with us too."

"That's great news, Mrs. Witt, but your husband still has a lot of explaining to do. He's broken at least a dozen laws that I can think of off the top of my head."

Ben takes the radio and replies, "I understand, sir, and I will surrender myself to your custody once we return home."

"And, by the way, you guys didn't have anything to do with setting a warehouse on fire, did you? The Puerto Vallarta fire department is still trying to put the blaze out."

"We might have," Bryan replies with a tinge of braggadocio in his voice. "Some of those flare guns just seem to have a hair trigger. We'll have the engineers at Engel Air Corp. work on that," he fibs.

Aurora and her parents spend the next few minutes on the radio with the FBI agent sharing details about the Russians' and Grossman's plans to extract technical design intel from Delano, at whatever cost to the Engels' health.

"There's no doubt in our minds, Agent Loudermilk, that Caroline and I would've been flown to Russia and probably never heard from again. We owe our lives to our daughter, Ben, and Bryan."

"Well, I'm sure we'll get this all sorted out in due course, and I'll make certain that we have proper security details assigned to guarding your homes and businesses."

"Thank you very much, Agent Loudermilk," Aurora says. "I know we've probably been a bit of a challenge for you, but things, well, things worked out."

They sign off, and the rest of the flight to San Antonio is somewhat quiet as the exhausted passengers recoup their sensibilities … and consider how close they all came to death.

Delano leans over and kisses his daughter on the cheek. "Thank you, honey. Your mother and I are very proud of you. When I first saw you at that warehouse, I thought that the Russians had captured you as well. You are indeed a very brave and clever girl!" Delano gives Ben's shoulder a fatherly squeeze. "And you, Benjamin, thank you too. Obviously, we need to talk more though."

Chapter 23

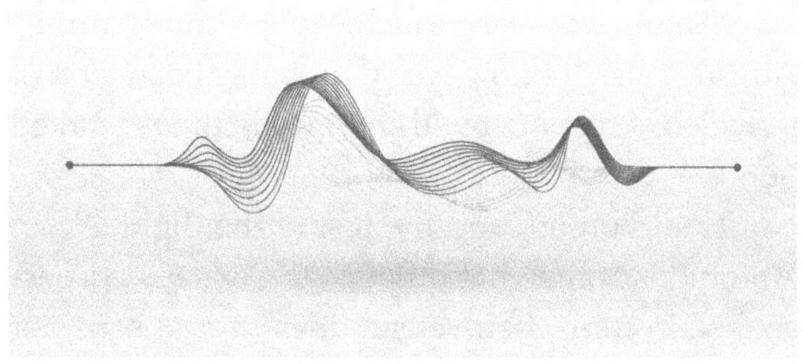

AFTER REFUELING THE Spartan Executive and getting something to eat in San Antonio, Delano takes over the plane's controls for the final leg of their journey back home. It's another eleven hundred miles before they arrive at Putnam County's airport.

"Ya know, as I think about it, when the Russians abducted Caroline and me, if the dummies had just searched my office a little, they probably would've found the patent details for all of our new technology. They would've had everything they wanted to get out of me."

"I still don't think that would've made a difference," Ben replies. "I understand what you're saying, but I think they also wanted to make a point that their reach is far and wide. They would've taken you and Caroline as trophies anyway, and perhaps to get even more of your money."

"That's a creepy thought, Ben," Caroline says, "but I think you're probably right. I wonder what their next plans are."

"Well, at least that jerk, Yuri Tabeshenko, won't be walking normally for a while after being on the receiving end of the flare."

"Yeah, that was a great shot, Bryan, and setting the warehouse on fire was pretty cool too!"

When they finally arrive in Putnam County, agents for the FBI are waiting to take Ben into custody, and to provide protection for Aurora and her parents. Aurora watches painfully as Ben is handcuffed and led away.

"Don't worry, sweetheart, we'll have him out soon since I don't plan on pressing charges against him. There are other legal issues he'll have to contend with, though, like stealing Grossman's files from NATO, and running from customs officials at Idlewild, and from the cops throughout Pennsylvania, Ohio, and Indiana. I've got to hand it to your husband, though, he's a pretty ingenious fellow. I'm still hoping he, Conrad, and Ty Irvin can help us recover the rest of our money."

"Yeah, I just want this to all be over, Dad, and for us to have the life we had before."

"Say hallelujah!" Caroline chimes in. "Let's go home!"

Aurora and Caroline part company with Bryan at the plane, and as Delano is walking out of the hangar, he tells Bryan he's giving him a hefty bonus. "Call it combat pay, my friend!"

"Sweet! Can I use the rockets next time?" he laughs.

"Fine by me," his boss affirms, "but let's try not to have a next time."

Aurora and her parents drive back home, and Caroline comments, "You know, everything looks just the way it should. What we experienced with the Russians and Grossman just seems like a very bad dream now. Hard to believe it really happened."

Delano puts his arm around her and pulls her close. "I'm so sorry you were in so much danger, both of you."

Delano and Caroline walk up the steps to the house and watch Aurora as she does the same at the carriage house. She stops for a moment at the Virtue bell and touches it fondly. "I'll never know how you and your sister bells do it, but I can't thank you enough for giving us such helpful guidance."

The Virtue peals softly, and she feels its message. *"I'm here for you, but be advised, all is not over ..."*

Aurora beseeches the bell for more information, but it remains silent. She tries to ponder the possibilities of what could come, but is too tired to even be scared. "Tomorrow's another day," she says under her breath. After waiting a few moments by the silent bell, she sighs and slowly walks inside.

At the Indianapolis field office of the FBI, Ben is confined to an interrogation room. His handcuffs have been removed, but given the high level of security at the facility, he knows he's not going anywhere unescorted. In truth, he's tired of being on the run.

He came clean with Aurora and her parents about being coerced, and his story was corroborated by none other than General Grossman, so he's content to be an upstanding citizen and answer all questions in a forthright manner.

Special Agent Loudermilk enters the room. "So, Mr. Witt, let's take it from the beginning again, shall we? Tell us about your relationship with General Grossman, and how the two of you collaborated in stealing $25 million from the Engel Charitable Trust."

Over the next two hours Loudermilk grills Ben about when he and the general became acquainted at NATO headquarters; how he got coerced through deadly threats to his family; how he was able to circumvent Conrad Zyer and Tyler Irvin in transferring the money to accounts in Mexico, Switzerland, and Russia; how he evaded law enforcement officials upon returning from Brussels; and how he decided to return home and help Aurora save her parents and steal $5 million back from the traitorous general. It's an exhausting process, but it's something that Ben knows he must endure if he's ever going to get a semblance of his former life back and hopefully reduce his jeopardy with jail time.

"There is another question that I just can't seem to understand, Mr. Witt, how was it possible for you and your wife to determine that the Russians had your in-laws tucked away in Puerto Vallarta, Mexico? It's just far too mysterious that you were able to figure that out. You see my dilemma with that, don't you, Mr. Witt?"

"Yessir, I do." Ben dodges the truth about guidance from the Virtue bell and the bell at Nuestra Señora de Guadalupe. "From the general's personnel file I stole from NATO, I learned that Grossman spent many vacations at a property he owned in Sayulita near Puerto Vallarta. It struck me as an ideal, familiar place for him to hide out, and since Aurora and I didn't have much else to go on, we followed that lead, and well, things worked out, didn't they?"

"Yes, they did, but I still have difficulty believing that there's not more to the story." Ben just shrugs and says nothing further.

Two hours of interrogation later Special Agent Loudermilk says, "I think that's about it for now, Mr. Witt. Your father-in-law has stated his willingness to forego legal charges against you, and to supervise you under house arrest until all legal issues are settled. Are you willing to comply with those parameters?"

"Absolutely, sir!" comes Ben's unequivocal reply.

"Okay then, your wife and in-laws just arrived from Greencastle, and they're waiting for you outside, but I warn you that any attempt to leave Putnam County or communicate with enemies of America will result in your swift incarceration. Are we clear on that, Mr. Witt?"

"Clear as a bell, sir, thank you."

Shortly thereafter Ben is escorted from the interrogation room to the field office's foyer where he's greeted by his lovely Aurora. He looks her in the eye, then holds her very close, neither of them wanting to let go. "Are you ready to go home?"

"Nothing would make me happier, sweetheart." They walk outside to the curb and climb into a limousine where Caroline and Delano are already seated.

"It's been one helluva ride, Ben," Delano says. "Did you ever think that moving to Greencastle, Indiana, would ever have so much drama?"

"Not in a million years, sir, and Aurora was originally concerned that I'd miss the action of a big city for easy-paced Greencastle. Right now I'll take quiet, small town livin' any day."

"It's a very good life, Ben, and we're still in a position to do well by our friends and neighbors. Del and I are delighted to have you back, and for you and Aurora to be together again."

"Thank you, Caroline. You've been great considering my transgressions against the family … and my conscience."

The foursome arrive home about an hour after leaving Indianapolis. "Why don't you two get settled and then come up to the house?" Delano suggests. "We still have about $20 million of our hard-earned money that's missing, and I want us to consider every option for getting it back."

"I have a few thoughts, Delano, but it'll require you alerting Connie Zyer and Ty Irvin that it's okay to communicate with me."

"Consider that done. I don't want to leave any stone unturned."

Aurora and Ben stand on the carriage house's porch as they watch Caroline and Delano walk across the yard to their home. The quietude of the moment is a welcome balm to them. Then, the

Virtue bell begins to toll, and they hear and feel its message deeply within their cores.

"Russia … Switzerland … seek and you shall find …"

"But, the FBI said you can't leave the county," Aurora warns.

"Yes, not physically anyway, but I have some ideas."

Chapter 24

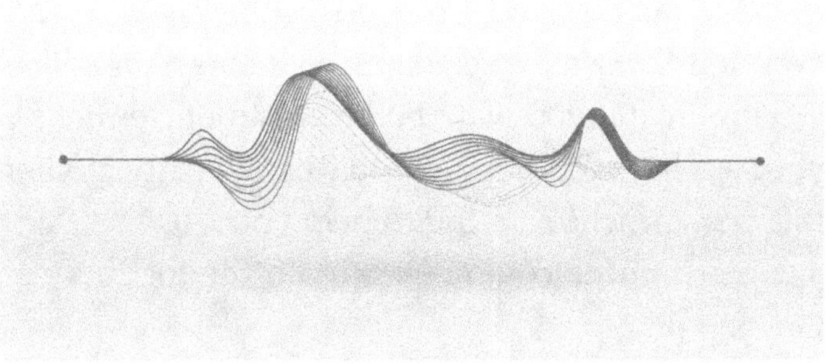

YURI TABESHENKO LIES prone on his hospital bed in Puerto Vallarta, Mexico. The serious burns his legs and crotch suffered when Bryan shot him with the flare gun will require some surgery and weeks to heal. To add insult to injury, he's having a dickens of a time communicating with his nurse. She doesn't understand Russian, and well, he's too uncomfortable and mean-spirited to be patient with his caregiver.

"Woman! Nurse!" he bellows. "Bring me more pain killer … and some damn vodka if you've got it!" She ignores his pleas since she just administered pain medication an hour before.

"What the hell are you hollering about?" Wendell Grossman scolds as he enters Yuri's hospital room. "If you want better treatment, either fly your ass back to Moscow, or try being a little politer to a person who's trying to help you."

Yuri mumbles an obscene Bolshevik curse at Grossman.

"See! That wasn't so difficult now was it, you turnip-eating communist!"

The two men, once sworn enemies and now allies joined by greed, look at each other, shake their heads, and laugh.

"Can you believe we got outsmarted by a bunch of amateurs. I thought we were better trained than that, Yuri."

"Me too," he confesses.

"So, what do the doctors say about her medical status and when you might be able to leave here?"

"The doctors say my burns are severe, and that I'll need some reconstructive surgery, especially with my private parts. Turns out they're not fireproof," he scoffs. "Essentially, I'll be able to travel back to a hospital in Moscow in a couple of days, and then I'll have to wait and see about returning to action. In the meantime, your new handler will be David Sapadinsky. Do what he says the first time he says it. He doesn't have the same level of patience and humor with traitorous generals as I do." He gives Grossman one of his frosty smiles.

"I hear you, Yuri. I appreciate the cautionary warning, but I expected as much from whomever is going to replace you. Looking ahead, though, may I please make a suggestion for us old war horses, comrade?"

"I'm all ears … and scorched tissue, Grossman, what're your sage words of wisdom?"

"You and I have been at this spy craft game long enough, Yuri, and I don't know about you, but I'm getting a little weary of this craziness. I say we let others decide about getting Delano Engel's technology secrets, and we just take the money we had that Witt kid steal for us and simply fade into the sunset. You release me from my obligations to Mother Russia, and you've always got a warm, sunny, quiet place to stay in Sayulita."

Yuri doesn't reply at first. He knows that Grossman's advice has a lot of merit, but he doesn't know if it's the general's attractive suggestion or the pain medication that's influencing his thinking.

"In a nutshell, Yuri, I say we cut our losses and take the money and run. Hell, you might even learn how to speak Spanish."

An hour after enjoying some long overdue conjugal bliss, Aurora and Ben depart the carriage house and stand by the Virtue bell hoping for more information about where to look in Russia and Switzerland, but the bell remains silent.

"C'mon, Ben, I don't know about you, but I could really enjoy a good stiff drink." They walk across the yard and enter their parents' house. "We're here. Where are you?"

"We're in the library," Caroline returns. "And, we've got a head start on you!" They enter the library and see Delano and Caroline sitting together on a loveseat with an ice bucket and a bottle of Four Roses bourbon on the cocktail table before them.

"Nothing like getting threatened by a bunch of lunatic Russians to test one's sobriety!" Caroline chortles, then hiccups. She reaches for the bottle to add a few more gulps to her glass, and Delano places his hand over her glass. "Uh, I think we've both had enough, darling." His wife hiccups again, then giggles. "Yippee for our team!" she fawns. She then looks curiously at her daughter and says, "My goodness, Aurora, you seem to have a very special glow about you this evening. Did you and this rascal you're married to just have sex?" She giggles again.

"Okay, darling!" Delano intercedes. "You're officially cut off!"

Ben and Aurora add some ice and three fingers of whiskey to two tumblers. "You'll have to excuse your mother," he laughs. "It's not every day that she comes close to dying."

"Yippee!" Caroline chirps! "Engel-Witt Team 1. Russkies 0."

Delano and Aurora roll their eyes in embarrassment while Ben remains politely silent. "That's if you don't count the $20 million we're still missing!" Delano adds. "While you were getting, uh, 'settled,' I placed calls to Connie and Ty to let them know what happened in Puerto Vallarta, and where we stand. They suggested that we have a conference call in a bit to discuss next steps. Ben, I told them that you have some ideas."

"Yeah, sounds good. A while ago when Aurora and I were standing by the Virtue bell, it communicated that we should 'seek and find' in Russia and Switzerland. I want to confirm the directions of the money transfers with Ty and Connie and see if that info can give us an opportunity to reverse any of the transactions."

"Do you honestly think that Grossman and the Russians would make it that easy for us?" Delano asks.

"We won't know until we get into the weeds, but sometimes people get lazy and overconfident when they get a ton of money."

Aurora and Caroline walk off to the kitchen to prepare something for everyone to eat while Ben and Delano organize their thoughts for their conference call with Conrad and Tyler.

"It probably goes without saying, but we need to view the transfer of cash to Russia and Switzerland separately. It was the approach I used to get the $5 million back from Grossman's bank account in Mexico. I didn't want to try to get the full twenty-five million back at one time, plus I really wanted to stick it to Grossman where he lives. Yuri Tabeshenko has a personal account at the Bank of Moscow, and we know that Grossman sent $10 million to that account from Mexico. It was the general's way of keeping the Russians happy and quiet. Grossman also transferred $10 million in cash to a personal account that he established in Geneva. With Ty Irvin's help, I believe I can home in on those bank accounts, and with some luck, perhaps uncover their passcodes. It'll be tricky, but I think Ty and his people are pretty clever."

"All right," Delano replies. "Let's get these guys on the phone, and see how clever and lucky we can get."

Shortly thereafter a conference call is set up among Delano, Ben, Conrad, and Tyler. "First, let me say that I'm delighted to have you safely back, Ben."

"I'll second what Conrad just said, Ben. I trusted you to be the upstanding guy you've always been, and you haven't disappointed."

"Thanks, Ty, you were there when I needed you, and I won't forget it. Now, let's see what we can do about swiping the remainder of the Engel Trust's money back."

Over the next several minutes Delano listens as Tyler shares the financial path that his analysts found on the $10 million that went to Russia. "As you know all too well, Ben, General Grossman leaned heavily on you to surreptiously transfer the $25 million to his bank in Sayulita, Mexico, and from there, he wired $10 million to the Bank of Moscow to keep his promise to the Russians. Does that sum that up accurately, Ben?"

"It does."

"Then," Tyler continues, "Grossman transferred another $10 million to an account in his name at the Bank of Geneva in Switzerland. Is that correct as well?"

"I assume that's correct if you say so. Remember, after I made that initial transfer of $25 million to

Grossman in Mexico, my hands were no longer on the money."

"Agreed," Tyler concurs.

Conrad Zyer has been quiet up to this point, and Delano asks his long-time financial advisor his thoughts.

"Well, I'm just a simple accountant from little ol' Chicago, but let's get to the heart of the matter: How are we gonna get Del and Caroline's dough back? Ben, Del said you have some thoughts."

"I do, Connie, but most of my thoughts relate to what Tyler's company can deliver via their banking contacts in Russia and Switzerland."

Ben's question hangs out there, and Delano asks, "So, what kind of contacts do you have in the banks in Moscow and Geneva, Tyler? You know, the banks illegally holding our money! Moreover, Mr. Irvin, why is it that it feels like we have to drag precious information out of you? We're paying you a boatload of money to do an important job for us, and I would've thought you'd be a lot more forthcoming with information."

"Uh, no! I mean yes, we have solid relationships with the leadership of both of those banks. They're clients of ours as well, but please don't misunderstand, Delano, we're enormously proud to be working on your behalf." An awkward silence ensues.

"Okay then, Ty," Ben begins. "Who do you know at those banks who'd be in a position to give us the specific account numbers, passcodes, and any other vital information allowing transfers of assets back to us?"

"Uh, I know the CEOs pretty well," Tyler admits. "I guess I could have a conversation with Mr. Badenov in Moscow and Mr. Bach in Geneva to see what they'd be willing to get for us."

"What they'd be willing to get for us?!" Ben hurls back at his once friend and associate. "You need to really think about where your loyalties lie, Mr. Irvin."

"I would also like to remind you that I tape record all of our conversations to ensure accuracy," Conrad adds.

"Yes, of course, when we hang up I'll check the time zones and begin calling the CEOs first thing in the morning."

"And, when can we expect to hear the results of your conversations with them, Tyler?" Ben asks.

"Immediately. The moment I get off the telephone with them."

Again, an awkward silence hangs briefly in the air.

"Okay, then, I think we're through for now," Delano concludes.

"I'm sure we're all keeping our fingers crossed, Mr. Irvin." They end the call.

Ben and Delano take sips from their whiskey glasses and look at each other. "So, what's your assessment of that call, counselor?" Delano asks his son-in-law.

"I think I'm thinking what you're thinking, and I'm stunned by Tyler Irvin's reticence to do more for us earlier. It's clear that he doesn't want to disturb his relationships with those bankers. Methinks he's working all of the angles to protect his own pocketbook."

"Yeah, and we don't need a magic bell to tell us that."

Just then Aurora reappears alone in the doorway.

"Where's your mother?" Ben asks.

"Oh, we had a few snacks, and then she told me it was time for her to go, uh, I believe her exact words were 'nighty night.' So, I put her to bed. She was snoring sweetly by the time I turned out the light and closed the bedroom door."

"Thanks, honey," her dad says. "She rarely drinks too much, but I think she earned it this time. Speaking of 'nighty night,' I think it's time for me to hit the hay too. Ben, you'll keep in close contact with Tyler Irvin, right?"

"You can count on it. Good night, Delano."

Aurora and Ben put the used glasses and dishes in the kitchen sink and slowly stroll across the lawn toward the carriage house. They stop at midpoint and Aurora turns to look at the house she grew up in. A golden glow emanates from the tower room and cascades down to the Virtue bell which rings softly as it senses their presence.

"I don't think I'll ever understand the magic of our home, but I guess I'm beginning to finally accept it for what it is."

"As an attorney I've been trained to follow the evidence, and all I know is that the Virtue bell and the Book of Tamberg have been there for your family in ways that are unfathomable, yet undeniable."

"I can't imagine where their mysteries will take us from here," Aurora says with wonder.

"Hopefully, to Moscow and Geneva and then back again to fuller lives in Greencastle, Indiana."

They kiss and hold each other in the bright tower light. Then, she leads him past the Virtue bell and up the steps to their front door.

"C'mon, Ben, let's crawl beneath the covers. Maybe 'fuller' includes a baby."

Chapter 25

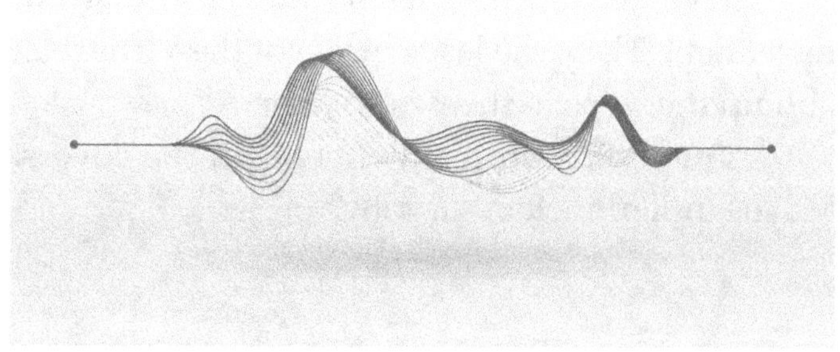

AT DAWN'S FIRST LIGHT Ben slips out of bed and quickly dresses. He glances at his beautiful Aurora who's sleeping peacefully and quietly moves to the kitchen and puts the coffee pot on to brew. He stares at the wall clock … 6:40 AM … probably too early to have heard anything back from Tyler Irvin, but he's disappointed nonetheless. He looks outside thinking that Delano might be up and wandering around the yard but doesn't see his father-in-law. A minute or so later he pours himself half a cup of coffee and walks outside to the porch in his stocking feet. It's chilly, but the steaming cup of coffee warms him within.

"Good morning, Virtue," he coos at the sentient bell. "And, did you sleep well or were you too busy protecting us mere mortals?" The bell chimes a gentle tone in return, but no important message is imparted. He leans on the porch railing and ponders what Tyler will learn from the bankers in Moscow and Geneva. He cringes when he thinks what the Russians and Wendell Grossman might do if Ben and his cohorts are successful in moving the Engel Trust's money back home. In the distance he hears the Putnam County courthouse bell chime seven times, and the Virtue bell rings once as if acknowledging a close friend. A moment later Ben sees Delano exit his house and head in his direction.

"Any word from Tyler or Connie?" Delano asks as he sets foot on the porch steps. Ben shakes his head negatively. "Well, it's obviously early yet. If we haven't heard from them by eight, why don't you give Connie a call? I prefer to let Tyler have a little more time to connect with his bank contacts before I get any more annoyed with him than I already am."

Ben shakes his head in agreement. "Why don't you come inside. I have coffee brewing, and Aurora should be up pretty soon."

They step inside and see Aurora wearing a bathrobe and slippers. "G'morning," she offers sleepily. "How's Mother doing this morning?"

"Still out cold. When I woke up I checked on her. She was dozing comfortably, but she's going to feel pretty hungover when she reenters the world of the living so I decided to let her sleep."

"Smart call," Aurora says. "We Engels have never been known as great drinkers."

A few moments later they hear footsteps on the porch followed by Caroline awkwardly staggering though the carriage house door.

"Coffee! I need coffee!" utters a bedraggled-looking woman with her shirt misbuttoned and her hair in disarray. "Coffee! Please!" she pleads again before plopping down on a chair."

"Oh my! You're just a mess, Mom, and your eyes look frightful."

"Well, my darling daughter, you ought to see them from my side!"

Delano fetches a cup of black coffee for his wife and helps her take her first sips. "Careful, dear, it's very hot!"

"Ah! Coffee!" she offers gratefully. "What'd I miss last night? I didn't sing, did I?"

"No, sweetheart, you didn't sing, but Aurora did have to put you to bed. As for what you missed, we had a conference call with Conrad and Tyler, and we're waiting to hear back from Tyler hopefully soon. He agreed to connect with his bank contacts in Moscow and Geneva to see if they can shed some light on accounts that received our money."

"Well, what the hell took him so long to do that?!" she blurts out soberly. "I thought we were paying him a lot of money to act on our behalf!"

"Our thoughts exactly, darling! Anyway, that's what you missed last night."

In the distance they hear the courthouse bell gong eight times, and Ben looks at Delano. "Time's up as far as I'm concerned. I'll give Conrad a call."

Conrad Zyer answers the phone on the second ring. "This is Zyer, it's only 7:00 AM here in Chicago, so I can only assume that it's Delano calling."

"Close enough!" Ben says, "but he's here with me. Have you heard anything from Tyler?"

"He called me about an hour after our conference call ended last night. Said he'd placed calls to both of the bank CEOs and would get back to all of us as soon as he has any news to report."

"Uh, huh,"Ben replies. "Delano and I are tired of waiting. We're going to rattle his cage a little more."

"Hold on," Conrad says. "I have a call on my other line. I'm going to put you on hold. Don't go away."

About two minutes later Conrad begins speaking again. "It was Tyler. He said that he'd spoken with the bankers in Moscow and Geneva, and that they'd acknowledged receiving the assets about a week ago from a General Wendell Grossman. Tyler said he told them that those assets were stolen from a charitable trust created by Delano and Caroline Engel, and that we need the money returned as soon as possible. He said both CEOs were sympathetic, but given the size of the transfers, they'd need more time to confirm that these transfers were actually ill-gotten. Tyler told me the conversation got a little heated, and he demanded that the money be transferred by the end of the day. He gave both bankers an account number and directions for the transfers. He then abruptly hung up."

"So, I guess we'll see if the Engel name and any future business relationships with us cuts any ice," Delano says evenly. "Not much more we can do now than just wait which is something I'm not very good at, especially when we're talking about another $20 million. Connie, thanks for staying on top of this. I know we'll hear from you as soon as you have anything further." They hang up.

After having their fill of coffee, Delano and Caroline stay for just a few more minutes and then head out the door. At the base of the steps they look at the Virtue bell.

"Thanks for helping us, my friend," Delano says warmly." The bell peals softly as if to say, *you're welcome.* Delano points to the tower room in their house, and he and Caroline see the golden glow they'd come to know so well from the Book of Tamberg twenty-five years earlier.

"I guess we should actually thank both of you," he offers.

"Amen to that," Caroline whispers.

Ben and Aurora clean up the kitchen, and she looks at the clock. "Wow, look at the time. I need to get to the office. It feels like I've been gone a lifetime. Thank goodness BJ is there to keep everything running smoothly in my absence. What're you gonna do today? Remember, you agreed to stay put."

"There's not much I can do other than stay put. Besides, I don't want to leave the phone in case Tyler or Conrad call. Your dad said he's gonna do some work in his study, and I owe several of my legal clients some important paperwork. Talk about feeling like I've been gone a lifetime. It seems like forever, and yet it's only been about ten days now. Yeah, I'm staying put."

Aurora scurries around getting ready for work and darts out the door. She pats the Virtue bell lightly as she passes it and climbs into her Lincoln for the four-minute drive to her office. Once there, her assistant, BJ, brings her mail and a list of telephone messages.

"G'morning, boss, glad to see you back in the saddle. Did you have a good trip wherever you went?"

"Don't ask," Aurora replies. "I'll tell you all about it someday. So, I see that Red Jergens has called a few times looking for any news to report in *The Banner*."

"Yes, he's been a good friend to the Engel Family and the Foundation, and I think we need to give him something soon."

"I'll call him in a bit. What else is there that's pressing?"

"You received a phone call from an older-sounding gentleman named Max Kindred. He wanted you to know that he's in the Evergreen nursing home recovering from a fall and is hoping you might pay him a visit if you get some time."

"Yes, of course, I will. Please don't let me forget, okay?"

Aurora spends the remainder of the morning returning phone calls and dictating replies to letters she received.

Meanwhile back at the carriage house, Ben occupies his mind by working on legal documents for his clients. He looks at his watch often wondering when he'll hear from Tyler Irvin. Hours go by, and still no word. He calls Delano at the house to see if he's heard anything, but he knows Delano would've contacted him immediately if he had. They agree to take a lunch break together and discuss some corporate legal issues for Engel Air Corp. Around 4:00 PM their patience is wearing very thin, and Delano picks up the telephone and calls Tyler's direct line. A recorded message comes on indicating that he's out of the office on business and will get back to the caller straight away.

"Trying to communicate with this man is maddening, Ben. How is it you ever decided to hire his firm in the first place?"

Clearly, his father-in-law is not amused by Tyler Irvin's lack of responsiveness. "I got to know him in law school where he was a star, and when he opened Irvin Financial Services, he was able to land some very high-end clients. I'm pretty embarrassed by his playing us off against his bank clients in Moscow and Geneva."

"All right, I've had enough of this crap. Let's just go around him and call the bankers ourselves.

Delano picks up the phone and calls Special Agent Loudermilk at the FBI's Indianapolis field office.

"Yessir, Mr. Engel, what do you have for us?"

"When we spoke with our financial advisor, Mr. Irvin, yesterday he said he'd lean on the banks that General Grossman transferred my money to. I haven't heard back from him directly, but Conrad Zyer said he'd received an abrupt message saying that Irvin had done so and had given the banks transfer instructions. Since we haven't received any further information, I'm hoping your people can give me direct telephone numbers for the CEOs at the Bank of Moscow and the Bank of Geneva. Their names are Badenov and Bach. I'm going to call them directly and see if I can move the needle on this."

"I'm sure I can get those numbers for you, Mr. Engel. Give me a few minutes, and I'll get back to you." They hang up. Fifteen minutes later Loudermilk calls Delano back. "Here are the private lines for Yvgeny Badenov in Moscow and Adolph Bach in Geneva. Let me know what you find out."

Delano dials the number for Badenov. "You realize that it's well after midnight in Moscow," Ben informs.

"Ask me if I give a donkey's derriere! This run-around has got to end now!"

A very drowsy sounding man with a Russian accent answers the phone. "This had better be good, whoever this is!"

"Mr. Badenov, this is Delano Engel in America. I know it's very early in Moscow, but I'm feeling very frustrated in getting answers about my family's money. Our man, Tyler Irvin, said he instructed you and Mr. Bach in Geneva to both transfer $10 million that was stolen from us back into our accounts. Can you tell me what the status of those transfers are?"

"Of course, Mr. Engel. Mr. Bach and I communicated at length earlier today, and we agreed that it appears that $20 million was stolen by this rogue general from your Engel Family Charitable Trust. As such, both of our banks transferred all of that money to the account that Mr. Irvin instructed us to use. I hope this is helpful, sir. The last thing our banks want to do is injure our reputations, especially with a person of your international stature."

"I appreciate that very much. So, just to be crystal clear, you and your Swiss colleague, Mr. Bach, have returned our money. Is that correct, sir?"

"Yes, Mr. Engel, every dollar, plus interest, that General Grossman originally transferred to us."

They hang up, and Delano and Ben stare at each other with frustration and anger etched on their faces.

"So, where the hell's Tyler Irvin, and why haven't we heard from him?!"

Chapter 26

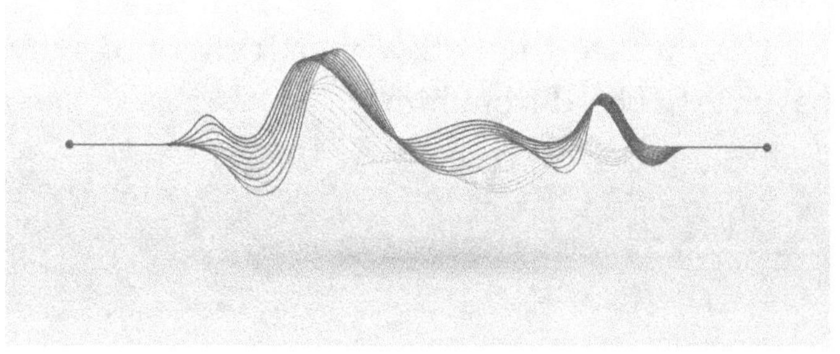

Yuri Tabeshenko lies in his hospital bed in Puerto Vallarta, Mexico, waiting to be released so he can return home to Moscow to receive reconstructive surgery. He peeks under the covers at his burnt flesh and cringes. A moment later the door to his hospital room swings open and an enraged Wendell Grossman strides in.

"My money's gone! All $10 million from my special account in Geneva. You didn't have anything to do with this, did you?"

"What are you talking about?" Yuri parries. "I haven't touched any of your effing money."

From the expression on the Russian's face, Grossman sees that he's probably telling the truth. "Well, you might want to check the status of your account, too, and I swear that if it's received my $10 million you won't any need reconstructive surgery because I'll choke the life out of you!"

"Calm down, Wendell, there's got to be a logical explanation to this." Yuri picks up the phone and dials a number to his contact at the Bank of Moscow. Yuri waits patiently for the international call to go through, and he finally connects with his bank officer.

"So, comrade, I'm calling to check on the status of my account. What is the balance?" Yuri waits as the banker pulls up his information. "Yes, Comrade Tabeshenko, your account balance is zero."

"What do you mean ZERO? You know I have much more than that!"

"But Comrade Tabeshenko, I followed your instructions when we spoke yesterday and transferred the entire balance to the new account, just as you instructed.

Yuri explodes with rage. "I never gave you any instructions to transfer my money anywhere. Get it back now!"

"I wish I could, comrade, but after I made the transfer, I destroyed all evidence that $10 million was ever in your account, along with all transactional details. You said it was a matter of national security, and who am I to argue with the KGB? Again, sir, our bank made the transfer and erased all the files just as you instructed."

A moment later, Grossman sees Yuri go totally cataplectic. "Aaarrggghh!" he screams in frustration. "My money's gone too! All of it … gone!"

"I'm sorry I doubted you, comrade. I swear to God, someone's gonna pay for this!" Grossman seethes. "The only question is who do we eviscerate first?"

Yuri picks up the phone again, and contacts his successor at the KGB, David Sapadinsky.

"Get me on the first plane back to that hospital in Moscow and mobilize our agents in America. Tell them to fly to Putnam County, Indiana, and await further instructions. General Wendell Grossman will meet them at the airport."

Over the course of the next thirty minutes, Delano and Ben continue to try to reach Tyler Irvin without success. They call Conrad Zyer in Chicago to see if he's heard anything from their investment advisor. Nada, zip, not a word!

Ben calls Aurora to tell her about the transfers of money from Moscow and Geneva and about Tyler's apparent disappearance. Then, Delano takes the phone and calls Special Agent Loudermilk.

"How'd you do with those bankers?" Loudermilk asks when he hears Delano's voice.

"The bankers did exactly as they were instructed by someone they thought was Wendell Grossman. In truth, it was Tyler Irvin impersonating the general."

"So, that's good news, right?" Loudermilk asks hopefully. "You've gotten your money back, right?"

"Uh, no," Delano replies. "The banks confirmed that $20 million was transferred, but we don't know where, and we don't have a clue where Tyler Irvin is. It appears that he's absconded with the dough."

"Dammit!" comes Loudermilk's response. "That also means the the Russians and Grossman are royally pissed off too. I'll send more agents and contact your local law enforcement folks to increase the security around your homes and businesses." They hang up.

"You knew Tyler pretty well in law school, Ben. Any idea where he might've gone into hiding?"

"Yeah, I knew him fairly well, but no place immediately comes to mind. I would imagine it's someplace that's remote and that he's very familiar with."

Throughout the rest of the afternoon Delano and Ben continue to call Tyler's number, hoping that their instincts about him are wrong, but they don't make contact.

"He can't actually believe that he can get away with this, can he, Ben?"

"He's a pretty clever guy, and that's one of the main reasons I wanted us to retain him to manage the trust. That's a decision I'll always regret."

About an hour later Aurora and Caroline pull into the driveway within minutes of each other. They meet for a quiet dinner at the main house and try to figure out Tyler's whereabouts. They know he could be anywhere, and that he now has the financial resources to change his identity, and to stay hidden for a long time. They clean up the kitchen after dinner and go into the library for a glass of port.

"None for me, thank you!" Caroline says. "I think it'll be a while before I wet my whistle again." They all smile and raise their glasses in a toast to her good judgment.

"C'mon, Ben, it's time to let these senior citizens go to bed." They say goodnight and get up and mosey onto the porch. Ben and Aurora look at the night sky and wonder if their lives will ever return to normal again. They see the golden light from the tower room emanating across the lawn to the carriage house.

"Well, that looks promising," Aurora says. They cross the yard and approach the Virtue bell. "So, Sir Virtue," Aurora begins, "any words of wisdom about where we search next?"

The bell is silent for a brief moment, and then it begins to reverberate, and Ben and Aurora feel its message deeply within. *"Go to Door. You shall find what you seek on the other side."* And then, it's silent again, and the golden light from the house's tower room fades into nothingness.

Aurora looks at Ben with a bewildered expression. "Any idea what it means by that?"

"Not a clue. Door? What door and what's on the other side? Doesn't make any sense to me." They go inside and get ready for bed.

———

Early the next morning Bryan Hilton arrives at the Putnam County Airport to begin his day. He makes a large pot of coffee and reviews the flight plans of planes that are scheduled to land before noon. As he scans the horizon and sips his coffee, the airport's radio squawks.

"This is Putnam County Airport," he says. "With whom am I speaking on such a lovely morning?"

"This is Logan Bridges out of Indianapolis," General Grossman lies, "requesting permission to land."

"Uh, yeah, Mr. Bridges, I don't see you as one of our scheduled arrivals this morning. Is this an emergency?"

"No, I work for a large commercial real estate company out of Indy, and my clients and I are looking for land for potential development. We could use some fuel and an aerial map of the county if you've got one. We're about a mile out from your location."

"Yeah, I see you now," Bryan responds. "Looks like you're flying an older military helicopter. Don't see many of them around here since the war ended."

He gives the pilot the proper heading for landing and greets the unmarked chopper as it lands adjacent to the county's modest terminal.

"G'morning, welcome to Putnam County. I noticed that your chopper doesn't have any visible markings. You know that's something that's required by the FAA, don't you?"

"Uh, I suppose so. Thanks for the heads-up. We rented the copter, and the owner told us that it's supposed to be repainted next week. He allowed us to use it just for today," Grossman prevaricates.

"I've got a pot of coffee available if you want some," Bryan offers. He notices that the people accompanying *Logan Bridges* don't speak, and that they appear to be rather tough looking characters.

"While I'm refueling for you, I've got some aerial maps in the terminal. You're welcome to have one. Any specific area in Putnam County you're looking for?"

"I think we'll recognize any potential locations once we're airborne again but thank you."

In truth, Grossman knows exactly where Delano and Caroline Engel's property is from when his team of thugs abducted the Engels several days earlier. While Grossman and his men are drinking coffee inside the terminal, Bryan begins refueling the chopper. He peers inside the cockpit and can't help but see Cyrillic letters on a knapsack.

"Hmm, Russian," he surmises. He looks further inside and is surprised to see large caliber weapons that make his hair stand on end. The Russian pilot comes outside to check on the fueling and slams the chopper's door shut to prevent any further looking.

"Almost got 'er done, sir. Which real estate company did you say you work for in Indy?"

The pilot looks him in the eye icily but does not answer. Grossman and the others return to the helicopter and climb inside.

"Well, have a nice day, gents. Hope you find what you're looking for." He hands them a bill, and Grossman pays it in cash. As soon as they're in the air again, Bryan picks up the phone and calls Delano at home.

"I've got a mighty bad feeling about four people who just took off from the airport. They're in an unmarked chopper with Russian-looking documents inside and several high-powered weapons. They've got an aerial map and sure don't seem to be the land developers they claim to be. Just in case, I urge the four of you to hightail it out of your houses for somewhere safe. My guess is that the Russians are gunning for you, and it won't take them long to get to your property. I'm going to get the Spartan Executive in the air just in case my worst fears come true."

They hang up, and Delano immediately calls Aurora and Ben in the carriage house. "Bryan just alerted me that we've got company flying our way in a helicopter, and he believes it's the Russians. You two need to meet Caroline and me in our new fallout shelter right away and bring your radio with you. The security cameras we've mounted throughout the property should give us good views of whoever's out there."

After their experience with the Russians in Puerto Vallarta, and knowing that the Russians and Grossman just got snookered out of $20 million, no one hesitates to move very quickly. Once safely inside the underground shelter, they manage to maintain radio contact with Bryan, and Delano alerts Agent Loudermilk of their imminent security threat. Subsequently, the FBI agent alerts local law enforcement to close in on the Engels' property.

"I'm in the air in the Spartan and heading in your direction. I'll let you know what I see when I'm over your position."

Four minutes later the undeniable sound of helicopter rotors fills the air over Carriage House Lane. The chopper lowers to just above the treetops, and two Russian KGB thugs rappel down ropes leaving Grossman and the pilot inside the copter.

"Search the house and the carriage house," Grossman commands. "If you see anyone, try to take them prisoner. If they don't go quietly, kill them!" The agents split up to search the buildings, but after several minutes of finding no one, the thugs radio Grossman.

"After completing a thorough search, meet us in the clearing in those ash trees. We'll land and pick you up. Then, we'll leave the Engels' property a charred mess. That'll teach them to screw with General Wendell Grossman."

When Bryan reaches Carriage House Lane in the Spartan, he sees the helicopter just above the trees. He notices that the copter's door is open with a Russian holding a grenade launcher.

He immediately radios Delano in the underground bunker. "Not a good scene from up here, boss. It looks like they're getting ready to do some serious damage to your property. Do you want me to wait for the police to get here? It may be too late if I do though."

"Our family has worked too hard over the years to build a beautiful home. I say we take matters into our own hands. Bryan, I suggest you use the prototypes that we've outfitted the Spartan with to defend us."

"Message received, boss. I'm signing off for now." As Bryan brings the Spartan about, he sees the Russian in the doorway launch a grenade that hits the Engels' barn. It explodes and the barn immediately goes up in bright orange flames.

"Dammit!" he hollers as he repositions the Spartan. He flips a switch on the control panel and hears a whir as rockets located under the wings are armed. He sees that the Russians are about to fire more grenades on the house and carriage house. He brings the Spartan around quickly until he's facing the helicopter from about seventy-five yards away. It's the first time Grossman and the Russians see their adversary.

"Quickly! Turn the copter ninety degrees so we can fire upon this bastard," Grossman commands, but their reaction time is too late. Bryan launches the rocket from under the starboard wing, and its flight is true. The copter explodes in midair raining flaming metal, glass, and body parts on the otherwise serene central Indiana property. The Russian thugs on the ground are consumed by the conflagration as well.

From inside the bomb shelter, Delano, Caroline, Aurora, and Ben watch as the security cameras show the immolated copter crash to the ground. No one speaks. No one cheers. The threat is over but at great cost to human life.

"Mission accomplished," Bryan evenly reports. "Chopper down. Heading back to the airport, boss."

As the Engels and Witts safely emerge from the underground bunker, they see the full extent of the carnage and know that no one in the helicopter or on the ground could've survived. Shortly thereafter, the police arrive on the tragic scene with sirens blaring and lights flashing wondering what in the world just happened. Ten minutes after that firefighters from the Greencastle Fire Department arrive and begin extinguishing the remaining embers of the Engels' barn and the wreckage of the helicopter.

Agent Loudermilk and an FBI contingent eventually appear on the scene, but all of the excitement is over by the time they arrive from Indy.

"So, how in God's name did you bring down a freaking helicopter, Mr. Engel? I thought you said you were underground in your fallout shelter."

"We were, but our man, Bryan Hilton, appeared just in the nick of time in our Spartan Executive and fired on them."

"With what?! He had to have more than a flare gun this time?"

"Yeah, well, it's something we've been developing for Uncle Sam. Actually, it was the first time our new rockets were put to use in a live combat situation. I have no doubt our home would've been destroyed had it not been for Bryan's fast action."

Agent Loudermilk smiles wryly. "You and your family are just full of surprises, aren't you, Mr. Engel?"

"More than you know, sir. More than you know."

Chapter 27

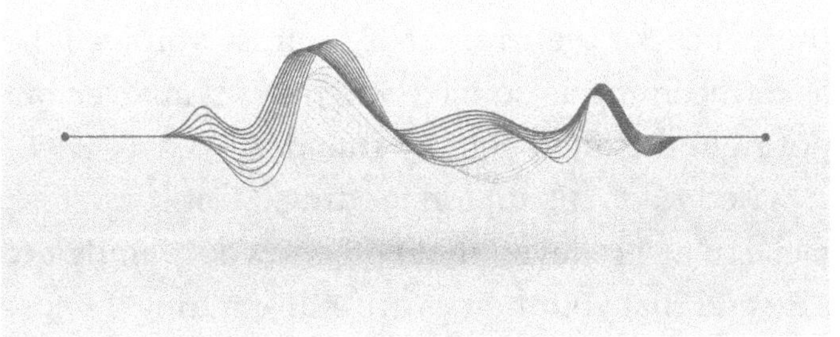

AN HOUR LATER THE Greencastle firefighters have put out the flames, and Delano and Ben have given their reports to the FBI, the Greencastle Police Department, and the Putnam County Sheriff's Office. Ben winces as he sees the charred remains of General Wendell Grossman and the Russian thugs placed in body bags for transport to the coroner's office. The only nonfamily member still on the scene is Red Jergens from *The Banner* newspaper. He snaps a few photos and asks Delano if he has any comments he'd like to offer for the morning paper.

"Not now, Red, I'm sure you can appreciate that it's been a very trying and emotional time for our family. May I suggest that you follow up with the police for their report? I promise you we'll be as forthcoming as possible when this is all over, but not right this moment, my friend."

Red nods his understanding. "Get some rest, Del. I'm just relieved that you and your family are safe and that your homes are still standing. I know you'll share everything you can when the time is right."

After Red leaves their property, Caroline, Delano, Aurora, and Ben walk over to the carriage house and settle into comfortable chairs. Ben pours coffee for each of them and says, "Thank goodness you had the presence of mind to build a fallout shelter. I shudder to think what would've happened if we hadn't had a safe place to hunker down, or if Bryan hadn't been astute about the Russians and Grossman when they arrived at the airport this morning."

"Yeah, we were darn lucky," Aurora concurs, and they hear the soft ringing of the Virtue bell in further acknowledgement.

"So, now what?" Caroline asks. "Hopefully, we're finished fending off nasty Russians and a greedy general." They all raise their coffee cups in a toast to that.

"There's still the matter of recovering the remaining $20 million. At this point there's little doubt that Tyler Irvin is the culprit. Now, we just need to figure out where he went. Earlier, the Virtue bell communicated with Aurora and me to go to a door and that we'd find what we're seeking on the other side. It was a very cryptic message, and we have no idea which door the bell was referring to."

"Well, it beats the heck out of me," Caroline says. "I don't know about you guys, but I've had enough excitement for one day, actually for a lifetime. Ready to head home, Del?"

"I am, sweetheart. The only other thing I want to do is to call Bryan to make sure he got back safely, and to thank him … for everything." They all raise their coffee cups in a final toast to Bryan, and Caroline and Delano exit the carriage house and stroll across the lawn to their house.

Ben and Aurora sit on their sofa and hold each other closely. They know their marriage vows had promised they'd be there for each other *for better or for worse,* but neither had any way of foretelling the life-altering challenges they'd face so quickly. They sit there staring out the window, talking about what they'd endured over the last two weeks: Ben being on the run after stealing the Engel Trust's money; letting so many people in their community down; rescuing her parents in Puerto Vallarta; and surviving the assault by Grossman and the Russians on their home.

"I swear you couldn't write a book about all of this. No one would be able to accept it as anything other than pulp fiction crap," Ben concedes. "So, where the heck is Tyler Irvin and the rest of the money?"

"I sure agree with you about the exhausting drama our lives have been embroiled in. All I want to do now is just be here safely with you."

Several minutes later Aurora falls asleep, and Ben gets up to turn the coffee pot off. When he returns to the sofa, he stares out the window again trying to recall anything that might give them direction in finding Ty Irvin. Through their closed windows he hears the Virtue bell ringing but doesn't feel its vibrations in any meaningful way. He puts his arm around Aurora and closes his eyes in hopes of having an epiphany when all of a sudden he bolts upright and says aloud, "Could that be it? Could that be where Irvin is holed up?"

He lightly touches Aurora's shoulder and arouses her from a nap.

"Huh, what?" she utters sleepily. "I must've fallen asleep."

"I think I may have it, Aurora. Thanks to the Virtue bell, I think I may know where Irvin is."

"That's great, dear, but I'm going back to my nap."

"No, wait, I want you to hear me out."

She sees how serious her husband is and shifts in her seat to face him.

Ben begins, " So when we were all in law school together at Northwestern, Tyler invited us up to his family's vacation home in Wisconsin one weekend. It was a beautiful old lodge situated on the bay that had been owned by his mother's family for years. You couldn't go because you had some family commitment or something, but a small group of us drove north with him past Milwaukee and Green Bay."

"So?" Aurora asks in confusion.

"When we got to Sturgeon Bay, we entered Door County."

Aurora looks at her husband wondering where he's going with his line of thinking when all of a sudden she bolts upright, too, as she recalls the Virtue bell urging them to find a door.

Ben smiles and nods his head affirmatively. "You get it, right?" he asks. "I'll bet you dollars to donuts that Tyler's in Door County, Wisconsin … and the bell said that we should go to a 'door' and that we'd find what we seek on the other side."

"So, what other side, Ben? Door County is a big place."

"I recall it took us a couple of hours to drive the length of the county until we finally arrived near the 'other side' of the peninsula just outside of Ellison Bay. I bet we can find him there if we can locate exactly where his family's lodge is located. Only trouble is I don't know his mother's maiden name, and the property is probably listed under it."

He reaches over to the end table and picks up the telephone.

"Who are you calling, Ben?"

He dials Special Agent Loudermilk's number. "The FBI never rests, and if anyone can figure the location out for us, it'll be them."

"This better be damn good!" Ben hears Agent Loudermilk's muffled voice say. "I'm in the middle of dinner."

Over the next two minutes, Ben shares his thinking with Loudermilk who has to admit that it's a possible lead. Ben chooses not to share the source of his epiphany because it would mean explaining that it came from a sentient old bell.

"Don't say anything about the bell," Aurora whispers the obvious to him. "They'll lock both of us up in a padded room."

Agent Loudermilk agrees to see what he can find out about property owners in that area of the bay and agrees to get back to them in a few minutes. In the meantime Aurora calls her parents.

"Sorry to interrupt you, but Ben's got an idea about Irvin's location that we think has a lot of merit. Why don't you pack a bag and get ready for another trip?"

Ben then contacts Bryan at the airport and asks him to get the Spartan Executive ready to go on another adventure. Thirty minutes later Loudermilk calls Ben back.

"Irvin's mother's maiden name is Rud, and according to Door County tax records the property's still listed in that name. It's located at 39 Garrett Bay Road. I've contacted the sheriff's office in Door County, and they'll meet you at an airfield called Mave's Lakeview Road Airport near Ellison Bay. Here's an officer's name and number you should call as you're preparing to land. They'll meet you there, and please, can you just let law enforcement personnel handle this one? In other words go easy with the rockets and flare guns, will ya?!"

Another twenty minutes later Aurora, Ben, Caroline, and Delano arrive at the airport and join Bryan who's already in the cockpit of the Spartan Executive. In the west they see the sun beginning to set over the horizon. Bryan shouts, "Strap in, everybody, because here we go!" He takes a final look around, engages the aircraft's throttle, and they take flight … into the unknown.

Chapter 28

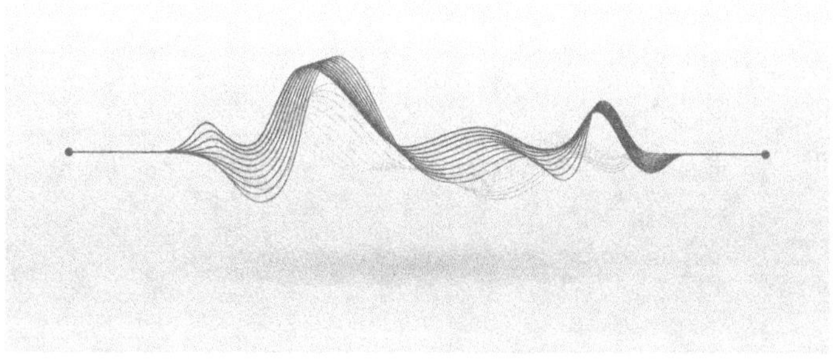

TYLER IRVIN LOUNGES ON the back deck of the lodge that's been in his mother's family for decades. It's where he spent many a summer as a boy learning to swim and fish with his father and grandfather, and to this day it's the place on earth that he cherishes most.

He watches the gulls rise and dive on the winds. He listens to the wind through the cedars, birches, and maples. He feels the sun warm his face, and he smells a combination of lake spray and forest conifers.

Now, he's $20 million richer having stolen money from his clients and friends. "So, why'd I do it?" he muses out loud. "I have plenty of dough already as it is. I come from a wealthy-enough family and had access to a superior education that helped set me for life. Most recently, it's been my financial services company that's enabled me to ride the wave of postwar business investments and the stock market. It gave me opportunities to work with clients like Delano Engel and Ben Witt. So, why'd I do it?"

He gets up from the lounge chair and walks inside the lodge to his office where he has a stock ticker rattling off quotations, similar to the one in his office at work. He smiles broadly as he sees the value of his $20 million continue to grow.

"So, I guess I could also ask myself 'where do I go from here?' I reckon I'm not as clever as I thought I was. Should've thought about a cozy place to hightail it to before I stole the money, but when the Russian and Swiss bankers gave me the keys to the vault, as it were, I guess greed and my sense of entitlement just got the better of me, and I opted to line my pockets and screw the others."

A brief pang of guilt hits him. Tyler wonders if he should give the money back and concoct some wack-a-doodle excuse for why he took it in the first place.

"Nope, I'm not doing that. Not at this point. The die is cast, and I'm not gonna go to jail for even a minute." He ponders a potential place to escape to. "Hmmm, Grand Cayman Island perhaps. I've heard it's a real up-and-coming place for ex-patriots with a lot of dough. Something to look into …"

After refueling the Spartan at an airfield near Milwaukee, Delano takes over the controls, and Caroline serves as his copilot. "Not like flying the old Curtiss Jenny, is it, Del?"

"No, it's not, but this Spartan Executive is about as fine an airplane as anyone can own now. I've read that the Spartan Company isn't going to manufacture any more planes, so our 1946 model is the last year they'll make them. I thought about our buying the company, but we've already got too many irons in the fire. It's interesting to think that our Flying Jenny was at the infancy of commercial aviation, and now twenty-five years later, this Spartan is state of the art. I'd never bet against American ingenuity."

Caroline reflects back. "I'll never forget the first time I went up with you in the Jenny, and we spotted our future home's roof tower sticking up through the trees. It looked magical to me, and little did we know that magic existed within the hidden tower room. Finding the mystical Book of Tamberg seems almost like a dream now."

Delano nods his agreement. "And now Aurora and Ben have their own magic with the Virtue bell. Who knows why our family was chosen in such mystifying ways or what the future may hold. I think Max Kindred's words to Aurora about just accepting the mysteries is sage advice."

An hour later Delano flies the Spartan over Green Bay, Wisconsin, with his instrumentation set for Sturgeon Bay near the southern end of Door County.

"Well, Ben, we've found the *door* as the Virtue bell advised. Now, we need to find who and what we're seeking on the other side. I sure hope your interpretation of the bell's message, and your rec-ollection of Tyler's family's property are correct."

"Me, too," he replies hopefully, "because without this lead, we'll be flying blind."

While Delano pilots their aircraft in a northeasterly direction, Caroline radios ahead to the Mave's Lakeview Road Airport near Ellison Bay to alert them that they'll be arriving soon. She then radios the number at the Door County Sheriff's Department that Special Agent Loudermilk gave them. The dispatcher connects her to Sheriff Sven Johannsen who's standing by to meet them upon landing.

"We'll have two vehicles available for my men and your party. Agent Loudermilk from the FBI told me you folks have a knack for, uh, taking matters into your own hands when it comes to confronting bad people. He wants us to keep you all on a very short leash."

"Of course, Sheriff, heaven forbid we'd ever get in the way of law enforcement," Caroline replies as she rolls her eyes. "See you soon."

A few minutes later Delano safely sets the Spartan Executive down on the only paved runway at the tiny local airport, and they all deplane and meet the Ellison Bay sheriff's deputies. As usual, Bryan stays with the plane to protect and refuel it, and to take flight quickly if Delano and company so instruct.

"So, Agent Loudermilk gave me a thumbnail explanation of your reason for being here. Why don't you fill me in a little more as we drive over to Garrett Bay Road," Johannsen says to Delano and Ben.

Johannsen's eyes go wide with surprise as Ben and Delano take turns filling in details about the theft of $20 million by their financial advisor, Tyler Irvin, and the role that Russian KGB agents played in that theft, the abduction of the Engels from their home to Mexico, their assault on the Engel and Witt's property resulting in multiple deaths …

"And that's just the tip of the iceberg," Caroline chimes in.

Sheriff Johannsen is a small-town constable, and he's nearly at a loss for words. "Uh, that's darn near unbelievable. I've got to tell you we're not accustomed to that kind of turmoil up here. I also need to tell you that the Rud/Irvin families have been part of the bedrock of this community for many decades. If it weren't for Agent Loudermilk confirming the veracity of your story, I doubt we'd be rendering any assistance at all."

"I understand," Delano replies, "because we come from a very sedate community as well. Having said that, we need to approach this situation with extreme caution. If Tyler Irvin is the crook we believe him to be, he's not likely to go quietly."

The two cars slow to a crawl as they approach the family lodge at 39 Garrett Bay Road. Delano and Ben ask Caroline and Aurora to remain in their vehicle with one of the sheriff's men. They park a hundred yards away, and Ben, Delano, Johanssen, and one of his deputies proceed on foot. "Let's fan out," Johannsen orders everyone when they're in eyesight of the lodge, "and no one approaches the lodge until you receive my order."

Tyler Irvin sits in his favorite easy chair looking out a large picture window at a few sailboats cruising the windy waters of Green Bay. Winter comes early in this part of the world, and a soft layer of snow covers the landscape. It's a scene that he's enjoyed for more times than he can count. He sips from his tumbler of bourbon and munches on a handful of cheese curds. "I'm gonna miss this place. Maybe I'll be able to return from time to time."

He's so engrossed in the serene view that he doesn't hear a barely audible click near a rear door, and then he turns his head and shivers in shock. He starts to get up, but immediately sees a very large handgun pointed at his face.

"Who the hell are you, and how'd you get in here?"

The reply comes with a thick eastern European accent. "Please don't move, Mr. Irvin, I'd hate to have to seriously wound you to get the information that I seek."

"I don't know what you could possibly want other than money. I have some locked away in my safe. You're welcome to it. Just take it and leave."

"Oh, that's most generous of you, Mr. Irvin, and yes, it is money that I'm after, but not the paltry few thousand you might keep for casual spending. No, how about the $20 million that you stole from your client, the Engel Family, and from a retired general and my colleagues in Mother Russia? You see, one of the hard parts of having a lot of money is hanging on to it, yes?"

"Who are you?" Tyler demands as he sits down again.

"My name is David Sapadinsky, and I recently learned about the Engels' money from my mentor, Yuri Tabeshenko. He sent me to retrieve what he views as his."

At the mention of Yuri's name, Tyler knows he's in deep caca.

As if to forestall the inevitable, Tyler asks Sapadinsky: "How did you find me? I thought I was totally off the grid up here."

"Yes, but remember that we KGB acolytes love nothing more than researching the backgrounds of all people we have, uh, interest in. So, as the financial manager for the huge Engel Charitable Trust, you were very much on our radar screen from the beginning. We know about you. We know about your business and family, and we know the properties you all own. So, here we are, yes?"

Sapadinsky offers Tyler a serpent-like smile and continues, "Research is something we do very well, and from years of spy craft, I learned that when people are on the run, they often assuage their anxiety by hiding in very familiar places they think no one other than the locals might know about. In other words, sir, when it comes to our *research*, the harder we work, the luckier we get. Now, get up, and no funny business! We're going down to the lake. Our boat is waiting."

Chapter 29

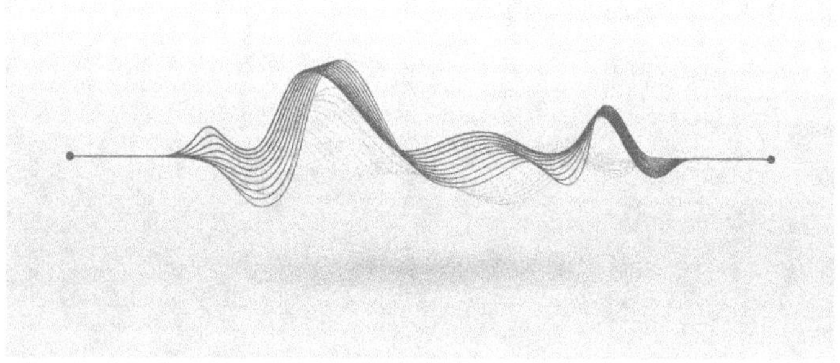

Ben and Delano circle around to the back of the lodge while Johannsen and his deputy approach the front door. The sheriff has known Mr. Irvin for many years, and they've never had any negative legal run-ins. In fact, The Rud and Irvin families have been very generous with local benevolent causes, including helping the sheriff's department. For years they've worked together during the holidays to make sure needy children have a proper winter coat and at least one toy. He's always admired these generous people, so he chooses to take a more genteel approach by simply knocking on the front door.

"Mr. Irvin!" he calls out as he knocks on the door again. "Need to speak with you, sir." There's no reply. He looks over at his deputy and says, "Cover me. I'm going in." Fortunately, Johannsen doesn't have to work hard at it. He simply turns the handle and heaves his broad Swedish shoulder against the door, and it yields. He calls out again to Tyler Irvin, but his voice goes unanswered. He steps inside and waves for his partner to join him. Together, they search the premises, but find no one at home.

"Looks like he was here very recently," his deputy observes. "His drink is unfinished, and the ice cubes haven't melted. Let's keep looking."

As Ben looks around the rear of the property, he hears a motor start down by the dock and sees two figures struggle to get a third person into the boat. He recognizes that third person as Tyler Irvin. He points the escape out to Delano and shouts to Johannsen. "Hey, get out here! They're down by the lake boarding a motor boat."

Johannsen and his deputy quickly join them outside on the back deck, and the deputy begins running down to the dock to try to stop them, but to no avail. They speed away in an inboard Chris-Craft.

"Where do you think they might be going?" Ben asks the sheriff.

"They could be going anywhere along the shoreline, but if I were a betting man, I'd say they'd be going to the airport on Washington Island. It's about fifteen miles or a fifty minute cruise from here." The sheriff radios his dispatcher to issue a call for all law enforcement personnel in the area to be on the lookout for them.

Delano says to Ben: "If they need to travel almost an hour to get to that airport, I think we might be able to intercept them in the Spartan. He radios Bryan at the Mave's Lakeview Road airport to get the plane ready for immediate takeoff.

"C'mon, sheriff, let's get over to the airport. We have a very small window of opportunity to catch them because if we don't, their plane can fly below radar and go anywhere including Canada."

The three men run back to the car and jump inside with Aurora and Caroline. It's only about a seven-minute drive to the airport, but with their siren blaring they make it in five."

"You ladies stay here," the sheriff advises. "We'll keep in touch with you via our radios." Aurora begins to protest their being left behind, but Caroline convinces her to do so.

"C'mon, Bryan, let's get this plane up in the air. Sheriff, call ahead to Washington Island and have them immediately clear the air space in a five-mile radius."

Bryan makes sure everyone is strapped in and then revs the engine and pushes throttle forward. Once airborne they all keep their eyes peeled for the Chris-Craft, but there are a good number of places to hide, and it's a challenge.

Bryan flies low over the water close to the shoreline in repeated circles, but there are plenty of niches for them to briefly hunker down under overhanging trees until any suspicious looking airplanes pass by.

Meanwhile in the Chris-Craft, Tyler is trying to make the Russians' getaway as difficult as possible. He kicks at Sapadinsky repeatedly until the Russian pistol-whips him with his handgun. He passes out from the brutal whipping.

Bryan flies the Spartan past Gills Rock at the northern tip of the Door County peninsula into the strait known as Porte des Morts, meaning the Gate of the Dead.

"Hardly an encouraging name," Delano mutters.

"Yeah, a lot of Indian skirmishes and shipwrecks in the straits between here and Washington Island over the years." The sheriff stares through his binoculars at the coastline trying his best to include boats that could be hiding near docks and boathouses. It's tedious work, but it pays off.

"Hey, I think that's them," Johannsen says, and Bryan sees where he's pointing and swings the Spartan in that direction.

"Let's see if I can get them to identify themselves." He radios on all frequencies. "Hello the Chris-Craft passing through Porte des Morts, this is Sheriff Johannsen. Request that you identify yourselves." There's no immediate reply from the boat. Johannsen radios again.

Finally, "Yes, this is the Chris-Craft. What do you want, Sheriff?" comes a very eastern European accent.

"I need you to pull ashore and prepare to be boarded when you reach Detroit Harbor at the southern tip of Washington Island. Do you copy?"

The boat driver feigns static on the radio and replies, "Your message is breaking up. Please repeat."

Johannsen is in no mood for their shenanigans, and he motions for Bryan to reduce his altitude and buzz the aircraft. As he does so, they see some turmoil on the boat as Tyler Irvin has regained consciousness and begins wrestling with Sapadinsky.

"Bryan, fire a rocket across their bow. Maybe that'll get their attention," Delano directs.

"Just try not to hit them" Johannsen commands. "I want us to take them alive if we can."

Bryan launches a rocket from beneath the Spartan's port wing. It's path is true, and it explodes when it hits the water about thirty feet in front of the boat.

"Holy shit!" Johannsen erupts. "How do I get some of those?" He tries to make radio contact again, but the radio remains silent, and the boat increases its speed.

Delano is about to tell Bryan to fire another rocket when they see Tyler and Sapadinsky in the middle of a furious struggle. The Russian attempts to shoot him, but his shot goes wide, and Tyler knees him in the groin and manages to grab the gun.

"All right, tell your man to steer us over to the shoreline now!"

"And, if I don't?" Sapadinsky replies with a Slavic sneer. The Russian sees Tyler hesitate, and he lunges at him. As if by pure reflex, Tyler fires the gun at point-plank range and kills the arrogant Russian.

"That was ugly!" Johannsen says. "Looks like one bad guy down, and two more to go."

Tyler regains his equilibrium and points the gun at the boat driver. They're about a quarter mile from Washington Island, and the Russian begins swerving the boat back and forth in an effort to knock Tyler off balance. It works briefly, but then he recovers and shoots the Russian in the back. The driver slumps forward onto the steering wheel, and the Chris-Craft appears on a collision course with the shoreline.

Finally, Tyler manages to get the boat under control, and he cuts the engine about a hundred yards from Detroit Harbor. Johannsen tries to raise the Chris-Craft on the radio again.

"This is Sheriff Johannsen. I order you to maintain your position and await further instructions. Do not attempt to flee or you will be fired upon again, copy?"

Tyler does not immediately respond, and Ben takes the radio and tries to communicate with his one-time friend and colleague.

"Ty, this is Ben Witt. Please do as the sheriff commands. No matter what you've done, it's not worth dying for."

"Hello, Ben, it's good to hear your voice, old buddy. Look, I don't think I'm emotionally capable of spending the rest of my days in jail with that unsavory class of people. I'm sure you understand. Listen, in all seriousness, I'm truly sorry for the upheaval I've caused, but I don't see any good way out of this, old friend."

"C'mon, Tyler, if you cooperate, maybe the court will show some leniency. We've both studied enough legal cases to know it can happen."

"Perhaps, but I don't think so, Ben," Tyler replies. "As a parting gesture for old time's sake, here's the account number and transaction code for the $20 million that I stole. Please tell Delano that I'm deeply sorry."

Ben begins to tell Tyler that he can say that to Delano in a few minutes, but then they hear the piercing sound of a gunshot and see Tyler Irvin drop dead from a self-inflicted wound.

"Oh no!" Ben shouts. "No, Tyler, no!"

Sheriff Johannsen radios the harbor master, and asks him to prepare a tender so they can secure the drifting Chris-Craft and retrieve the bodies. The mood within the Spartan is very subdued, and Delano says softly: "Caroline and I always wanted our money to support good causes. I never would've dreamed in a million years that so much death and destruction would result instead."

Some ten minutes later, the Spartan Executive has landed, and while Bryan refuels it for the return flight, Johannsen, Ben, and Delano borrow a car and drive a few miles south to Detroit Harbor where the sheriff oversees the extraction of the bodies. It's a heartbreaking and gruesome scene, and the steel-gray skies and blustery wind make the scene even more somber.

Ben radios Aurora and Caroline at Mave's Lakeview Road airport and reports what's transpired. "It's pretty grim up here, three dead men and a lot of blood. We should be back to you in about an hour, and then I want us to return home. The sheriff needs to stay here to wrap things up."

"Are you and Dad okay, Ben?" Aurora asks sympathetically.

"Yes and no," comes her husband's frank reply. "None of this should ever have happened, and I'll always believe that my initial theft from the Engel Trust set so many tragedies in motion."

Delano hears him say that to Aurora and says, "Everything you did was for the right reason, Ben. None of us will ever hold you responsible for the awful behavior of others, so please don't be too hard on yourself. We're all safe, and thanks to you we're getting all of the money back."

"Thanks, Delano, I appreciate your kind words more than you know. All I want now is for all of us to go home to Greencastle and continue living the lives we set out to do." Ben talks a few moments longer with Aurora, and then they hang up.

The flight back to Greencastle, Indiana, is long. Everyone is physically and emotionally spent. Bryan pilots the first leg of their return, and they refuel in Milwaukee and grab some dinner. Delano pilots the next leg of their journey swinging wide of Chicago's airspace and landing for more fuel and to stretch their legs near Crown Point, Indiana. From there, Brian retakes the controls, and they finally arrive back home at their Putnam County Airport early the next morning. They bid adieu to Bryan at the airport and finally pull into Carriage House Lane around three in the morning. With the exception of the charred remains of their barn and the scattered remnants of the Russians' downed helicopter, everything looks quiet and serene.

"I think we'll sleep in tomorrow, I mean today," Ben says wearily, "and then I need to confirm the successful transfer of the $20 million back to the Engel Trust's account. I'm sure it'll be a welcome relief to Conrad who must be wondering where we all vanished to."

Caroline and Delano slowly walk across the yard to their porch and and enter their home through the kitchen door. Aurora and Ben watch until they're safely inside, and then hold each other for the longest time. As they turn to enter the carriage house, they both lightly run their hands along the curvature of the Virtue bell.

"We couldn't have done it without you, dear friend," Aurora praises. "However you do it, just know that we're grateful beyond words." The bell reverberates a soft, embracing peal, and the young couple steps inside their home.

Chapter 30

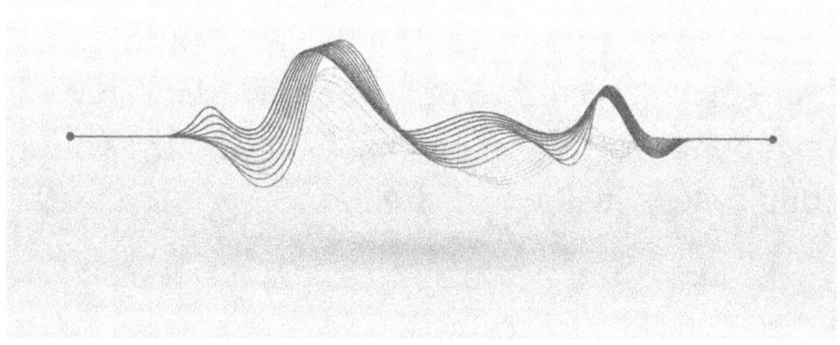

A COUPLE OF DAYS LATER the lives of the Engels and Witts already seem to be returning to some semblance of normalcy. It's Christmas Eve and a feeling of hope and healing and goodwill is in the air. As usual, Delano is very focused on major issues at work. His engineers are making great strides in jet propulsion and highly technical weapons systems. The government's purse strings are wide open to them.

Caroline is in her glory with her fellow volunteers working on decorations to help make Christmas in Greencastle truly special this year. Colorful Christmas lights adorn storefronts on the courthouse square and holiday music welcomes shoppers wherever they go.

There's a lovely blanket of snow covering the landscape, and the view reminds Aurora of a winter Currier and Ives scene. The red carriage house looks almost like a large Christmas tree ornament, and the Virtue bell wears its soft snow cover like an ermine cap.

The only sad news is that Max Kindred has passed away. At the moment of his death bells all across the community reverberated their doleful peals in tribute to a very fine man.

"You know, we only got to know him relatively recently," Aurora laments, "but he had such a positive impact on our family. I'm so glad we've been able to keep his precious 'ringers' on his property and allow others to share in his dream."

On a more sober note Ben has already met with federal prosecutors in Indianapolis to discuss any legal charges they're considering filing against him for grand theft, stealing documents from NATO, fleeing law enforcement in multiple states, and a host of minor offenses. With Aurora, Caroline, Delano, and FBI Agent Loudermilk speaking on his behalf, Ben is able to retain his license to practice law, and to serve as a trustee for the Engel Family Charitable Trust. As a penance, however, he is ordered to serve six months of community service which he's more than happy to do.

To the welcome relief of her assistant, BJ, Aurora returns to her office at the Engel Family Charitable Trust. She and her team are busier than ever trying to wrap things up that need to occur before December 31st. The stack of phone messages and paperwork waiting for her is immense, but she knows that focusing on good works will help replace the recent fear and anger that consumed her and her family.

"First things first, BJ, can you please see if you can get Red Jergens on the phone?"

Aurora and Red talk for a long time, and she's very happy to report that the $25 million corpus of the Engel Charitable Trust has been returned. She outlines the next wave of monetary grants that community organizations will receive and discusses how they hope to expand a "culture of giving" in Greencastle.

"Ben tells me that concepts like the United Way and community foundations are growing by leaps and bounds in cities across America, and that we should try to accelerate that process in smaller communities like ours. Grassroots giving!"

"That's wonderful news, Aurora! Your family is certainly leading in ways that make us all proud." He hesitates a moment. "But going back to the theft of the $25 million, how much of the story aren't you telling me, Aurora?" he asks curiously.

"Plenty, and I give you credit, Red, for trying to get more details out of me. Truth is, there are some major national security issues involving foreign adversaries that I'm not at liberty to discuss with you.

"Russians?" he prompts.

"Off the record, Red?"

"Off the record, Aurora."

"Yeah, Russians and a rogue NATO general. That's all I'm comfortable telling you right now, and I probably shouldn't have even said that. Besides,

Red, my family and I would far prefer that you share the great news about the Engel Trust and its commitment to helping make Greencastle a stellar, world-class community."

The next day the large headline in a special edition of *The Banner* newspaper says it all:

Engel Family Regains Trust

Later that evening Delano and Caroline join Aurora and Ben on the porch of the carriage house for light snacks and hot spiced cider. They have a nice blaze going in their fire pit, and everyone feels cozy despite the winter temperature.

"Here, Aurora, your dad and I are planning a little holiday soiree for some of our friends and associates. I've brought a list of names I want us all to go over together. We sure don't want to leave anyone out."

Aurora and Ben take their time perusing the list that contains some seventy-five potential guests. Many names they recognize, but there are several others that are new to Greencastle, and the Engels want them to feel welcomed to the community.

"Looks like a pretty comprehensive list. Where do you plan on holding the party?"

"Your mother has already spoken with Gwen at Almost Heaven, and we've reserved the entire upstairs dining room for New Year's Eve."

"Wow, sounds great, count us in!" Ben confirms.

"There is one name not listed here that we should definitely include, however …"

"Oh?" her mother asks. "Who?"

A golden glow appears from the house's tower room and beams down on them, and the Virtue bell begins to reverberate as if heralding new life. It's joined by a chorus of bells ringing vibrantly all across Greencastle and beyond.

Ben and Aurora lean lovingly against each other and smile warmly at her parents.

"Our soon-to-be baby daughter and your very first grandchild, Bella Kindred Witt."

~ The End ~

About the Author
Stuart Fabe

DURING HIS ADULT LIFe Stuart Fabe has enjoyed a couple of meaningful careers, but none more personally fulfilling than being a storyteller. He began his professional life in the early 1970s working with delinquent and at-risk children who appeared before the Hamilton County Juvenile Court. He then focused on organizing and conducting successful fundraising campaigns for vital organizations such as Cincinnati Children's Hospital, the Jewish Hospital, and the Cincinnati Zoo. He helped raise millions of dollars over a span of twenty-five years.

Throughout the decades that he raised charitable funds, Stuart always maintained a photographic darkroom where he escaped the rigors of his daily work to print fine art photographs that he exhibited at art shows and galleries primarily throughout the Midwest.

In 2005 he moved away from Cincinnati, Ohio, to Putnam County, Indiana, to concentrate on creating art full-time, including intricate weaving on hardshell gourds, and photographing the Milky Way and the night sky. It wasn't until ten years ago, however, that he began writing suspense novels in a serious way. He readily admits that the first few stories weren't his best work, but he was fascinated by doing research for his books and creating compelling stories with fascinating characters.

Kindred Spirits is a sequel to *The Write House* and is his ninth novel in ten years. He enjoys the solitude of living in the bucolic countryside near Greencastle with his life-partner, Marla, and together they contribute to the health and well-being of their family, their community, and their animals and friends.